The Hindered Hand

The Hindered Hand

Sutton E. Griggs

MINT EDITIONS

The Hindered Hand was first published in 1905.

This edition published by Mint Editions 2021.

ISBN 9781513296821 | E-ISBN 9781513298320

Published by Mint Editions®

MINT
EDITIONS

minteditionbooks.com

Publishing Director: Jennifer Newens
Design & Production: Rachel Lopez Metzger
Project Manager: Micaela Clark
Typesetting: Westchester Publishing Services

Contents

Tuning the Lyre

I n the long ago when the earth was in process of formation, it must have been that those forces of nature most expert in the fashioning of the beautiful were ordered to come together as collaborators and give to the world Almaville!

Journeying toward the designated spot, they halted on the outskirts of the site of the contemplated city, and tossed up a series of engirdling hills, whose slopes and crests covered with verdure might afford in the days to come a beautiful sight to the inhabitants when riding forth to get a whiff of country air. These same forces of nature, evidently in love with their work, arranged, it seems, for all the beautiful clouds with their varying hues to pass in daily review over the head of the city to be born.

In all that appertains to physical excellence Almaville was made attractive, and somewhere, perhaps behind yon hills, the forces rested until man set his foot upon the soil and prepared to build. They so charged the air and all the environments with the spirit of the beautiful, that the men who later wrought in building the city found themselves the surprised and happy creators of a lovely habitation.

On an eminence crowning the center of the area whereon the city is planted, the State has builded its capitol, and from the tower thereof one can see the engaging network of streets, contemplate the splendid architecture of the buildings, and gaze upon the noble trees that boldly line the sidewalks, and thus testify that they are not afraid of civilization.

Even in the matter of climate Almaville is highly favored, it would seem. Her summers are not too hot nor her winters too cold, and many a fevered brow finds solace in her balmy breezes.

The war gods saw and admired her, and decreed that one of the famous battles of the Civil War should be fought within her environs, that their memory might ever be cherished here.

Philanthropy, it seems, singled out Almaville for special attention, granting unto her opportunities for learning that well might cause proud Athens to touch her crown to see that it was still there and had not been lifted by her modern rival.

A murky river runs through Almaville and a dark stream flows through the lives of all of us who dwell upon its banks. But yonder! yonder! is the ocean! Where?

THE AUTHOR

I

Occurrences That Puzzle

To the pagan yet remaining in man it would seem that yon railroad train plunging toward the Southland is somehow conscious of the fact that it is playing a part in events of tremendous import, for observe how it pierces the darkness with its one wild eye, cleaves the air with its steely front and causes wars and thunders to creep into the dreams of the people by whose homes it makes its midnight rush.

Well, this train now moving toward Almaville, queen city of the South, measured by the results that developed from that night's journey, is fully entitled to all its fretting and fuming, brag and bluster of steam and smoke, and to its wearisome jangle of clanging bell and shrieking whistle and rumbling wheel.

It was summer time. A Negro porter passing through a coach set apart for white passengers noted the fixedness with which a young woman with a pretty face and a pair of beautiful blue eyes was regarding him. Her head was inclined to one side, her hand so supporting her face that a prettily shaped ear peeped out from between her fingers. In the look of her eye there was a slight suggestion of immaturity, which, however, was contradicted by the firm outlines of her face. As the porter drew near her seat she significantly directed her look to a certain spot on the car floor, thence to the eyes of the porter.

Having in mind the well understood dictum of the white man of the South that the Negro man and the white woman are to be utterly oblivious of the existence of each other, this Negro porter was loth to believe that the young woman was trying surreptitiously to attract his attention, and he passed out of the coach hurriedly. In a short while he returned and again noted how intently the young woman regarded him. This time he observed that she had evidently been weeping and that there was a look of hopeless sorrow in her eyes. Again the young woman looked at him, then upon the floor and up at him once more. The porter looked down upon the spot indicated by her look, saw a note, stooped and picked it up. He returned to the coach or rather to the end of a coach, set apart for Negroes, took a rear seat and surveyed the car preparatory to reading the note which the young woman plainly indicated was for him.

"I don't want white girls passing me notes," thought the Negro, clutching the note tightly and continuing to glance about the coach in a half-frightened manner. He arose to hoist the window by which he sat, intending to utilize it to be rid of the note in case the occasion should demand it. His fears had begun to suggest to him that perhaps some white man had noticed his taking cognizance of the young woman's efforts to attract his attention.

As the Negro section of the coach was the forward section and next to the baggage car, any person coming from the section set apart for the whites would be to the back of the Negro passengers. The porter therefore changed his seat, going forward and taking a position where he would be facing any one coming from the coach for whites. He raised the window by which he sat and his eye wandered out into the darkness amid the sombre trees that went speeding along, and there arose to haunt him mental visions of a sea of angry white faces closing around some one dark face, perhaps guilty and perhaps innocent; and as he thought thereon he shuddered. He felt sorely tempted to toss the note out of the window unread, but remembering the pleading look on the face of the young woman he did not follow the promptings of his fear.

"In case of trouble, this crew in here couldn't help a fellow much," said the porter, moving his eyes about slowly again, taking note one by one of those in the section with him. There was the conductor, who though a white man, seemed always to prefer to sit in the section set apart for the Negroes. There was the newsboy, also white, taking up two seats with his wares.

"As well as they know me they would go with the other gang. A white man is a white man, and don't you forget it," mused the porter.

There were two male passengers sitting together, Negroes, one of whom was so light of complexion that he could easily have passed for white, while the other was of a dark brown hue.

"A fine looking fellow," thought the porter concerning the dark young man.

Across the aisle from the two young men mentioned, and a seat or so in advance of them, sat a young woman whose face was covered with a very thick veil. The perfect mould of her shoulders, the attractiveness of her wealth of black hair massed at the back of her head—these things were demanding, the porter noticed, many an admiring glance from the darker of the two young men.

The porter seemed about to forget his note in observing with what regularity the young man's eyes would wander off and straightway return to rest upon the beautiful form of the young woman, but an incident occurred that brought his mind back very forcibly to the note. The door from the section for the whites opened and two white men entered.

The porter's hand in which the note was held cautiously crept toward the open window, while he eyed the two white men whom he feared had come to accuse him of an attempted flirtation with a young white woman. One of the men reached behind to his hip pocket and the porter half arose in his seat, throwing up his hands in alarm, expecting a pistol to appear to cover him. The white man was simply drawing out a flask of whiskey to offer his companion a drink.

Ensal Ellwood, the dark young man, looking around to see if the parties who had entered had closed the door behind them (for the adjoining section was the white people's smoking apartment, and care had to be exercised to keep smoke and tobacco fumes out), saw the two white men about to take a drink. He arose quickly and advancing to the two men, said quietly, urbanely and yet with an air of firmness,

"Gentlemen, the law prescribes that this coach shall be used exclusively by Negro passengers and we must ask that you do not make our first-class apartment a drinking room for the whites."

The two men stared at Ensal and he looked them frankly in the face that they might see that in a dignified manner he would insist to the last upon the rights of the Negro passengers. The justness of Ensal's request, his unostentatious, manly bearing had the desired effect. The two men quietly turned about and left the car.

The porter who had been standing during this little scene now sat down, opened the note and read as follows:

> MR. PORTER
> When this train is within a fifteen minutes' run of
> Almaville please pass through this coach and so announce.
> Then stand on the platform leading from this coach to the
> coach in which the Negroes have their section.
> FROM THE GIRL THAT LOOKED AT YOU

The first part of this request the porter concluded to comply with, but he registered all sorts of vows to the effect that he would never be found waiting on any platform for any white girl. He murmured to himself.

"My young lady, you may sign yourself, 'From the girl that looked at you;' but with all due respect my signature is 'The boy that wasn't there.'"

Again he looked out of the window at the same sombre trees and into the gloom of their shadows, and he put his hand in his collar as though it was already too tight.

"No, my God!" he said softly. Tearing the note to shreds, he fed it to the winds, lowered the window and began to whistle.

When the train was in the designated distance of Almaville the porter entered the coach for whites in which sat the young woman who wrote the note. "Fifteen minutes and the train pulls into Almaville," he exclaimed, as he walked the aisle in an opposite direction to that desired by the young woman. She at once understood and saw that she must depend upon herself.

The fragile, beautiful creature arose and by holding to the ends of the various seats staggered to the door. She opened it and by tenacious clinging to the iron railings on the platform managed to pull herself across to the adjoining coach. Passing through the smoker for the white men she entered the Negro section. With a half stifled sob she threw herself into the lap of the Negro girl and nestled her face on her shoulder.

The young woman from the coach for the whites now tossed back the veil of the Negro girl and the two girls kissed, looking each other in the eyes, pledging in that kiss and in that look, the unswerving, eternal devotion of heart to heart whatever the future might bring. The young woman now slowly turned away and went toward the coach whence she came, assisted by the wondering conductor.

From large dark eyes whose great native beauty was heightened by that tender look of the soul that they harbored, the Negro girl stood watching her visitor depart. The grace of her form that was somewhat taller and somewhat larger than that of the average girl, stamped her as a creature that could be truthfully called sublimely beautiful, thought Ensal. Whatever complexion on general principles Ensal thought to be the most attractive, he was now ready to concede that the delicate light brown color of this girl could not be surpassed in beauty.

If, incredulous as to the accuracy of the estimate of her beauty forced upon one at the first glance, an effort was made to analyze that face and study its parts separately, each feature was seen to have a beauty all its own.

"So sweet and beautiful a face and so lovely a form could only have been handed to a soul of whom *they* are not even worthy," thought Ensal.

A sober look was in Ensal's eye and some kind of a mad gallop was in his heart. There was more than soberness in the blue eyes of Earl Bluefield, Ensal's companion. When Ensal looked around at his friend he was astonished at the terribly bitter look on his face.

The train emptied a number of its passengers and rushed on and on and on, as if fleeing from the results to be anticipated from its deposit of new and strange forces into the life of Almaville.

II

His Face Was Her Guide

T his is a rich man's war and a poor man's fight." Such is said to have been the character of the sentiment that was widespread in the ranks of the Confederate army during the late Civil War.

Be that as it may, it is very evident that the highest interest of the "poor whites" who bore the brunt of the fighting was to be conserved by the collapse rather than the triumph of the cause for which they fought with unsurpassed gallantry. For, with the downfall of the system of enforced labor, the work of the world became an open market, and the dignity of labor being restored, the "poor whites" had both a better opportunity and a more congenial atmosphere to begin their rise. Thus the stars in their courses fought for the "poor whites" in fighting bitterly against them.

At one time the Negroes of the cities of the South had almost a monopoly of the work of transferring passengers and baggage to and from the depots, but white men organized transfer companies, placed white agents on the incoming trains to solicit patronage, employed white men to drive the transfer wagons and thus largely wrested the business from the hands of the Negroes. But the Negroes would yet drive up to the station, hoping for some measure of success in the spirited contests that would arise in attempts to capture such gleanings as the advance agents of the transfer companies had left behind.

So, when the train on which we rode into Almaville poured its stream of passengers upon the platform of the car shed and they had ascended the steps to the depot platform, they were greeted with a series of shouts from the Negro hackmen and expressmen standing at the edge of the platform, the preponderance of the chances against them lending color to their cries.

Ensal Ellwood and Earl Bluefield boarded a street car, while the Negro girl who had occupied the coach with them, not knowing anything about the city, went in the direction of the clamoring hackmen, hoping that some one of them might tell her where she could find proper entertainment for the night. As she drew near, the line of hackmen bent forward, with hands outstretched for traveling bags, each man eyeing her intently as if hoping that the character of the look bestowed upon her might influence her choice. One man pulled off his hat, hoping to impress her with a mark of respect not exhibited by the others. The remainder of the hackmen quickly pulled off their hats, determined that no one should have the advantage. The young woman tossed back her veil that she might see the better.

A young man better dressed than the hackmen was standing behind them. The moment he caught sight of the young woman's astonishingly beautiful face he pushed through the crowd, walked rapidly to her side, gently took hold of her satchel, and said quietly, "You will go with me. I will see you properly cared for."

The young woman looked into his face and recoiled. His tone was respectful and there was nothing affronting in his look or demeanor, yet the young woman felt utterly repelled.

"That's right, lady. Don't go with him. Go with any of the rest of these men in preference to him," said a genial faced young man, slightly below medium height, rather corpulent and very dark.

The young woman looked in his direction and was favorably impressed with his open, frank expression.

"I'll trust myself to your care," said she, pulling away from the well dressed young man.

Leroy Crutcher, for such was his name, cast a look of malignant hatred at Bud Harper, the successful hackman and muttered something under his breath. He also scowled at the young woman whose utter disdain of him had cut him to the quick.

"I will get even with the pair of them, if it takes me the balance of my life," said Leroy Crutcher to the group of hackmen, after Bud Harper and the young woman had driven away.

The men looked at him in sullen, contemptuous silence, loathing and yet dreading him more than they did a serpent, for he conducted a house of ill-repute for the exclusive use of white men and Negro girls, and, being diligent in endeavoring to bring to his home any and all Negro girls to whom his white patrons might take a fancy, had great influence with this element of whites.

Noting the indisposition of the men to talk to him, and rightly interpreting their contemptuous silence, Crutcher drew from his pocket a wallet full of greenbacks. Taking out as many one dollar bills as there were hackmen, he threw them on the platform and said, "I am a gentleman, myself. Money talks these days. Help yourselves, gentlemen."

The men did not look at the money. Each one returned to his vehicle and journeyed to his humble home, leaving Crutcher alone upon the platform. If the hackmen had taken his money it would have served as proof to him that they were no better than he, that they were not in a business like his simply because they lacked his skill and finesse.

The action of the hackmen intensified his resentment at the treatment accorded him by Bud Harper and the young woman, and, meditating vengeance, he now walked toward his den of infamy where his mother had reigned in her day and where he was born of a white father.

The human race has not thus far even approached the point of constructing such habitations as would render mankind indifferent to rumblings underground, nor has society such secure foundation that it can think lightly of its lower elements.

In the long run the LeRoy Crutchers will be heard from. It is inevitable.

III

WHEREIN FORESTA FIRST APPEARS

When the young woman who had committed herself to Bud Harper's care awoke the next morning she saw standing near her a tall, slender, Negro girl, of a dark brown complexion.

"My name is Foresta," said the girl, showing the tips of her beautiful white teeth. Her lips were thin, her nose prettily chiseled, her skin smooth, her brow high, her head covered with an ample supply of jet black hair. "Excuse me, please," said Foresta, "but mama told me to tell you that breakfast would soon be ready."

Foresta having delivered her message, for which she was thanked, did not at once turn to leave. Her pretty brown eyes nestling under equally pretty eyebrows, looked lovingly into the stranger's face. Without saying more, however, Foresta left the room. A little later she brought the young woman's breakfast, clearing the center table to make room for it.

"We eat in the kitchen. It is mighty warm in there, though, in the summer time with fire in the stove. We thought we would do a little better by you than that," said Foresta apologetically. She sat down to keep the young woman's company while the latter was eating.

"That was Bud Harper that brought you here last night," said Foresta, unable to repress a smile over some pleasing thought that was passing through her mind.

The young woman looked up from her breakfast. "My!" she said, "Your eyes are pretty. They are such a lovely brown."

"I'll swap hair with you," said Foresta, feeling of her own hair and looking admiringly at the wealth of beautiful black hair on the young woman's head.

"You would cheat yourself. Your hair isn't as long as mine, but it is so black and lovely," said the young woman.

Looking at Foresta from head to foot, plainly but neatly dressed, the young woman remarked, "You are a pretty girl, Foresta—and a good girl," pausing between the former and the latter complimentary reference.

Foresta's kindly face lighted up with joy at the compliment. For some time she had felt, without knowing what it was that she felt, the need of a confidante—some one with a fellow-feeling to whom she could talk.

"Something funny happened once about Bud Harper and—"

"Yourself," said the young woman, with a sweet, knowing look.

"Yes," admitted Foresta with a light laugh, pleased that the young woman was entering so readily into the spirit of the recital. "Bud had a brother Dave that looked just like him," said Foresta. "Almost, I mean," she added, remembering that nobody was to be put on a level with Bud. "Poor Dave is dead now," she said in sad tones, looking the young woman fully in the face as if making a further study of her.

Satisfied with the result of the inspection, Foresta now said in a confidential tone: "Dave died in the penitentiary. He and a white man got in a fight. Dave killed him in self-defense. Dave could have come clear, but it wouldn't have done any good. He would have been lynched. His lawyers advised him to take a twenty years' sentence to satisfy the clamor, and said they were sure they could get him a pardon. All of Dave's friends thought it was better to take his chances with a good governor rather than a mob."

Foresta's eyes now filled with tears. "It did hurt poor Dave so to go to the penitentiary. He was such a good-hearted boy. He died there in about a year and a half. It may be he's better off." Foresta now paused an instant. Shaking off the spell of sadness she said, "But that's not what I started out to tell you."

"I know it isn't," said the young woman, smiling sadly.

"Don't be too sure you know what I have to tell," said Foresta, laughing. "It is really something funny."

"I am listening," said the young woman.

"One night Bud went to church with me. You know our church is called the 'high falutin' church,' and a good many of the poorer and plain people don't like to go there. Well, Bud isn't a highly educated boy and he doesn't like our church for anything. He likes the preacher all right. He will hardly ever go in and sit with me. He walks about out doors till church is out, then comes back home with me. You are tired listening to my foolishness, aren't you?" asked Foresta.

"Not at all. I am interested," said the young woman reassuringly.

"Well, Bud is a sort of a bashful boy. Dave was just the opposite. Dave was full of nerve. Bud kept a 'hemming and hawing' trying to, trying to er—"

"Well, just say that he was trying to," said the young woman, and the two laughed heartily.

"Dave kept after Bud to speak out, but Bud was afraid that he would spoil matters," resumed Foresta. "They rigged up a scheme to find out where I stood without Bud's risking too much. Now, remember, Bud and Dave looked just alike, almost. Many a time I have taken one for the other. When little they often got scolded and beaten for one another. Their father never could tell them apart. Bud came to church with me one night, and he and Dave agreed that Dave was to carry me home without my knowing it was Dave. Dave was to make out that he was Bud and make a dash of some sort to find out how Bud stood with me. On our way home Dave didn't talk much. That helped to fool me, because Bud and I have gone along not saying a word; only looking at each other now and then. But that night Dave, whom I was taking to be Bud, was unusually quiet. And I thought then that he was meditating something. When Dave got home with me, he stood between me and the gate and said, 'You must pay toll to get in.' I knew he was asking me to kiss him. 'If you don't let me by I will call mama,' I said, mostly for fun, for I knew that Bud thought mama was against him. You ought to have seen Dave stepping aside to let me in. I didn't say another word, but walked into the yard and upon the porch. I knocked. Mama came and unlocked the door and went back. 'Good night,' said I. But Dave wouldn't move. He was so afraid that he had spoiled things for Bud. I stood there and thought a while. It came to me that it might not be wise to treat Bud's first attempt to say what I was willing for him to say, too coolly. And yet I didn't want to appear too anxious. You know what I mean," said Foresta appealingly.

"I understand you, perfectly, though my time hasn't come yet," said the young woman.

"So I stood on the porch," continued Foresta, "looking away from Dave, thinking and thinking how I could save myself and not hurt Bud too much. Womanlike, I suppose, I decided to make a sacrifice of myself. I opened my door a little. Quick as a flash, but so he could plainly see what I was doing, I threw a kiss and darted in the house. Dave fairly flew to where Bud was waiting for him. Dave told Bud all about it and the two boys liked to have hugged each other to death. Dave having opened the way, Bud grew bolder very fast. After everything was understood between us and the time set, Bud told me all about the trick. And I boxed his ears for him. If you are here I want you to come to my and Bud's wedding."

Foresta now arose to go. Holding up a finger of warning, she said, "We haven't told the old folks yet."

IV

The Ways of A Seeker After Fame

This world of ours, thought of in comparison with man the individual, is so very, very large; its sons and daughters departed, now on hand and yet to come, form such an innumerable host; the ever-increasing needs of the living are so varied and urgent; the advance cry of the future bidding us to prepare for its coming is so insistent; the contest for supremacy, raging everywhere, must be fought out among so many souls of power—these accumulated considerations so operate that it is given unto but a few of those who come upon the earth to obtain a look of recognition from the universal eye; and fewer still are they who, by virtue of inherited capacity, proper bent, necessary environment and the happy conjunction of the deed and the hour, so labor as to move to admiration, sympathy or reverence the universal heart, an achievement, apart from which no man, however talented, may hope to sit among the earth's immortals.

The fact that enduring world prominence is an achievement rarely and with great difficulty attained operates upon different individuals in different ways. Some grow weary of the strenuous strife, give up the contest with a sigh and retire, as it were, to the shade of the trees and with more or less of yearning await the coming of the deeper shades of the evening eternal. Others, fully conscious that they have been entrusted with a world message, confront a mountain with as much courage as they do a sand dune, and press onward, whether the stars are in a guiding or a hiding mood.

Mrs. Arabelle Seabright, aspirant for world honors, sat in a rocking-chair in her room in the Domain Hotel, Almaville, the stopping place of the wealthiest and most aristocratic visitors. Her small well shaped hands were lying one upon the other, resting on the back of an open book which was in her lap, face downward. Slowly she rocked backward and forward, tapping first one foot and then the other upon the floor. It was very evident that she was thinking, but a glance at the face was all that was needed to tell one that this thinking was not due to irresolution or uncertainty of purpose.

Nothing was ever more plainly written upon the human countenance than that this woman knew her own mind and knew the course which she was to pursue. Her thinking now is with a view to making travel along the elected course as agreeable as possible. The door to her room opened and there entered a young man of medium height with delicate, almost feminine features. His face was covered with a full beard that was so black as to appear almost uncanny, and it seemed so much out of place on one so young, the wearer not being over twenty-five at most.

"You have come to say 'yes,' my boy," said Mrs. Seabright, rising to meet her son.

The young man had really come to say "no," but that firm, unyielding look in his mother's eyes halted him. Instead of the determined stand which he had resolved to take, in the presence of his mother's imperious will, all he could say was, "Mother, I—I—I—had hoped otherwise."

His mother shook her head and looked him directly in the eyes. She wanted him to see the determination written in her own eyes.

He saw and collapsed. "I will go, mother," said he. "Be seated, mother," he requested.

Mrs. Seabright, directing a look of inquiry at her son, sat down.

He now dropped on his knees and rested his head upon her lap. "Mother, say to me the prayer that you taught me in my childhood—days when you were not this way. Lead me back there once more, for something within tells me that life is never more to be life to me."

Mrs. Seabright did not at all relish the sentimental turn of her son's mind, but she began in as tender tones as she could summon:

"Now I lay me down to sleep."

"Now I lay me down to sleep," repeated the young man.

"I pray the Lord my soul to keep," his mother continued.

"I pray the Lord my soul to keep," said he.

"If I should die before I wake," the mother said.

"If I should die before I wake," said the son.

"I pray the Lord my soul to take," concluded the mother.

"I pray the Lord my soul to take," the son repeated lingeringly.

"Mother, truly I am laying me down to sleep. I am putting my life, my soul away. When I awake from this sleep into which your influence as a mother has lulled me, I shall awake to look into the face of my Creator."

The young man now arose and turning upon his mother, he said out of a burning heart: "Oh, mother! May your soul meet God. As I leave you, let me tell you it takes that to reach your case!"

"You are not the son of your mother," quietly said she.

The young man now rushed from the room to get out of the presence of one who, though his mother, possessed nothing in common with his own soul. In spite of the manner of his leaving, Mrs. Seabright knew full well that he would perform unto the utmost all that she had exacted of him.

Mrs. Seabright resumed her seat and rocked to and fro complacently for a few moments. Arising, she went to a rolling door, leading to a room adjoining her own. There, coiled upon the bed, lay the beautiful young woman whom we first saw endeavoring to attract the attention of the Negro porter to a note. Her hair lay wildly about her pretty brow, there were tear stains upon her cheeks and her eyelids were closed. A fear seized Mrs. Seabright that her daughter might be dead. Rushing to the bedside, she called, "Eunice! Eunice!"

The young woman opened her blue eyes into her mother's, sat up and began to sob violently. The mother put her arms around the young woman, but the latter jumped from the bed and pulled herself away.

"Now, Eunice, don't act in that way. You can't see how bright a future I have mapped out for you. If you only knew!"

The young woman shook her head in rejection of all that the mother might offer.

"I will let you see her as often as you choose, Eunice!"

"Will you?" almost shrieked the young woman, stamping her foot upon the floor, a wild look of joy leaping into her eye.

"If you will let me plan your future I will not interfere with your relations with her whatever."

"Mother, mother," said the young woman rushing to Mrs. Seabright and throwing her arms about her neck. Between sobs she said, "Mother, mother, do with me what you will, just so you allow me to be with her when I choose. Oh, mother, how I wish you were now what you were before the adder bit you."

Mrs. Seabright, unmoved by this outburst, gently released herself from her daughter's grasp and returned to her rocking chair.

"I shall yet harness to my cause the two forces that are the most potent yet revealed in shaping the course of human society," said she. Going to her window, she looked out into the skies and whispered in confidence to the stars:

"I shall be remembered as long as you shall shine."

Hard by the house of fame sits the home of infamy. Those who offer too strange a price for the former are given the latter.

V

RATHER LATE IN LIFE TO BE STILL NAMELESS

On the morrow following our ride into Almaville on the passenger train, toward twilight Ensal Ellwood sat upon the front porch of his pretty little home, a sober look in his firm, kindly eyes. By his side sat his aged mother, whose sweet dark face of regular features was crowned with hair that was now white from the combined efforts of time and sorrow. Her usually placid countenance wore a look of positive alarm. She had just been a listener to a conversation between her son and Gus Martin.

Gus Martin was a Negro of brownish hue, whose high cheek bones, keen eyes, coarse black hair and erect carriage told plainly of the Indian blood in his veins. Gus was a great admirer of both Ensal and Earl Bluefield and the three had gone to the Spanish-American war together, Ensal, who was a minister, as chaplain, Gus and Earl as soldiers. These three were present at the battle of San Juan Hill, and Gus, who was himself notoriously brave, scarcely knew which to admire the more, Ensal's searching words that inspired the men for that world-famous dash or Earl's enthusiastic, infectious daring on the actual scene of conflict.

Gus could read and write in a fashion, but was by no means as well educated as either Ensal or Earl, his friends, and consequently looked to them largely for guidance.

Earl had made efforts to secure promotion upon the record of his services in battle, but had failed, because, according to common opinion, of the disinclination of the South to have Negro officers in the army. Gus Martin took Earl's failure to secure promotion more to heart than did Earl himself. Gus was a follower but not a member of the church of which Ensal was pastor, and he had come to pour forth his sentiments to Ensal anent the failure of his friend Earl to be rewarded. Ordinarily the well-known tractability of the Negro seemed uppermost in him, but this evening all of his Indian hot blood seemed to come to the fore. His voice was husky with passion and his black eyes flashed defiance. He questioned the existence of God, and, begging pardon, asserted that the Gospel was the Negro's greatest curse in that it unmanned the race.

As for the United States government, he said, "The flag aint any more to me than any other dirty rag. I fit fur it. My blood run out o' three holes on the groun' to keep it floatin', and whut will it do fur me? Now jes' tell me whut?"

Ensal endeavored to show that the spirit of the national government was very correct and that the lesser governments within the government caused the weakness. He held that in the course of time the national government would mould the inner circles of government to its way of thinking.

"Excuse me, Elder; but that kind o' talk makes me sick. You are a good Christian man, I really think; but like most cullud people you are too jam full o' patience an' hope. I'll be blessed if I don't b'lieve Job was a cullud man. I ganny, I got Indian blood in me and if they pester this kid they are goin' to hear sump'in' drap."

It was to this conversation that Ensal's mother had listened with disturbed feelings. She believed firmly in God and her only remedies for all the ills of earth were prayer and time. Therefore it ruffled her beyond measure to have a new spirit appearing in the race.

"Ensal, there isn't any good in that Gus Martin," said she, in earnest, tremulous tones, nodding her head in the direction of the departing Gus. "I may be dead, my son, but you will see that the devil will be to pay this side of hearing the last of him," she continued.

Ensal did not look in his mother's direction, but stole one of her thin worn hands and placed it between his own. He felt that his mother's prediction with regard to Gus Martin was only too likely to be fulfilled.

At this juncture two young women appeared at the gate and entered. They were Foresta Crump and the young woman whom we saw taken to Foresta's home on the preceding evening. Being informed that the stranger desired a conference with him, Ensal retired to his study, lighted the room and invited her to enter. Foresta remained upon the porch and entertained Mrs. Ellwood, with whom she was a favorite, because of her peculiarly lovable disposition and her attention to the aged.

When the young woman was seated, Ensal took a seat and looked in her direction, saying, "Consider me at your service, please." There was an air of unnatural calm about the young woman. She now removed her hat from her head and Ensal noted that her hair was so arranged as to allow her face to fully stand as nature gave it to her, unrelieved. He also noticed that her attire was of a simple order throughout, though good taste and ample means were needed to produce the results attained by her dress. The light of the train that had told Ensal that she was beautiful, had only hinted at the attractiveness of form and feature as disclosed upon closer inspection.

The young woman seemed in no haste to begin the conversation about the matter that had brought her there, and chatted with Ensal in a desultory manner. She was studying Ensal and was affording him an opportunity to study her. Ensal had been so highly spoken of to her, and in her present state of mind she was so anxious to meet such a person as he was represented to be that she was calling into requisition all the powers of intuition of which her soul was capable.

At length an instant of quiet on the part of his visitor told Ensal that she was now to approach the matter that had given rise to her call.

"Mr. Ellwood," began the young woman, "it sometimes happens in the course of human life that we are compelled to appeal to the faith that people have in us. Life is more or less a matter of faith anyway, but ordinarily there is some sort of buttress for our faith in surrounding circumstances. Tonight, I bring not one shred of circumstance, not one bit of history from my past life, and yet I appeal to you for faith in me, absolute unquestioning faith."

Her earnest tones and the pleading look in her beautiful eyes and the trembling of her form burned those words into Ensal's memory:

"I have the necessary faith," said Ensal, earnestly and quietly.

"I have come to Almaville to begin life anew. This has become necessary through no act of my own. This is all I care to say on that point, and I do not promise to ever break the seal of silence with regard to the past. I wish to find a name and I wish to find friends among the really good people of Almaville, the good Negroes. I am lately from New York and I am your friend. With these facts and only these, can you name me, can you place me in touch with your friends?" said the young woman.

"Name you?" enquired Ensal.

"Name me as I was named when a babe. The name that I have borne shall know me no more," replied the young woman.

As pastor of a Negro church at a period when almost the entire leadership of the race was centered in that functionary, Ensal was accustomed to having all sorts of matters placed before him, but the present requirement was rather unique in all of his experience as a pastor. He arose from the chair and began to walk slowly to and fro across the room, having asked the indulgence of the young woman for resorting to his favorite method of procedure when engaged in serious reflection. If we must tell the truth of this young man, the question which he was debating most was somewhat at variance with those raised by her requests.

Ensal had come to the conclusion many years previous that marriage was not for him, and hitherto woman had had no entrance into the inner chambers of his thoughts. And this beautiful stranger, nameless and homeless, had almost wrested the door of his heart from its hinges, without even an attempt thereat, and the young man was trying to grapple with the new experiences born into his consciousness.

Finding that he lost ground by trying to reason with his heart, Ensal let the wilful member alone and engaged in the more honest task of naming his visitor. Turning toward the young woman, glad that he had something to say, so that he might look into her beautiful face again, he said:

"I name you Tiara."

Ensal assigned the name with so much warmth that Tiara dropped her eyes, and the faintest symptoms of a smile appeared on her face.

"You have forgotten the latter part of my name," she remarked.

Ensal resumed his walking. Happening to look up at the top of his desk he caught sight of a sculptured bust of Frederick Douglass. He paused, and pointing to the bust, said:

"Behold one whose distinctive mission in the world was to serve as a harbinger for his race! A star of the first magnitude, he rose in the night of American slavery, attracted the admiring gaze of the civilized world, and so thrilled the hearts of men that they broke the chains of all his kind in the hope of further enriching the firmament of lofty human endeavor with stars like unto him. I name you Tiara Douglass."

Ensal turned to Tiara, his face enkindled with enthusiasm. He stepped back, threw up his hands, and plainly showed in his eyes the unbounded surprise which he felt at the way in which Tiara had received his suggestion for a surname. There Tiara sat, tears evidently long pent-up freely flowing and her body shaking with, emotion.

To find a word expressive of Ensal's bewildered state of mind is a problem to be handed over to the type of man engaged in the search for perpetual motion and does not come within the purview of a simple author. Man who tames the lion, harnesses the winds, makes a whimperer of steam and cowers the lightning—this same vainglorious, triumphant man is simply helpless in the presence of a woman's tears! Ensal stole quietly to his seat and sat there in a state of amazement.

Tiara looked up through her tears, a few pretty locks of hair having now fallen in beautiful disorder across her brow.

"Mr. Ellwood, I cannot endure the name Douglass and I cannot explain," said she.

Ensal now perceived that this name Douglass had somehow made the girl's thoughts touch upon the very core of her life's troubles.

"Douglass, Douglass, Douglass; no not Douglass," repeated Tiara in passionate tones, evidently trying to accept the name for Ensal's sake and yet being unable to do so.

"Your name shall be Tiara Merlow," said Ensal.

"Merlow—Merlow. I like that," said Tiara.

"I will arrange for you to stop with Mrs. Helen Crawford," said Ensal.

"Thank you," said Tiara.

Tiara now arose to go, but it was evident that there was something yet unspoken. As she reached the door of the room she turned around and looked Ensal directly in the face. Ensal had been following her to the door, and the two now stood near each other.

"She is just tall and large enough to be grand in appearance, which, coupled with her beauty of face and symmetry of form, make her fit to set a new standard of loveliness in woman," mentally observed Ensal.

"Mr. Ellwood," said Tiara, "I perceive that you are an admirer of Frederick Douglass. Do you approve of his marriage to a white woman?"

Ensal was about to answer, when something in Tiara's look told him that he was somehow about to pass final judgment upon himself. He looked at Tiara to see if he could glean from her countenance a hint of her leaning, but her countenance was purposely a blank. He now tried to recall the tone in which she asked the question, but as he remembered it, that, too, was noncommittal. He was not seeking to divine Tiara's opinion with a view to shaping his own accordingly. If it was apparent that he and she agreed, he was of course ready to answer. If they were to differ, he preferred to postpone answering until such a time as he might be able to accompany his answer with his reason for the same.

Ensal now said smilingly, "Practice suspension of judgment in my case. In some way I may let you know my views on the matter later on."

"All right," said Tiara, slowly turning to leave.

It was evident to Ensal that further progress in her favor was largely contingent upon his answer, and the marriage of Frederick Douglass to a white woman became an exceedingly live question with him. He accompanied Tiara and Foresta home and the moonlight and starlight never before appeared so glorious to him or nature so benign.

After all the heart makes its world.

VI

Friendly Enemies

It has always been a mooted question with Ensal as to whether he did or did not sleep the night of Tiara's call at his residence. But he has ever stood ready to take oath or affirmation that, whether waking or sleeping, Tiara was constantly in his thoughts that night. And when turning his face toward the window the following morning he saw streaks of golden sunshine stretched across the floor, and realized that there was a nameless something within him which that sunlight could not match, he knew that the crisis in his life had come.

After a frugal meal with his mother, and the planting of a kiss of unusual warmth upon her cheek, Ensal stepped forth for his day's duties. As he went out of his gate he noticed a white man across the street acting as though he was sketching his (Ensal's) home. Feeling that he was warranted in having as much interest in the man as the man seemed to have in that which pertained to him, Ensal walked somewhat obliquely across the street, coming near enough to the man to receive an explanation, if the man desired to give one, or, at any rate, near enough to have a good view of the sketch taken.

The white man took advantage of the opportunity to get a full look at Ensal, who felt a little uneasiness at the intense interest which the man's whole countenance showed that he had in him. The man's eyes had an earnest, pained expression. His cheeks were hollow and seemed to indicate that he was just going into or emerging from a hard spell of sickness. His hat was a faded brown derby and his suit of clothes was of a tough, coarse fibre and much worn. Standing by him on the sidewalk was what appeared to be a much battered drummer's case to which the man's eye would revert oftener than the utmost caution would seem to have rendered necessary. Ensal passed on, but somehow this strange white man came into his mind and demanded a share in the thoughts which would otherwise have gone undividedly to Tiara.

Ensal called at the home of Mrs. Crawford and made it possible for Tiara to arrange for a home with her, an alliance which would at once afford Tiara an entrance into the social life of the best Negro circles.

This much accomplished, Ensal started in the direction of the Crump's to apprise Tiara of the arrangements.

"Why so much haste?"

Ensal turned and looked into the face of his friend, Earl Bluefield.

"Was I walking fast?" asked Ensal.

"Fast!" exclaimed Earl. "If you can induce the saints in your church to give the devil half as much trouble to catch them as you have given me, why they will be saved all right. Really a person who didn't know would have thought that your mother-in-law had died and that you were hurrying to make arrangements for her funeral," said Earl.

"By the way," said Ensal, "I am glad that I met you. A-a friend of mine from New York, a Miss Merlow, Tiara Merlow, is in the city. I wish you to pay her a call with me tomorrow evening. May I make the engagement?"

Earl dropped his head in meditation. His brain was exceedingly active. Beneath this apparently simple proposal of Ensal's lay hidden many possibilities.

Ensal and Earl represented two types in the Negro race, the conservative and the radical. They both stood for the ultimate recognition of the rights of the Negro as an American citizen, but their methods were opposite. They intuitively assumed, it seemed, opposite sides on every question that arose pertaining to the race, and championed their respective sides with much warmth and vigor. Yet they remained friends, were great admirers of each other, and lived each in the hope of converting the other to his way of thinking.

On the question of racial connection Ensal was really proud of the fact that he was a Negro, and felt that had he been entrusted with the determining of his racial affinity he would have chosen membership in the Negro race. Earl accepted the fact of his connection with the Negro race as a matter of course, had no desire to alter the relationship, and felt neither dejection nor elation on account thereof.

Ensal felt that the acceptance of slavery on the part of the Negro in preference to extermination was evidence of adaptability to conditions that assured the presence of the Negro on the earth in the final wind up of things, in full possession of all the advantages that time and progress promise. Earl rather admired the Indian and felt that the dead Indian refusing to be enslaved was a richer heritage to the world than the yielding and thriving Negro.

Ensal held that the course of the Negro during the Civil War in caring for the wives and children of the men fighting for their enslavement was a tribute to their humanity and would prove an invaluable asset in all future reckonings. While thoroughly approving of the Negro's protection of the women and children of the whites from violence, Earl was sorry that the thousand torches which Grady said would have disbanded the Southern armies were not lighted. Ensal deprecated all talk and thought of the sword as the final arbiter of the troubles between the races. Earl had his dreams—and his plans as well.

The procuring of the full recognition of the rights of the Negro was such a passion with Ensal that Earl relied upon it to finally bring him from the ranks of the conservatives to the radicals. Earl was fully convinced within himself that all of Ensal's hopes of a satisfactory, peaceful adjustment of matters were to be dashed to the ground, and knowing how thoroughly Ensal's soul was committed to the advancement of the race, he really expected Ensal to develop into the leader of the radicals. But this looming into view of a young woman, a friend of Ensal's, was liable, Earl thought, to complicate matters.

Earl had all along rejoiced in Ensal's determination to remain unmarried, fearing that family life might add to his conservatism. This accounts for the fact that Ensal's simple invitation to call on a Miss Tiara Merlow on the following evening so deeply affected Earl.

"Yes, yes, I'll go," said Earl slowly, almost as much to himself as to Ensal.

Ensal knew Earl so well that he could have told him the character of his (Earl's) thoughts.

On the following evening as Ensal and Earl sat in the parlor of the Crawford's chatting, Tiara parted the curtains shutting off an adjoining room, and stepped in. Her hair was arranged in two rich black braids tied up so as to extend only to her shoulders. The hair on the front part of her head was allowed to come forward, but not enough to forbid glimpses of a well rounded, beautiful forehead. As she stood there, symmetrical in form, just large and tall enough to be commanding in appearance, Ensal again inwardly declared that she was the most beautiful woman he had ever seen, heard of or dreamed about. Her eyes would have made a face of less regular features appear beautiful. As for Tiara, they made her beauty simply dazzling.

When Earl's wits, swept away by Tiara's beauty, slowly returned, it dawned upon him to his great astonishment that he was face to face with the young woman who had ridden into Almaville with Ensal and himself.

"If she was Ensal's friend, why did he not make himself known to her on the train?" asked Earl of himself. But this query was soon dislodged from his mind by one of far more interest to him, to wit: "Is it not likely that I may utilize this young woman as a means of bringing to me a second glimpse of that girl that paid us a visit from the coach for whites?"

Earl was introduced in due form and joined in the conversation now and then; but it was evident to Ensal that he was, for some cause, ill at ease. Tiara and Ensal, however, enjoyed the evening, each intently weighing the remarks of the other.

They say that Cupid is blind. This may be true of him at some stage of the proceedings, but when he is looking for a spot at which to let fly an arrow, he could play schoolmaster to Argus, of the many eyes.

Ensal and Earl departed, Ensal going home to live the evening over through the night, while Earl called upon Leroy Crutcher and engaged him to use Tiara Merlow as a clue to trace the unknown young woman.

"Is this honorable, this forming an alliance with Leroy Crutcher, this placing of a surveillance, as it were, on the movements of my friend's friend?"

These questions came to Earl more than once that night and the answer of the hot blood of his soul was: "Conditions have made me an outlaw among my kind. Rubbish aside, am I not as much of an Anglo-Saxon as any of them? Does not my soul respond to those things and those things only to which their souls respond? He that is without the law shall be judged without the law."

Judged! That is a solemn and sometimes an awful affair with nature.

VII

Officers Of The Law

H old on, there!" said one of a group of white boys on their way to school. The command was addressed to a Negro lad fourteen years of age. "Where are you going?" asked the self-appointed spokesman of the white boys. The Negro lad looked sullenly at the white boy.

"No need of clouding up; you can't rain," said the white boy. "Don't you know the law? The school board said for you niggers to get to school a half hour before we white children. What do you mean by hanging around and going to school on our time?"

"It is none of your business," said the Negro.

"I guess you had better skip, Mr. Coon," said the white boy. The group now sat down on the curbing, while the Negro walked away. The white boys gathered stones preparatory for battle.

The race problem had at last reached the childhood of the two races. In former days the children of the whites and the Negroes had played together, and ties of friendship were formed that often survived the changes of later years when one playmate became a master and his fellow became his servant. But that friendly commingling of other days was practically all gone now, and clashes between the white and Negro children became so frequent that the school authorities had decreed separate hours for the opening and closing of the schools of the two races, so as to lessen the friction as much as possible.

"Fly, you black face nigger, you," shouted a white boy.

"My face ain't near as black as your heart," rejoined the Negro, adroitly dodging the stones thrown by the white boys. The Negro threw his books to the sidewalk and soon had a handful of missiles. The rock battle was now on in earnest, the white boys feeling sure that their superior numbers would soon put the lone warrior to flight. The Negro entered into the battle with his whole soul, and was vigorous and alert. It was his idea that the injuring of one or two of his opponents would bring the battle to a close. A policeman rounded a corner leading to the street in which the rock battle was raging. The Negro's back was to the policeman, while the other boys were facing him. They dropped their stones and assumed a pacific and frightened attitude in time to impress the policeman that they were being needlessly assaulted by the Negro.

The Negro who did not see the policeman, ascribed the capitulation of his opponents to his own vigorous campaign, and now picked up his books, a look of exultation on his face. When he turned he found himself in the arms of the policeman. One of the boys, it developed, had been slightly bruised by one of the Negro's rocks. The Negro was put under arrest and locked up in the station house for the night.

The next morning as Tiara was perusing the paper, she noticed that a Negro boy, Henry Crump, had been arrested on a charge of assault and battery.

"Henry Crump—Henry Crump—Crump—Crump! That name is familiar to me," said Tiara, laying aside the paper to see if she could recall why the name sounded so familiarly to her. "I have it," said she, springing to her feet. "Why, I stayed with the Crumps the first night that I was in Almaville. And it is their little Henry in trouble. I'll help the little fellow out," said she.

Tiara observed that little Henry's case was set for ten o'clock that morning and it was then nine. She dispatched a note to Ensal, who immediately responded in person to accompany her to the place of the trial.

"This," said Ensal, "is but a symptom of a growing disease. In the days before the war the young master and the Negro boys played together and there was undoubtedly a strong tie of personal friendship between the slaveholding class and the Negroes on their plantation. But all is changed now. Rarely do you find white and Negro children playing together, and the feeling of estrangement grows apace with the years."

"What is pending?" earnestly asked Tiara, turning her large, anxious eyes on Ensal.

"Heaven alone knows," replied Ensal. "Just think! In order to have peace here between the children of the two races, the school authorities provide that there shall be a difference of an half hour between the respective hours of going to and coming from school," continued Ensal.

They were soon at the police station. Climbing the flight of stairs they entered a room crowded with Negroes from the lower stratum. The great majority of the women, it could be seen, had made some effort at respectability in attire. Some of the occupants of the room were there as witnesses in cases, others because of interest in parties to be tried, while the majority were there to pass judgment on the judge and learn as best they might the ways of the court and the law. Here and there was a sprinkling of respectable people who had by means of some mischance been caught in the drift.

One by one parties charged with offenses were called forward, fined and ordered released or passed back. At length the case of Henry Crump was called, and he came forward at a rather brisk pace, looking confidently at his mother and Foresta who had come prepared to lift him out of his trouble. On the same seat with Foresta and her mother sat Tiara and Ensal and their presence somehow gave added assurance to Henry.

Henry made his statements, the witnesses were examined and in the monotone with which the police judge went through with all of the cases, he said, "Fined twenty dollars and costs."

Foresta half arose, shocked at the amount, and Mrs. Crump crouched back in her seat in despair. Foresta had in her hand a crisp ten dollar bill which the family had raised, not dreaming that the fine would go above that amount.

"Pass him back," said the judge. Henry cast an inquiring look at Foresta and his mother. Tears were in Foresta's eyes and Henry knew that they were helpless. It simply meant that he was to have a pick on his leg and work the streets of Almaville. He dropped his head disconsolately, nervously fumbled his hat, and tears appeared in his eyes. The sting went deep into his boyish soul as he walked away.

"Wait a minute!" rang out Tiara's voice, and going up to the judge's desk, she put down a fifty-dollar-bill, saying, "Take the amount of the fine and costs out of this."

The judge looked up somewhat surprised. Tiara's act, born purely out of sympathy for the youthfulness of Henry and of sentimental regard for the first family that harbored her in Almaville, was totally misunderstood by the court officials. They fancied they scented a race contest in the matter and felt that Tiara was simply trying to show that it was all right for a Negro boy to stand up against white boys. They now decided to punish Henry to the limit of the law.

"Release the prisoner," said the judge.

Henry was released and Foresta and her frail looking mother rushed to Tiara to thank her. While they were doing this the deputy sheriff stepped up and rearrested Henry.

"Pardon me," said Ensal, interrupting the felicitations of the ladies. "We are not through yet. I see they are taking the boy over to the County Court."

"That isn't right," cried Foresta, as she followed the group.

The Criminal Court was then in session, and Henry's case was not long in being called. The deputy sheriff was seen to whisper a few words aside to the judge. The jury brought in a verdict of guilty and the judge assessed his punishment at ten months on the county farm.

Henry was now placed on the bench, where sat the row of convicted prisoners awaiting the pleasure of the sheriff, whose duty it was to deliver them to the places assigned them. As the boy took his seat on this bench to await the issue of other trials, when the sheriff would carry all the prisoners over together, there began to crowd to his mind all that he knew of Negroes on the county farm. He had heard of the indecent manner of whipping Negro women practiced out there. He saw one woman whose eye had been knocked out by an overseer. He had seen a petition emanating from the colored people containing sworn allegations setting forth a multitude of horrors.

Henry remembered having seen one boy return whose foot was frost-bitten and had to be amputated as the result of exposure at the farm. It was summer now, but ten months would carry him fully through the winter at the farm. The thoughts of a stay there was too much for him. Arising quickly he sprang up into the court house window. An officer rushed toward him to intercept him, but it was too late. Out of the window he jumped, dropping to the pavement below. He dashed out of the side gate of the court house yard and ran southward across the square, in the center of which the court house stood. Coming to the street which led to the bridge over the river that intersected the city, he turned eastward and started across the bridge with all the speed at his command.

The court officials were now in hot pursuit of the fleeing lad, one officer seizing a buggy, another jumping upon a street car and ordering the motorman to proceed at his utmost speed.

Henry had almost covered the full length of the bridge when the cry of the officers, caught up from one to another, had about come up with him. When he had all but reached the farther end of the bridge, in order to avoid an officer whom he saw standing awaiting him with a drawn pistol, he leaped over the railing and dropped about twenty feet, striking the embankment reared up for a resting place for the end of the bridge.

This officer of the law saw Henry leap and ran to the steps which were not far from the spot whence he had jumped. The officer reached the steps in time to see Henry sliding toward the water's edge. The officer began running down the steps, shooting as he ran. The people on the bridge crowded to the side over which Henry had leaped and witnessed the race between Henry and the shooting officer. Henry fell and it was thought that he was hit, but he arose and continued his running. He turned under the bridge and ran along parallel with the waters of the river. After passing fully under the bridge, Henry plunged into the stream and ran somewhat diagonally toward the center of the river until he was up to his neck in water.

"Move a step further out and I will kill you," said a bareheaded officer, who had at last reached the river bank, brandishing his pistol as he spoke.

By this time hundreds, perhaps a thousand or so, of people had gathered on the bridge. Henry stood in the water tossing his arms up and down. He feared to come ashore and was equally afraid to try to swim further out, feeling that he would be killed in any event. Some one on the bridge lifted a revolver to the railing, leveled it at Henry's head and fired.

"Shame! Shame! Shame!" was the word passed from lip to lip, as the noise of the shot was heard. Henry threw up his hands and fell, his arms upstretched above his head as he disappeared beneath the surface of the water. No one of the thousands stirred. In breathless silence they watched the spot where the lad had sunk out of sight. Some felt that Henry had simply dived and in due time would rise. Second after second passed, on the brief moments of time flew, while the eager eyes of the multitude were fastened on the murky waters of the river. Henry did not rise. He was dead. When it was known that life must be extinct, officers of the law rowed out to where he was last seen and fished his body out.

Ensal who had followed the chase now returned to the court house. Tiara, Foresta and Foresta's mother had heard the shooting and formed an awe-struck group, fearing that something had happened and yet hoping against hope. Ensal's sad countenance told them that their worst fears were realized.

"Henry is dead, mama," moaned Foresta, as she threw her arms about her frail mama's neck. "He is dead, mama; let's go home," wailed Foresta again.

Ensal and Tiara returned to Mrs. Crawford's.

VIII

A Messenger That Hesitates

Mrs. Crump sat in her room, her elbows propped up on her knees and her cheeks resting on her hands. The death of Henry, her only boy, was indeed a severe blow to her, but at this particular moment she was bearing up well under it, reserving her strength by a supreme effort of her will to the end that she might comfort her husband when he became aware of the tragedy.

Foresta had gone for her father with the understanding that she was not to tell him what had occurred, but was to allow her mother to break the news to him upon his arrival home.

Every step that Foresta took on her sorrowful journey was accompanied by a rain of tears. As she drew near the place where her father was at work, she stopped and tried to remove all traces of sorrow. She wiped and wiped her eyes, but the tears persisted in flowing. Her father was at work in a quarry as a rock breaker.

The city was using small stones as a sort of pavement for the streets, and aged Negro men were given the work of breaking rocks into fragments to be used in that way. The occupation was not an ideal one, as employment was of a fluctuating character, and the sitting on the ground, often damp, was not conducive to health. The amount earned in proportion to the labor performed was very small. But aged men unable to move about very much found this to be about all that they could do. So, the rock pile grew to be the accepted goal of all the Negro men who wore themselves out in other service without laying aside a competence or establishing themselves permanently in the good graces of their employees.

There were many who did thus establish themselves, and Ford Crump would have been such a one but for the following chain of circumstances, to which account you may give heed while waiting on Foresta to feel self-possessed enough to approach her father.

Soon after the Civil War Mr. Arthur Daleman came to Almaville and entered business. Ford Crump, Foresta's father, then a young man, was his first Negro employee. The business grew until Mr. Daleman was rightly classed as a very rich man.

For several years after Mr. Arthur Daleman's marriage, no children had come to bless their home. Early one morning, as Mr. Daleman was crossing the bridge, he saw a young white girl acting rather suspiciously, peering up and down the bridge. Drawing near, he found that she had an infant wrapped in a bundle. Fully believing that it was the intention of the girl to drown the babe, he asked that she give him the child. This the young woman very gladly did. As the child grew, Mrs. Daleman's heart warmed to it and after several years of anxious thought and observation of the child the couple decided to adopt it as their son. Within a year after this was done a beautiful little girl, whom they called Alene, was born to them.

When Mr. Daleman grew wealthy, he decided to travel through the North and induce capital to invest in the South. He felt that the commercial tie between the sections would be of the greatest possible value and it was said of him that he brought more outside capital into the South than any other one man. He turned his business over to his adopted son, Arthur Daleman, Jr.

Arthur Daleman, Jr., did not like Negroes, and though Ford Crump had been with the business from its infancy, his presence was not desired by the new manager. When Ford Crump got so that he was not as active as was desired, he was summarily dismissed and his place given to a young white man. Arthur Daleman, Sr., whose interests were now immense, never came near the store, and, as a consequence, did not know the fate that had overtaken his faithful employee.

Ford Crump did not appeal to Mr. Daleman, Sr., in the matter, partly through pride and partly because he could not bear the irritating tone of the younger Daleman, which was in such striking contrast to the kindly manner of the elder Daleman. He had saved his earnings and bought a little home, and he was now willing to take his chances in the world even at his advanced age. It was thus that he found his way to the rock pile.

We now return to our messenger. Foresta sees that she is not going to be able to appear before her father free from signs of sorrow, and she decides on another course. Picking up a stone she rubbed it violently on the back of her hand, tearing the skin and causing blood to flow. She now hurried to the spot where her father sat, and said,

"Papa, mama wants you!"

The tone of Foresta's voice caused her father to look up quickly and anxiously.

"What are you crying about, my dear?" asked Mr. Crump.

Foresta made no reply, but held out her hand so that her father could see it.

"Poor thing; how did you hurt it?" he asked.

"Don't think about that. Mama wants you. Come on!" said Foresta, averting her face.

The father and daughter trudged along home, the father trying to say comforting things to Foresta and she weeping the more bitterly the while. At length it occurred to Mr. Crump that Foresta was more deeply touched than would have been the case if her trouble had been merely that of a bruised hand. Stopping, he said,

"Say, now, Foresta, is your mama hurt?"

"O no, papa! Mama is not hurt. Come on!"

"Is Henry—"

Foresta perceived the coming question, and ran to avoid it. They were now near home. Foresta rushed in and threw her arms around her mother. Hearing her father's footsteps, she ran into the kitchen, leaving her mother to break the news.

"Ford, we haven't any little Henry now!" said Mrs. Crump in sad, soothing tones.

Ford Crump whirled away from his wife and walked rapidly out of the room through the kitchen into the back yard. Little Henry's chief task was attending to the chickens, and Mr. Crump stood at the fence running across the yard to form an enclosure for the fowl.

"Chicks, your best friend is gone," said he.

"My head! my head!" he cried.

Foresta and her mother heard his cry and reached him just in time to break the force of the fall, but not in time to prevent his answering the final summons.

IX

A Plotter Is He

Neighbors came and took charge of the body of Ford Crump. The body of Henry was brought home and received the same kindly attention. Foresta and her mother now set forth to make arrangements for the burial. The undertakers asked for a lien on their place as a guarantee of the payment of the debt.

Upon investigation it transpired that the place had been purchased by Arthur Daleman, Sr., in his own name. Mr. Crump had paid him in full for the place but the proper transfer had never been made. Mr. Daleman was not in the city and Arthur Daleman, Jr., refused to have anything to do with the matter. He also intimated that unless Mrs. Crump could show a clear title to the place, she would be charged rent.

This intimation did not worry Mrs. Crump, for she knew Arthur Daleman, Sr., to be the soul of honor and knew that he would do what was right, title or no title. But her personal confidence in Mr. Daleman could not be converted into cash, and she had to look elsewhere for money.

There infested Almaville scores of loan companies that charged exorbitant rates of interest and had their contracts so arranged that a failure to pay put them in possession of the household goods of the party in debt. It was also held to be a criminal offense punishable by a term in the penitentiary for a person to borrow money from more than one company on the same items of furniture.

Little Henry had always asserted that he was going to be a merchant when he became a man, and made it a custom to pick up and preserve such business cards as were thrown into his yard. From his pile of cards stacked in a corner Mrs. Crump learned the location of these loan companies and decided to resort to them for the money needed. Getting a small sum from each, she had borrowed from fifteen companies when she at last got the amount demanded by the undertaker.

Arthur Daleman, Jr., was not making money as fast as he desired in the business turned over to him by his father, so he had resorted to the loan business. Knowing that people would often borrow from more than one loan company in spite of the regulations forbidding it, and reasoning that such borrowers would be even more sure than others to pay, because of fear of the penitentiary, he had ten loan companies of his own operating in different buildings under various names.

It happened that on the evening that Foresta and her mother made the rounds borrowing money, he was on an inspecting tour of his loan companies. Mrs. Crump borrowed money from five of Arthur Daleman's companies without, of course, knowing it. Arthur Daleman, Jr., himself was present in two places when she was borrowing the money. On each of these occasions he had taken more than a passing interest in Foresta. Her beauty was by no means diminished by the mourning attire, and Arthur Daleman, Jr., found himself admiring her, notwithstanding his hatred of her race. When the papers were signed in the second loan transaction which he witnessed, he said to himself with a feeling of satisfaction: "My way is tolerably clear."

With the money procured from the various loan companies little Henry and his father were given what the people called a nice burial. Within a week after the interment Arthur Daleman, Jr., made his appearance at Mrs. Crump's home. Foresta was at school when he called, and when she reached home she found her mother standing, facing him, with an angry and excited look in her eyes. Foresta read in her mother's countenance that she was angry and that the advantage in whatever matter it was, was not altogether on her side.

"What is it, mama?" asked Foresta.

"This man wants you to hire out in his family after you graduate."

Foresta looked at the man in surprise. The thought of going into the service of the whites was utterly foreign to her ambition.

"You may take your choice," said Arthur Daleman, Jr., sure of his ground.

"What choice?" asked Foresta, alarmed by the man's tone of assurance.

"It is this way. Negro servants are not up to what they used to be. They are getting squeamish, and you have to be so careful how you speak to them or they will leave you. We are kept always on the lookout for a servant girl."

"What on earth have I to do with that?" asked Foresta, her eyes widening with astonishment.

"This much—I am going to have a measure of stability in my family service somehow. Your mother here is in a tight box. All I have to do is to speak the word and to the penitentiary she goes!" said Daleman.

Foresta grew weak, her lips slightly parted and she backed to the wall for support.

Arthur Daleman, Jr., continued: "Borrowing money from loan companies takes the form of a sale, as you can see by reading any of the contracts. Now you can't sell a thing to two different people at the same time. The law does not allow such. It is a penitentiary offense. See?"

Foresta rushed to her mother and threw her arms about her and sobbed bitterly.

Mrs. Crump said, "I'll go to the pen. Come after me when you get ready! but Fores' shall never work for you."

"Take your choice," said Arthur Daleman, Jr., and walked from the room.

Foresta tore herself from her mother's arms and rushed out of the room after him. "Mister! Wait!" she called. "Don't do anything to mama. I'll come and do the work faithfully," said Foresta trying to smile.

"All right," said Daleman, smiling, "Be a good girl and you won't have a better friend than I am," said he, in a significant tone, trying to awaken Foresta to the real situation.

If she understood it her impassive countenance did not reveal the fact.

The world at large has heard that the problem of the South is the protection of the white woman. There is another woman in the South.

X

ARABELLE SEABRIGHT

A rabelle, I am not going to have a thing to do with this whole matter. Suppose the bottom falls out and we are detected. Just imagine *my* fate."

"Detected?" hissed Mrs. Arabelle Seabright, turning a scornful gaze upon her husband. "You talk as though we have committed or are about to commit some crime. You just stay in your place, please, and leave matters to me."

"Do you mean to tell me that I need not meet the man?" asked Mr. Seabright eagerly.

"Yes!" replied Mrs. Seabright.

He leaped out of his chair and waltzed across the room, kissed his wife and darted through the door.

"Fool!" she muttered between her teeth.

Mrs. Arabelle Seabright in her room in the Domain Hotel was now awaiting the arrival of a newspaper reporter, the next victim to be bent to her will. It had been on her programme to have her daughter Eunice and her husband present during a part of the interview with the reporter, but as they were not entering enthusiastically into her plans she was rather glad that they had declined to be present.

It was not long before a Mr. Gilman, reporter for the "Daily Columbian," was ushered into Mrs. Seabright's room.

"Let us understand each other at the outset, if possible," said Mrs. Seabright, with a smile, directing a kindly gaze in the direction of the young man. Mr. Gilman bowed deferentially, but said nothing.

"I am ambitious." said Mrs. Seabright.

"Ambitious people are the ones that carry the world forward," ventured the young man modestly.

"I have an unbounded ambition,—an ambition to live in history as long as a record of human affairs is kept. Oh! I hate death!" said Mrs. Seabright with a shudder, stamping a foot upon the floor for emphasis. "I have money with which to further my ambitions. I am aware of the traditions of your paper, the 'Columbian.' I shall not ask you to violate them. But if you will put your heart in your labor and be an incessant worker in my interest, your ambitions will be gratified. A fair exchange is no robbery. You put me on the way to attain my ends and I shall do the like for you. Is it a bargain?"

"Whatever I may be able to do consistently, I shall certainly do, and shall be duly appreciative of whatever may result in my favor in consequence of work worthily done," said the young man with so much fervor that Mrs. Seabright knew that she was well fortified in that direction.

Bit by bit the Almaville public was educated as to the Seabrights. They were descendants of sires that took a prominent part in the affairs of the Colonies during and succeeding the period of the American Revolution. Mr. Seabright inherited a large fortune which a keen business sense had enabled him to increase very materially. He had now moved to Almaville to found one of the largest furniture manufacturing establishments in the country. He was so absorbed in business pursuits that he did not relish social affairs much, but his charming wife was such a dispenser of hospitality that she made up for his deficiency.

Eunice, reputed to be the sole heir to the Seabright millions, was a girl of great beauty, highly accomplished, and the center of attraction of any group of which she formed a part.

A valuable tract of land had already been purchased for the manufacturing establishment and a contract for the construction of the plant had been let. As soon as a suitable location could be found, Mr. Seabright was going to erect a mansion in Almaville that would be the pride of the South. An option had been taken on a piece of property in the West End that about measured up to the requirements, and the likelihood was that the residence would be constructed there.

The mere prospect had caused the prices of the property in that vicinity, already valuable, to soar much higher.

The public soon perceived that the conservative, the reliable "Columbian," the paper of the Southern aristocracy, was favorably impressed with the Seabrights as a valuable addition to the commercial and social life of Almaville, and even the most exclusive circles prepared to make room for the newcomers.

The Hon. H. G. Volrees sat in his law office with his chair tilted back, his chestnut brown hair much rumpled upon his large Daniel Webster looking head. Here was one of the most astute legal minds of the state and the real head of the Democratic party of the state. He was now forty-five years old and unmarried. He had never held public office but was seriously considering entering the race for United States Senator. A venerable senator was to retire within about three years and the position could be his if he but indicated a willingness to accept.

The Hon. H. G. Volrees had large ambitions. He was anxious to restore the old time prestige of the South in the councils of the nation. He was a well-to-do man but did not have the money to gain an assured social position at the nation's capital. He fancied he detected the flavor of ambition in those flattering notices concerning the Seabrights.

"It may be that my hour has come," said Mr. Volrees, picking up the paper and looking again at the published picture of Eunice. He closed his desk and went to his hotel.

Mrs. Arabelle Seabright's net had caught its fish. And what had the fish caught? Now *that* is the vital question.

XI

Unusual For A Man

Never in all of human history was an ambitious woman more satisfied with the progress of her plans than was Mrs. Arabelle Seabright. In due time the Hon. H. G. Volrees had formed her acquaintance and it was not long before they had come to an understanding. Eunice demurred not in the least when it was made known to her that she was to be Mrs. H. G. Volrees.

At an opportune time the Hon. H. G. Volrees announced his willingness to accept a seat in the United States Senate and long before the time of the election party leaders vied with each other in declaring in his favor. When the success of his candidacy was assured he approached Mrs. Seabright with a view to laying claim to his bride. The announcement of the engagement was made, the date of the marriage was set and preparations for the great event went on apace. Eunice appeared to enter heartily into all the plannings, and was seemingly happy to an unusual degree.

The "Daily Columbian" did its share in stimulating interest in the forthcoming marriage. Almaville as a whole seemed to be particularly well pleased with the proposed wedding, involving, as it did, a union of the wealth and beauty of the North with the brain and chivalry of the South.

As for Mr. Seabright, the more his family attracted social attention the more uneasy he grew. At first he did make out to accompany his wife to church and to theaters; but he had such a way of staring at the ceiling, avoiding the gaze of people, and hurrying away to escape introductions, that finally she was glad to leave him at home. Many brilliant social functions were given at his home, but he was always absent.

A Mrs. Marsh, in whom curiosity was more strongly developed than even in the rest of her kind, was determined to find out something about this eccentric Mr. Seabright. She managed to get on intimate terms with Mrs. Seabright, and was very free in moving to and fro in the Seabright residence. Her intentions were not however hidden from Mrs. Seabright. She knew that Mrs. Marsh was planning to get closer to her husband as a matter of curiosity, and she was glad of the experiment, hoping that Mrs. Marsh would eventually succeed in making him at home in the social circle.

There was a sort of turret-shaped cupola crowning the Seabright residence and Mr. Seabright made this his retreat. It was fitted up with a telephone connecting it with the rest of the house and with his place of business. It also had connections with a long distance system. The door to his den was always locked, and no one could gain admission without first calling him up over the telephone.

One day Mrs. Marsh, who was a good mimic imitated the voice of a foreman in Mr. Seabright's factory and caused him to open the door of his den. When Mr. Seabright caught sight of a woman's face and form he made a quick attempt to close the door, but Mrs. Marsh apprehending such an attempt, thrust a foot in so as to prevent this.

"Will you kindly withdraw?" asked Mr. Seabright, excitedly, holding the door as nearly closed as the foot would allow.

"No, thank you; I have had too hard a time getting here," said Mrs. Marsh cheerily. "To be frank, Mr. Seabright, would you allow a lady to be able to truthfully charge you with discourtesy?" asked Mrs. Marsh naively.

Mr. Seabright opened the door in despair, intending to dart out of the room as soon as Mrs. Marsh entered.

Mrs. Marsh was looking for just such a step and forestalled it by closing the door and pocketing the key. She now took a seat and bade Mr. Seabright to do likewise. Seeing that he had an unusual character to deal with, Mr. Seabright sat down resignedly to await the further pleasure of his female captor.

Mrs. Marsh looked directly at Mr. Seabright, and said, "I have broken through all rules of propriety in order to get to you. I wish to say to you, Mr. Seabright, that this plea of absorption in your business is all humbug. You have other and secret reasons for not desiring to appear in our social circles."

The perspiration broke out in great beads on Mr. Seabright's face.

"You have treated your wife and daughter shamefully, refusing to honor their social affairs with your presence," continued Mrs. Marsh.

The tone of reproach in this remark, indicating that Mrs. Marsh did not approve of his absence from social functions, caused Mr. Seabright to feel slightly better, as she evidently did not think that the secret reasons governing his course were to his discredit personally, else she would not have lamented his absence.

"You are from the North and rate the Southern women as being beneath your notice, do you?" inquired Mrs. Marsh.

"O no! no! no!" said Mr. Seabright. "On the contrary, I very much admire—," he did not finish the sentence, some fresh thought checking him in the midst of the utterance.

Mrs. Marsh waited for him to finish, but he did not go on with the remark. Finally, finding herself unable to make any headway with Mr. Seabright, Mrs. Marsh eventually arose to go.

"I would be very thankful if before you leave you will sign a statement that I shall draw up," said Mr. Seabright eagerly, going to his desk to do the writing.

Mrs. Marsh looked at him a much puzzled woman. His phenomenal success as a business man gave proof of his sound mental condition, and yet he acted so queerly about everything else.

"I wonder what sort of a statement he wants me to sign," thought she.

The paper ran as follows:

"This is to certify that I was in the presence of Mr. Seabright unaccompanied for a few moments and can testify that his treatment of me was in every way exemplary."

Mrs. Marsh smiled in an amused manner. "You are making me testify to the fact that I deserved my cool reception. I will sign." So saying she attached her signature to the paper and departed.

Mr. Seabright folded up the statement and put it among his most valuable papers. "This may save two hundred and eight bones from being broken. I think that is the number of bones in the human body," said he, double-locking his door.

XII

A Honeymoon Out Of The Usual Order

The much heralded Volrees-Seabright marriage is at last a reality, and a morning train is now bearing the distinguished couple through the beautiful mountain scenery of the state, en route to an Atlantic seaport, whence they are to set sail for an extended tour through the Old World.

As the porter passed through the coach in which Eunice sat, he recognized her and she likewise recognized him. Eunice perceived that the porter remembered her and she was glad of it, for it simplified the work before her.

In order that they both might look directly out of a window Eunice insisted on taking a seat behind Mr. Volrees. Taking advantage of her position she wrote the following note.

> MR. PORTER
>
> "Enclosed you will find a one hundred dollar note. For this you must see to it that this train stops after it has gone a few hundred feet into the long tunnel. Now you had better do as I tell you or else I will see that you have trouble. You know that any white woman can have a Negro's life taken at a word. Beware! Do as I tell you and say nothing to any one!"

The porter took the note and read it with much anxiety. There came to his mind instance after instance in which white women had given innocent Negro men great trouble. He had heard how that Negro tramps begging for food had been greeted by such a show of fear and excitement on the part of those approached for food that the tramps had been overtaken and lynched for alleged attempts at heinous offenses, when the real offense was that of begging for bread. He recalled one case particularly that took place on a farm adjoining the one on which he was reared.

The father of a girl seriously objected to the attentions being paid his daughter by a white man, and he cautioned his old faithful Negro servant to keep a watch upon the movements of the daughter with a view to preventing an elopement. Seeing that there was not much hope of outwitting the father without first getting rid of the Negro, the girl decided to get him out of the way. The Negro was so loyal to his employer and so faithful in the discharge of his duties that the girl knew that she could not attack him from that quarter. One morning before day she was found lying upon the front porch of her home, her dress covered with blood. When after much effort she finally spoke, she laid a grave charge at the door of the Negro servant. He was apprehended and a mob was formed to lynch him. The father of the girl, however, doubted her story and insisted that the Negro be given a trial. Within a very few days the girl eloped with the suitor so unacceptable to her father. After her marriage she testified that the Negro was innocent, that the blood found on her was the blood of a chicken sprinkled there by herself and that she concocted the whole story of the outrage to get rid of the surveillance of the faithful Negro servant.

The perturbed porter canvassed in his mind the stock of alleged facts circulated secretly among the Negroes setting forth the manner in which some white women used their unlimited power of life and death over Negro men, things that may in some age of the world's history come to light. After thoroughly considering the situation, the porter succumbed to the temptation and concluded to stop the train according to Eunice's directions.

Eunice read in the porter's eyes his acquiesence and her spirits rose high. She was all life and animation and the Hon. H. G. Volrees was regaling himself with thoughts of his home as the social center of the life of Washington.

"Let me bring you a drink of water," said Eunice laughingly.

"And where does Southern chivalry take up its abode while you do that?" asked Volrees.

"In the granting of the first request of a newly made and happy bride," said Eunice, playfully pulling Volrees down in his seat and tripping gaily out to get the water. She used a cup which she had brought along and into which she had dropped a drug of some sort.

Volrees drank the water suspecting nothing. As the day wore on he found himself growing very sleepy, but did not associate it with the water which he had taken. In order to get his business in such shape that he could leave it, he had not found much time for rest of late and felt that his tired body was now calling for rest. Eunice arranged a tidy little pillow for his head and watched him sink into a profound slumber.

Toward nightfall the train reached the designated tunnel. Eunice under cover of the darkness, incident to passing through the tunnel, went to the door of the coach without attracting much attention. When the train made the stop prearranged with the porter, Eunice dropped off of the coach step and stood with her back pressed against the tunnel wall. The train soon pulled out, the officials concluding that it was the shrewd trick of some tramp "riding the blind baggage" (between the baggage and the express car), who desired an easy way for alighting.

On and on rolled the train bearing the sleeping Mr. Volrees. When he awoke the sunlight of the day following the one on which he went to sleep was falling in his face. Tied to his wrist he saw a letter. Looking about for Eunice and missing her, he concluded that she was playing some joke, and with a smile he took the note from his wrist and read:

DEAR MR. VOLREES

Pray act sensibly in this trying period that has come in your life. Think well before you act. I am a sincere friend of yours and really like you. Now it will pay you to do just as I am going to tell you to do. Continue your journey to the Old World. From each point mapped out for a sojourn send back the appropriate letter from the batch which I have written and am leaving with you. I have read much of the places which we have planned to visit and I am sure that my letters have enough of local color to pass for letters written on the scene. Send these letters back to be passed around and read by my friends.

"In some foreign country telegraph back that I am dead. Your ingenuity can supply the details. By this time mother knows all and will join me in my advice to you. When you return to this country come as a widower and enjoy the money which comes to you through your marriage with me. By all that is sacred in earth and in heaven, I swear that I shall ever remain dead to you and will in no way directly or indirectly cross your path. Nor shall any one save my mother know that I am alive and she shall never see or hear from me again.

EUNICE

It was not long before Mr. Volrees was handed a telegram which read as follows:

"For God's sake do as the girl directs. So much is involved!
ARABELLE SEABRIGHT

The Hon. H. G. Volrees' wrath knew no bounds. "What do they take me to be, a knight errant of hell and a simpleton withal? I swear by every shining star that I shall probe to the bottom of this matter if it shakes the foundations of the earth," said he. He took the first train back to Almaville, his spirit crushed within him, though he bore his sorrow with an outward calm. He utterly refused to discuss the affair, as did also Mrs. Seabright. Almaville society had not received so profound a shock since the unexplained course of Sam Houston in returning his young bride to her parents and disappearing among the Indians.

XIII

Shrewd Mrs. Crawford

Between Tiara and Ensal there existed a barrier which had seemingly prevented a development of the ties that all who knew the two expected with full assurance.

The attitude of a Negro on the social question as between the races was no child's play with Tiara. It struck at the very root of the deepest convictions of her soul, and she was firmly resolved to allow no Negro into the inner circle of her friendship of whose views on that question she was ignorant. She had, as she felt, practiced "suspension of judgment" with regard to Ensal, and assured herself that he was making no progress in her esteem. She also impressed Ensal that he was a decidedly stationary quantity, no further advanced in her esteem than on the occasion of their first meeting.

This situation did not displease Ensal altogether. He felt that so long as Tiara did not and would not take more than a passing interest in him, he could continue to keep in abeyance that grave question as to whether, in view of the drift of things, a young Negro, absorbed as he was in the question of the condition of the race, should form family ties. So he journeyed along cherishing an ever-increasing attachment, but content for the present to worship her at a distance.

Mrs. Crawford, with all her quietness, was an exceedingly wise woman. She did not know exactly what it was, but she knew as well as did Ensal and Tiara that there was an artificial barrier between them. She also knew that if ever a man loved a woman, Ensal was in love with Tiara. And she knew more. She knew that Tiara was self-deceived; that Tiara herself would be the most astonished person imaginable when she awoke to find out how much she really cared for Ensal.

Mrs. Crawford knew Ensal's reasons for hesitating to form family ties, but did not regard them as substantial. She was determined that Ensal and Tiara should marry; her whole heart was set upon the project. Never in her whole life had she met a couple more clearly designed for each other than this pair, as she viewed the matter. She knew how firm of mind both Ensal and Tiara were and how useless it would be to attempt to talk to either of them. In view of the secret barrier, Tiara would have given her to understand that the matter was not worthy of a second's consideration. As for Ensal he could not have been brought to think that Tiara came any nearer being in love with him than with the rankest stranger, for in all their conversations, not being settled upon the question of marriage, as a matter of honor he had neither sought to develop nor to test the strength of Tiara's regard for himself.

Mrs. Crawford felt fully justified under the circumstances in forcing matters to an issue. She perceived that to do this involved a great sacrifice on her part, the temporary loss of Tiara's friendship; but she decided that the purchase was worthy of the price.

One night as Tiara was about to retire to rest, Mrs. Crawford dropped into her room for one of their customary chats. After talking on various topics she brought the subject around to Ensal.

"Now there is a young man that inspires many people with contempt," said Mrs. Crawford, in a manner to suggest that she, too, was one of that many.

Tiara almost fell, clutching the footboard of the bed for support.

"How can any one possibly have such an opinion of Mr. Ellwood?" asked Tiara, in tones of deepest injury.

Mrs. Crawford merely shrugged her shoulders.

"I have never met a nobler man," continued Tiara.

"Oh, some people have faith in the fellow," said Mrs. Crawford sneeringly.

"You seem to have changed, Mrs. Crawford. It hasn't been so long since I heard you speaking of Mr. Ellwood in the highest possible terms."

"We learn more of people from time to time and must revise our estimates of them in keeping with our more extensive knowledge," replied Mrs. Crawford.

"Be specific, Mrs. Crawford; Mr. Ellwood is a friend of mine," said Tiara, now thoroughly aroused.

"Oh, if you are that much of a friend, you might not be competent to weigh the evidence in the case," said Mrs. Crawford, smiling and arising as if to go.

"Would you cast aspersions upon a person's character and treat the matter so lightly?" asked Tiara, a flush of anger appearing on her face.

"Things other than moral blemishes inspire contempt sometimes. I do not care to say more about the matter. Good night," said Mrs. Crawford.

Tiara went no further with her preparations for retiring. She stowed away all of her possessions in her trunk and locked it. She then sat down and wrote a note to Mrs. Crawford, thanking her for her many courtesies and expressing regret that she found it beyond her power of endurance to longer stay under her roof.

Tiara now went to the telephone in the hallway and called for a carriage. It was not long in coming and she was soon being whirled in the direction of Mrs. Crump's residence.

Mrs. Crump was glad to receive Tiara and she was again assigned to the room in which she slept on the night of her arrival in Almaville. Tiara did not go to bed, but rocked to and fro, anxious for day to break, eager, so eager to see Ensal. At length the question crept into her consciousness: "Why are you so enraged? Are you as anxious to see every one whom you have defended as you are to see this one?"

"My God! I love the man!" said Tiara, rising from her chair and throwing herself face downward across the bed. "Oh, I must never see him again. He might read this awful, this maddening love in my eyes."

Early the next morning, Mrs. Crawford sent for Ensal.

"Mr. Ellwood, I wish you had been more frank with me," said Mrs. Crawford.

"Please explain," said Ensal.

"I took occasion to discuss you rather freely last night, and I seem to have given mortal offense to Miss Merlow, who appears to be madly in love with you."

Ensal was perplexed and knew not what to say.

"Where is Miss Merlow?" asked Ensal.

"She became so indignant that she left my house last night. When you win people's love to such a degree as that, you ought to post your friends so that they may be careful. Miss Merlow has gone to Mrs. Crump's. I shall offer you no explanation of my course until you have heard from Miss Merlow. Now leave me and go to her." Much mystified at the strange turn of events, Ensal took his departure.

The postman early that same morning had left the following note at Mrs. Crump's for Tiara.

"Ensal Ellwood is a noble young man. You loved him and did not know it. I have opened your eyes. Forgive me, dear, but I could not see two, whom I regard so highly, so far apart. As for Ellwood, the lad has never had his right mind since he first met you.

MADGE CRAWFORD

That day a telegram came to Mrs. Crawford's for Tiara and she carried it to the latter forthwith. When the two met there was a mischievous twinkle in Mrs. Crawford's eyes and the light of happiness in Tiara's. When Tiara read the telegram she appeared much disturbed. That night she left Almaville. When she returned she bought her a home on the outskirts of the city, took Mrs. Crump to live with her, and denied herself to all her former Almaville friends, Ensal included. Eunice Volrees or Seabright, had come to stay with Tiara and the latter had for the sake of Eunice shut herself out from all her friends.

XIV

ALENE AND RAMON

A lene Daleman and Ramon Mansford stood within the vestibule of the former's home. Ramon's arm was around Alene's waist and her beautiful black eyes were upturned to his, as if to say, "Fathom the love we tell of, if you can." Down stoops Ramon and plants a fervent, lingering kiss upon the lips of the girl he loves, saying, as he stroked her hair,

"The last token of love until the minister has his say."

"Let me have a last, too," said Alene, tiptoeing to plant a kiss upon Ramon's lips, and thus the two parted.

Light of heart, Alene went tripping to Foresta's room and said:

"Foresta, as you know, the house is full of people who have come from a distance to attend my wedding. You need not stay here tonight. I will occupy your room."

Foresta was very glad indeed, as an early release enabled her to carry out some plans of her own.

"MAMA," SAID FORESTA, HER FACE buried in her mother's lap, "I have something which I wish to tell you."

Her mother stroked her hair, and said, "Tell me, dear."

"You know Mr. Arthur Daleman, Jr., threatened you with the penitentiary, but compromised the matter on the condition that I should work for him."

"Yes, dear," said Mrs. Crump, beginning to breathe fast through the force of increased excitement.

"He pretended that he would not cancel the matter, in order that he might be sure to hold me as a servant," said the girl.

Foresta paused and her mother said, "Go on; I am listening."

"He had dark purposes, mama," said Foresta.

"Yes," said Mrs. Crump, rather feebly, fearful of what was to come.

Foresta, detecting considerable anxiety in her mother's voice, looked up quickly.

"Now, mama, don't look so scared and troubled; it isn't anything awful, now." So saying, she buried her face again and continued her recital. "He pretends to love me, mama. He has tried many times to kiss me. I knew what kind of a sword he held over you, and while I resented his advances, I sought not to enrage him for your sake."

"Well!" said Mrs. Crump, thoroughly alarmed.

"I kept him in his place by threatening to tell Miss Alene. He thinks lots of her and that scared him. He wouldn't care about anybody else."

Foresta took another look into her mother's face, then resumed her former attitude. Continuing, she said:

"Miss Alene leaves tomorrow, and I am afraid to stay there with him. You know a colored girl has no protection. If a white girl is insulted her insulter is shot down and the one who kills him is highly honored. If a colored girl is insulted by a white man and a colored man resents it, the colored man is lynched."

Mrs. Crump let a tear drop and it fell on Foresta's cheek. Foresta felt the tear and raised herself and said.

"Now, you bad mama, you! What's the use crying? I'll take care of myself," a fierce gleam coming into her pretty eyes.

Having wiped her mother's cheeks free from tears, Foresta buried her face again.

"I am not going back any more. I am going to get married tonight. Bud and I are going to get married. And Bud has saved up enough money to pay us out of debt."

Mrs. Crump now understood why Foresta was hiding her face. She remembered her own feelings when the question of marriage had to be broached to her mother. She bent over and kissed Foresta.

"Bud and I are going to run away and get married. Run away from you," said Foresta laughingly. "And you must be awfully surprised when we come back. We are going to do this to avoid a lot of useless expense in getting up a big wedding. That money can go to help us get rid of those eating cancers, those old loan men."

Mrs. Crump knew how much Foresta's heart had always been set on a fine wedding, and she knew that Foresta was making that sacrifice for her sake.

"My sweet Foresta, you have been such a dear child—God will reward you," said Mrs. Crump, burying her head on Foresta's shoulder. "This is not what I had planned for my darling; but God knows what's best. His will be done."

At the appointed hour Bud Harper was standing at Foresta's gate. Foresta soon joined him and they took a train for a nearby town where they were made man and wife.

In the meantime some awful things were happening at the Daleman residence. Leroy Crutcher, of whom we caught a glimpse or so in an earlier chapter, happened to be passing along the sidewalk that ran parallel with the side of the Daleman residence. As he reached the alley at the rear of the yard, he saw a man standing on a rock looking over the back fence. The two men glared at each other. The moon was shining brightly and they could see each other well.

Leroy turned away and walked along the street, saying to himself, "I ought to have shot that scoundrel, Bud Harper, then and there." Reflecting a little he said, "No, I must get him without hurting myself."

The man about whom Leroy had thus spoken climbed over the fence and crouched in the shadow of the coalhouse. His eyes were fixed on Foresta's room and his vigil was ceaseless. At about eleven o'clock Arthur Daleman, Jr., emerged from the hallway of the second story, paused a few moments and crept toward Foresta's room.

"Yes, its true," muttered the Negro, between gritted teeth, the look of a savage overspreading his face. He clambered over the fence saying, "Wait a few minutes, happy couple."

In the meantime Arthur Daleman, Jr., had unlocked the door to Foresta's room and stood as if rooted to the spot. There upon the bed lay Alene instead of Foresta, as he could plainly see by the dimly burning light. Fearing that Alene might awaken and see him, he quickly turned out the light and stepped from the room. In his haste he left the door slightly ajar. What took place thereafter the morning revealed.

XV

Unexpected Developments

According to previous engagement, Mr. Arthur Daleman, Sr., Alene's father, and Ramon Mansford, her affianced, went forth together for an early morning walk. Arm in arm the somewhat aged Southerner and the young Northerner sauntered forth.

"My boy," said Mr. Daleman, "I have thought to have a talk with you concerning the dark shadow that projects itself over our section, the Negro problem. Not that I would infect you with my peculiar views, but that those of us and our descendants who abide here may have your sympathy."

"My love for Alene invests all that is near to her with my abiding sympathy," said Ramon with quiet fervor.

"Yes, but the mind must be informed if sympathy is to be intelligently directed. To begin with, men of my class, families like mine have no prejudice against Negroes nor they against us. We know them thoroughly and they know us. There is never the slightest trespass on forbidden ground by us or by them. It is a boast of many Negroes that they can tell a 'quality' white person on sight, and practically all Negroes ascribe their troubles to a certain class of whites."

"I have noticed the kindly relations between your people and all the Negroes that have had dealings with them," interposed Ramon.

"My class was humane to the Negro in the days of slavery and under our kindly care developed him from a savage into a thoroughly civilized man. But I am glad slavery is gone. Under the system bad white men could own slaves and their doings were sometimes terrible. They were the ones who made Uncle Tom's Cabin possible and brought down upon us all the maledictions of the world, Like 'poor dog Tray,' the humane class were caught in bad company and we have paid for it. But all of that is in the past. A word about the present and the future," said Mr. Daleman.

The two men were now in a grove of trees in the suburbs of the city. Mr. Daleman took a seat on a stump and Ramon, unmindful of the dew, threw himself at full length on the grass, and looked up intently into the face of his prospective father-in-law.

Mr. Daleman now resumed: "The radical element at the South has always given us trouble. The radicals hate the Negro and nothing is too bad for them to do to him. We liberals like him and want to see him prosper. Such of us liberals as labor to keep the Negro out of politics do so, not out of hatred of him, but for his own good, as we see it. We hate to see him the victim of the spleen of the radicals and they do grow furious at the sight of the Negro in exalted station. In your Northern home bear in mind these two classes of Southerners and remember that some of us at least are anxious for the highest good to all."

Mr. Daleman now paused and a sad look came over his face.

He resumed: "One of the hardest tasks among us is the suppression of lynching. In the very nature of things, as conditions now exist, there cannot be such a thing as a trial of a charge of outrage by a Negro man upon a white woman. Often in cases of that nature the crime charged is disproved, by proving another offense involving collusion. Well, no lawyer can be found who would set up such a defense for a Negro client if the white woman in the case objected, for he would be killed, perhaps, and, furthermore, collusion is punished in the same way as outrage. So lynching is here fortified. Tolerated and condoned for one thing it spreads to other things and men are lynched for trivial offenses.

"If a departure could be made from the custom of public trials and jury trials in such cases, relief might be found. The trials could be secret and before a bench of judges. Care for the feelings of the woman and her guardians, and things will be better. There is no pronounced sentiment among the better classes in favor of lynching for other causes and it can be put down. There is marked improvement in this matter, and it may be that lynching may be stopped without the changes in jurisprudence which I suggest."

Mr. Daleman now arose from his seat, saying, "Come, my son. They will be awaiting breakfast for us, I fear. Tell the North that down in this Southland there is an element of as noble men as the world affords; men with a keen sense of justice and an unfaltering purpose to lift our section to a position of high esteem in the estimation of the world. We may seem to work at cross purposes with you of the North; we may be overwhelmed by waves of race prejudice from time to time, but we are here, and I claim to be one of them. I challenge the man, white or black, rich or poor, to say that I ever mistreated him by word or deed."

"You need no vindication. Time was when practically all Southerners were classed together by the outside, but that day has passed."

The two men walked back home in silence, Mr. Daleman thinking about the future of his home without Alene, and Ramon thinking of his own future home with her. When they got back to the house breakfast was ready and they were soon seated at the table.

"Tell Alene to come down. I know the child is a little shy this morning, but I must have her by my side this once more. Go for her, Arthur," said Mr. Daleman, Sr., to his son.

Arthur involuntarily drew back slightly at the request and his father cast an inquiring look at him.

"I hate to disturb the child's slumbers. I doubt whether she slept much last night," said Arthur, in somewhat husky tones.

"He hates to see Alene leave him," thought Mr. Daleman.

Arthur ascended the stairs and, coming to Alene's door found it slightly ajar. He knocked, but received no response. He knocked harder, then again and again. He knew that he had knocked hard enough to awaken one from sleep, so he concluded that Alene must be up and in some other part of the house. As she had left the door open, Arthur decided that the room was prepared for entering. He had a secret desire to step in and glance around the room in which, on the previous night, he stood in such imminent danger of exposure. Pushing the door open, he stepped in quickly, but far more quickly stepped out, terror stricken. Upon Foresta's bed lay the beautiful Alene, her face covered with blood and her hair falling over her face, dyeing itself a crimson red.

Arthur was speechless with horror. He ran his fingers through his hair, brought his hand down over his face as if seeking by that means to clear his brain so that he could answer the question as to whether he himself had not committed the murder. Recovering his self-possession in a measure, he dragged himself down stairs to where Mr. Daleman was. There was such an awful look upon his face that Mr. Daleman was thoroughly aroused.

"What is the trouble, Arthur?" asked Mr. Daleman.

Arthur said nothing, but made a motion in the direction of the room that looked to be as much a sign of despair as of direction.

Mr. Daleman rushed up the stairway and into the room. A glance told him the awful story. The kindly light that always lingered in his eyes died out and a cold, keen glitter appeared. His form showing the slight curvature of age, now stiffened under the iron influence of his will and he stood erect. The tears tried to come, but he tossed the first away and others feared to come. No more bitter cup was ever handed man to drink; but he quaffed it, dregs and all. One awful unnamable fear, involving the motive of the crime, haunted his soul. The family physician was sent for and said tenderly, as he came from the room of the murdered girl, "It might have been worse." Through the dark sorrow of Mr. Daleman's soul there shot a gleam of joy. The two men clasped hands in silence. The horror was less.

The whole city was soon in a furor of excitement. Bloodhounds were put on the trail and about noon a Negro who had been tracked was apprehended, sitting quietly on a bridge a few miles out from the city. He made no effort to escape, and manifested no surprise when caught.

"Have they killed anybody else?" was his first and only utterance to the officers who took him in charge. His captors did not deign to make reply. The Negro was handcuffed and led back until the party arrived at the outskirts of the city. The patrol wagon was telephoned for and the Negro was soon safe in the station house. News spread like wildfire that the criminal was in the prison and soon the street was full of thousands. A mob was formed and an assault was planned upon the prison. The chief of police came out on the steps of the building and, with drawn pistol, declared that the majesty of the law would be maintained at all hazards. He then retired within.

Nothing daunted the mob surged forward. The chief of police came forth again and in a manner that left no room for mistake, declared that only over his dead body could they take the prisoner. His long record as a daring and faithful officer was well known and the mob now hesitated.

The sheriff of the county was out of the city at the time and one of his deputies was in charge of affairs. This deputy had been laying plans with a view to being the candidate of his party for the office of sheriff at the next election, and he fancied that he now saw an opportunity to curry favor with the masses. He elbowed his way through the crowd and held a whispered conference with the leader of the mob. Thereupon the leader took his place on the steps and harangued the mob as follows:

"Fellow citizens, do not despair. The voice of the people is the voice of God, and your voice shall be heard this day. I assure you of this fact. I beg of you, however, that you now disperse. You shall meet again under circumstances more favorable to your wishes."

The persons in front passed the word along, and knowing that some better plan of action had been agreed upon, the crowd dispersed into neighboring streets.

The deputy sheriff, armed with the proper papers, appeared at the station house and demanded and secured the prisoner, as the city had no jurisdiction over murder cases. When he had proceeded about a block with his prisoner, a group of men who understood the matter raised a mighty yell. The mob which had dispersed now reformed.

The prisoner was taken from the deputy sheriff, and was hurried to the bridge connecting the two parts of the city. A rope was secured and the Negro was dropped over the side of the bridge. As his form dangled therefrom, every man in the crowd who could, and who had a pistol, leaned over the railing and fired at the Negro. The rain of bullets made the Negro's form swing to and fro. The crowd finally dispersed, leaving the body suspended from the bridge.

Gus Martin had kept up with the mob from the beginning, walking about with folded arms, betraying no trace of excitement save, perhaps, the rapid chewing of the tobacco which was in his mouth. His blood was stirred, but its Indian infusion contributed stoicism to him on this occasion.

When the whites were through with the body, Gus went to the side of the bridge and drew it up. Calling to his aid another Negro, he procured a stretcher and bore the body to Bud Harper's home.

XVI

An Eager Searcher

Up and down the street on which he lived, Ramon Mansford, the affianced of Alene Daleman, walked as one in a trance. Night was coming and as the shadows deepened the bitterness deepened in his soul.

"Think of it! my father sleeps in an unmarked grave somewhere in the South, and I know that the hope of freeing the slave actuated him to enlist in the army. For the Negro, my father buried his sword to the hilt in the blood of his Southern brother and in turn received a thrust, all for a race from which this vile miscreant has crept to murder Alene, my Alene."

In the darkness of his own calamity distinctions between right and wrong began to fade away, and he found his hatred of the Negro race assuming a more violent form than that manifested by the native Southerner. In his heart there was the harking back to times more than a thousand years ago—to times when his race was a race of exterminators. At this particular time it seemed to him that nothing would have suited him better than to have taken the lead of forces bent on driving every black face from the land. Now and then he would pause and ask himself:

"Is all this horror true? Is the sweet Alene gone? Was the dear one foully murdered while I slept? Great God of heaven, can all this be true? Must I go through life unsupported by the brave heart of Alene on which I was depending for strength to conquer worlds?"

He sat down upon the curbstone and buried his face in his hands.

About twelve o'clock that night a Negro woman came rushing along at full speed. Ramon seized her and she uttered a loud scream, falling in a helpless heap at his feet. With a tight grip on her arm he said,

"Have you, too, blighted somebody's happiness? Have you murdered some one?"

With terror stricken eyes the woman looked up into his face and said, "Mistah, please lemme go, please sah!"

"What have you done?" sternly asked Ramon.

"Nothin' sah," said she. "I'se been roun' ter Dilsy Harper's, settin' up ovah Bud Harper's daid body, whut wuz sent home frum de bridge.

Wal, sah, ez shuah ez dis here chile is bawn ter die, while we wuz settin' up ovah Bud's body, Bud hisself walked in. We looked at Bud, den at de body, en we wuz skeert ter death. Den de livin' Bud, went up an looked down on de daid Bud, and de daid Bud skeert de livin' Bud, and de livin' Bud fairly flew outen dat house. Den, bless yer soul, honey, dat ole house wuz soon empty."

This weird tale furnished the needed diversion to Ramon's overburdened mind. His thoughts began to run in another direction.

"Was the mob mistaken? Is the man thought to have been killed yet alive? If one mistake has been made, who can say that two haven't been made? Is her real murderer yet alive?"

Such were the thoughts that went crashing through Ramon's mind and his grip on the woman's arm slackened. The woman wrenched herself loose and continued her journey with increased speed.

As late as it was Ramon hurried to the Harpers' home and found the Negroes standing about at a distance from the house, discussing the sudden reappearance and disappearance of Bud Harper, when there, all agreed, lay Bud before their very eyes.

Ramon returned to his home strangely becalmed, and though late in the night he sat down and wrote the following letter to his home in the North.

My Dear Norfleet

I am in the throes of an overwhelming sorrow. My Alene has been foully murdered. A mystery surrounds the case. We cannot fathom the motive of the crime. Today (rather yesterday now, for it is two o'clock in the morning) a man accused of murdering her was lynched. Tonight the man who was supposed to have been lynched made his appearance at his home. But the mother sticks to it that the real murderer, her son, is the corpse, and appearances seem to bear out the contention. Now it may be that Alene's murderer is yet alive and that an injustice has been wrought upon somebody. My heart is more firmly knit to my Southern white brethren than ever before. I fling ambition to the winds. Tell my friends that I shall not make the race for Congress, and thank them for me for the way in which they have always seconded my aspirations. It pains me much to not be in a position to attempt to scale the heights which their loving hearts fancied

I could make with ease. I shall walk with my kith and kin of the South in the shadow, for in the furnace of a common sorrow, my heart has been melted into one with theirs. We of the South (you see I call myself one of them), know not what the future has in store for our beloved section, but we face the ordeal with the grim determination of our race. If you believe in prayer, pray that I may be just and may even in darkness do the right.

RAMON, 'THE MAD'

When Alene had been laid to rest, Ramon, after lingering in Almaville for a few weeks, disappeared completely, leaving behind no trace of himself. He had previously given Mr. Daleman and friends assurances that he would do no violence to himself. So while they knew not where he was nor what was his mission, they were not unduly apprehensive as to his welfare.

Ramon Mansford had simply stained himself a chocolate brown and had thus passed from the Anglo-Saxon to the Negro race. He had gone to fathom the mystery of Alene's murder.

XVII

Peculiar Divorce Proceedings

"Dilsy Brooks, would you 'low me er few wurds wid you?"

Dilsy Harper, Bud's mother, paused in her knitting, pulled her spectacles a little further down on her nose, and peered over them at Silas Harper, her husband, who had just entered her room and stood with his hat in his hand. He was low of stature, small and very bow-legged. A short white beard graced his chin, while his upper lip was kept clean shaven. His head was covered with the proverbial knotty, wool-like hair, which was now the scene of a struggle for the mastery between the black and gray. Since the moment that the news was brought to him that Bud was accused of Alene's murder he had been acting rather queerly, even after all things were taken into consideration, thought Mrs. Harper.

The tone of Mr. Harper's voice and his sober face led his wife to believe that he was now about to unbosom himself. As he had seen fit to call her by her maiden name, Mrs. Harper did not deign to reply.

"I is willin' ter 'cept yer silunce fer cunsent, as I feel I mus' say whut air in me," Mr. Harper resumed. Continuing, he said: "Yer been 'ceivin' me, Dilsy; yer been 'ceivin' me."

Mrs. Harper could not stand that impeachment of her honor and she quickly hissed,

"Yer air jes' a plain, orternary liah, Silas. I is er hones' 'oman myself. But out wid yer pizen. I been knowin' 'twuz in yer."

"I 'peats ergin whut I dun sed. Yer hez been 'ceivin' me, Dilsy; yer been 'ceivin' me, an I ken prove it."

Mrs. Harper cast a withering look of contempt at her husband, folded her arms and leaned back in her chair, more puzzled than ever at his queer course.

"Now, Dilsy, let me ax yer some queshuns. W'en I wuz a lad in slabery time, didunt I dribe my young missus 'bout whar' eber she went? An' she wuz safe. Didunt dis heah same Silas do dat?" said he, his voice rising to a high pitch in his earnestness. "W'en de yankees wuz fightin' our folks and our mens wuz ter de front in battul, didunt dese hans er mine hole de plow dat brung de corn ter feed my missus? At night did

I sleep er wink wen dare wuz eny t'ing lackly ter pester de wimmins?" said he in the same high tones.

"De wimmins befoh de wah an' since de wah an' in de wah hez allus hed a pertectur in old Uncle Silas, an' yer knows it!" said he, pointing his index finger at his wife. "Wal, I'm comin' ter de p'int. Bud's done kilt er 'oman. He ain't no blood uv min'. You ain't been er true wife ter me. He's sumbody else's boy. He aint mine. My blood don't run dat'er way."

Not a muscle in Mrs. Harper's face moved as she listened to this indictment on the part of her husband.

"An', now," he continued, "you needunt min' 'bout sayin' eny ting 'bout dis. I aint gwine ter say nothin' 'bout yer ter skanderlize yer. I am gwine ter nail up de doh 'twixt you an' me. You aint no wife er min' fur Bud an me aint got de same blood. He kilt er 'oman."

Mrs. Harper looked steadily at her husband, her anger gone, now that she understood all. She leaned forward and parted her lips as if to speak. She seemed to take a second thought and slowly leaned back in her chair. It was evident that a debate was going on in her mind.

"No, he talks too much," said she to herself. She adjusted her spectacles, picked up her knitting and resumed work, a gentle look of forgiveness upon her face.

Silas Harper with bowed head, and shoulders more stooped than common, walked from the room. Procuring a hammer and nails he soon had the entrance from his room to that of his wife securely barred. And every lick that he struck was like unto driving a nail into his own heart, for he loved Dilsy, the love of his youth, the companion of his earlier struggles after slavery, the joint purchaser of their four-room cottage, and the mother of the two boys whom he had hitherto regarded as his sons.

XVIII

Mists That Vanish

In his far away peaceful Northern home, Norfleet, friend of Ramon Mansford, received the following letter:

My Dear Norfleet

I am about at the end of one of the most shocking and most mystifying affairs known to the human race. In keeping with my resolve I disappeared into the Negro race for the purpose of fathoming the mystery of the murder of my beloved Alene. The fact that I could so disappear is one of far-reaching significance. It shows what an awful predicament the Negroes are in. Any white criminal has the race at his mercy. By dropping into the Negro race to commit a crime and immediately thereafter rejoining the white race, he has a most splendid opportunity to escape. And men who commit the darker crimes are not failing to take advantage of the open door; but I picked up my pen to tell you my weird story.

"Well, I actually became a boarder in the home of Aunt Dilsy, the mother of the man accused of murdering my Alene. By mingling with the Negroes I came in contact with three persistent beliefs which I investigated.

"First of all, the Negroes were practically a unit in holding that Bud Harper had not committed the crime.

"On the next point to be mentioned the popular belief was divided. The more intelligent class held that the Negro lynched was not Bud Harper, but some strange Negro resembling him. When confronted with the fact that Dilsy Harper accepted it as the body of her son Bud, they shrugged their shoulders and said that that report came from the white officers who would pretend that a Negro had said just anything and that Aunt Dilsy would hardly know Bud after the mob got through mutilating him. They believed that Bud was living and that he had come home while the body supposed to be his was lying there. The more superstitious among them held that Bud was unjustly killed and his ghost had come to the wake, and that it could be seen almost any night on the bridge.

"I found whispered around in a rather select circle the belief that Arthur Daleman, Jr., had killed Alene. It was thought that Arthur was secretly in love with his foster sister and in a fit of uncontrollable jealousy had murdered her. A Negro woman, who went to the Daleman's to care for the house, was reputed to have found in Arthur's room appliances for making one assume the appearance of a Negro.

"Now all of these rumors I investigated and I came to the conclusion that the truth of the matter was as follows:

1. Bud Harper did not kill Alene.
2. Bud Harper was not hanged.
3. Bud Harper and not his ghost appeared at his home.
4. Dilsy Harper accepted the body as that of Bud to prevent a further quest of Bud.
5. Arthur Daleman, Jr., bore some relation to Alene's murder.

"The fifth conclusion was forced upon me by the guilty hangdog appearance of Arthur Daleman, Jr., which some people mistook for sorrow over Alene's death.

"Now let me tell you the strange manner in which I received confirmation of these things. On taking up my abode at Dilsy Harper's I noticed that she and her husband had no dealings with each other, though they lived in the same house. Today I came home and found the door unbarred and Silas Harper sitting in his wife's room, his face all wreathed in smiles. Mrs. Harper had been called away and he proceeded to unfold the cause of his previous strained relations with his wife and his present happy state. He had separated himself from her by the process of the barred door, because she had borne him a son that stood unpurged of a charge of having murdered a woman. While thus separated from his wife, brooding over the disgrace brought upon his name by his reputed son, he became very sick. His wife offered to nurse him, but he refused her services.

"In order that Mrs. Harper might be near her husband in his affliction, she gave him information that actually cured him—lifted him from his bed. She explained to him that she would have told him before, but feared that he would tell abroad what she confided to him, and thereby occasion more trouble. He promised to never divulge what she had said and kept his promise by telling me, the first man that he had seen since he was told. And here is the strange story that disentangles a deep mystery and solves a question which I was determined to probe to the bottom. I give in my own words the story told me by Silas Harper.

"This couple, Silas and Dilsy Harper, had had two sons so very much alike that hardly anyone save Mrs. Harper could readily distinguish them when they were attired alike.

"Dave was one day walking along the street with a young lady when a policeman collided with them. Words passed between them and in the fight that ensued Dave wounded the policeman and was sentenced to prison for twenty years. Another lad, a consumptive was sentenced the same day for two years. The guard that took them to the prison did not know one from the other, and at the suggestion of the consumptive the two exchanged names and sentences. When Dave Harper's name was called the consumptive stepped forward and registered, and when the latter's name was called Dave stepped forward. The prison officials, not dreaming that a man with a two years' sentence would exchange with one having twenty years' sentence, the matter was arranged without difficulty. In less than a year's time the consumptive, regarded as Dave Harper, died and was buried as such.

"The real Dave Harper served the consumptive's two years' sentence and was duly released from prison. He was so chagrined over the disgrace that his incarceration in prison had brought upon his family, he did not make himself known at home when released. Desiring to live in Almaville and yet be free from the danger of being identified as Dave Harper, he found employment in a saloon patronized only by whites. It was here that he overheard Arthur Daleman, Jr., telling his companions of a pretty 'coon,' Foresta Crump, whom he had slated for his next victim. Knowing that Foresta was Bud's fiancee he determined to look into the matter. As he watched the Daleman residence he saw Arthur Daleman, Jr., enter the servant girl's room. Judging that Foresta was favorably receiving his attentions Dave determined upon the killing of them both. Thus it was that my dear Alene lost her life. She received a blow that was drawn to her by the wicked plannings of her foster brother.

"Dave Harper supposing that he killed Foresta and Arthur Daleman, Jr., ran by home, made himself known to his mother and confessed all to her. He told his mother that Leroy Crutcher had seen him and no doubt mistook him for Bud and that he would therefore be compelled to hover near the city so that he might return and confess to the committing of the crime in case Bud was about to be made to suffer for his deed.

"Such are the facts as they came to me from Aunt Dilsy's husband. I have confronted Arthur Daleman, Jr., with the matter and he has confessed to his part of the awful tragedy.

"I have now changed back to the white race. In my capacity of a white man I have assured Aunt Dilsy that Bud Harper shall not be molested and have assured Mrs. Crump that it is safe for Foresta to return. The two women are happy souls. I have succeeded in locating Bud and Foresta and shall leave at once for the purpose of restoring them to their families and their friends.

"My dear Norfleet, in view of the terrible way things get twisted down here, don't you think it is an awful shame that this weak and often hated race is denied the right of trial by jury?

Ramon

XIX

THE FUGITIVES FLEE AGAIN

When Bud Harper and Foresta, on the night following their elopement, returned to Almaville, Bud took Foresta by her home to break the news to her mother, leaving her at the gate, while he went to his home to tell his mother. Finding a corpse in his house and noting the terror that his appearance seemed to inspire, Bud left and ran back to Foresta's home. In the meantime Mrs. Crump had explained the situation to Foresta, who now told Bud. With bowed heads and troubled hearts the three sat in deep study as to what to do.

The white people were under the impression that Bud had committed the murder. They had killed another man thinking that it was he. In case they now apprehended him, would the popular feeling be that there was a mistake in the lynching or a mistake as to Bud's having committed the murder?

Bud felt fully able to demonstrate his innocence, but the ruthless mob would hardly give him time to collect his evidence, he feared. Thus, though innocent, he decided that it was best for him to leave Almaville and remain in hiding for a time at least. Foresta asserted her determination to go with him it mattered not where he went.

Bud gave to Foresta the privilege of choosing their exile. For a number of years the condition of the Negroes in the cotton states farther South had been weighing heavily on her mind. She had read how that under the credit system, the country merchant, charging exorbitant prices for merchandise for which the crops stood as security, was causing the Negro farmer to work from year to year only to sink deeper and deeper into debt. She had read of the contract system under which ignorant Negroes, not knowing the contents of the papers signed, practically sold themselves into slavery, agreeing to work for a number of years for a mere pittance and further agreeing to be locked up in a stockade at night and to pay for the expense of a recapture in case they attempted to escape. She had heard much of the practice of peonage, how that planters and contractors would enter into collusion with magistrates and convict innocent Negroes of crimes in order that they might get Negro laborers by the paying of fines assessed on these trumped up charges. She had read accounts of investigations of the prison system of the South, showing that the various states made the earning of money by the prisoners a prime consideration, and detailing how brutal overseers were wont to maltreat convicts leased to them by the state. These things coupled with the absence of reformatories for youths were destined, Foresta felt assured, to produce a harvest of criminals. What to her mind added to the hopelessness of the plight of the Negroes was the fact that an emigration agent was required to pay such a heavy tax and stood in such a danger of bodily harm from the planters that nothing was being done toward pointing the inhabitants of the blighted regions to better lands.

Foresta concluded to choose Mississippi, a state in which conditions were in some respects so thoroughly forbidding, as their future home. Two things influenced her in making a choice, a desire to use her education for the amelioration of the ills of which she had heard so much and the thought that a land reputed to be so destitute of hope for the Negro would be searched last of all for Negro refugees. So the two had gone forth in the darkness and journeyed southward.

With money that Bud had saved they bought a small farm near Maulville, Mississippi. It was not long before Foresta's quiet influence was felt throughout that region. The whites who had been preying upon the more ignorant of the Negroes were not long in tracing this new influence to its source. It was agreed among them that the Fultons (for such was the name assumed by Bud and Foresta) were rather undesirable neighbors and a decision was reached to put them out of the way. The thousands of individual murders, and lynching by mobs, had so blunted the sensibility of these whites that they reached this decision without any qualms of conscience. Sidney Fletcher was agreed upon as the man to rid the settlement of Bud and Foresta.

On this particular afternoon, Foresta's hair was hanging down her back in girlish fashion. A small cap sat upon the top of her head, while a blue gingham apron protected her dress. She had finished the milking and was walking toward the house when Sidney Fletcher, the owner of a neighboring farm, approached her.

"Where has Tobe Stewart gone?" asked Fletcher, in a very gruff manner, inquiring about a Negro lad who had run away from him.

Foresta looked at him steadily without replying.

"You—wench, you, you can't speak can you? You and that dad blasted man of yours have got the big head, anyway," said Fletcher, drawing his pistol and starting toward Foresta.

Foresta dropped her milk pail and ran into the house.

Fletcher took a seat on a bench in the yard and awaited the coming of Bud Harper, Foresta's husband, who was out hunting and was not due for some time yet.

Foresta stole out of the door on the other side of the house and reached a patch of woods without being observed by Sidney Fletcher. By a circuitous route she was able to place herself in Bud's pathway so as to intercept him before he reached home.

"Oh, Bud," said Foresta, greeting her husband, "Old Sid Fletcher is at our house waiting for you with a drawn revolver."

A frown came over Bud's face. "The jealous knave," said he. "Ever since we bought this farm he has had a dislike for me and I have been expecting trouble from him."

"Yes, Bud; but we must stay out of trouble. A colored man hasn't a dog's show in this part of the world."

Bud sat down on a stump and Foresta dropped at his feet.

"Let's stay away from home tonight. We have had trouble enough, Bud," said Foresta pleadingly.

Bud looked down on her tenderly, and said, "It is a shame for a peaceful, industrious man to have a home and not be able to go to it."

Just then Sidney Fletcher was seen coming in their direction.

"Get behind a tree; nobody knows what will take place," said Bud to Foresta. She obeyed and Bud now calmly awaited the approach of Sidney Fletcher.

When Fletcher got in shooting distance he deliberately opened fire on Bud. After the third shot Bud raised his gun to his shoulder and fired and Fletcher fell backward a corpse. Bud and Foresta now looked at each other aghast. They knew the penalty attached to the raising of a black hand against a white man, even when that man unjustly sought the life of the black.

Rushing to their humble little home, Bud and Foresta hastily gathered a few things into a bundle, seized whatever food there was in the house, armed themselves and went forth as fugitives, Foresta attiring herself in man's clothing. By day and by night, through fields and forest, swamp and morass, avoiding the sight of man the unhappy couple fled.

The news of the killing of Fletcher was not long in getting abroad and a mob of several hundred whites was soon organized to give chase. The news agencies acquainted the whole nation with the situation and day by day the millions of America scanned with eagerness and with sad forebodings the progress of the chase. Several Negroes who happened to be found in the pathway of the mob that was sweeping the country were shot down or hung according to the whim of the pursuers.

The two in turn relieved each other at watching, whenever the exhausted condition of one or the other imperatively demanded sleep. It became Foresta's time to sleep and the two took a position behind a huge fallen tree, Foresta reclining her head upon Bud's lap. Soon she was asleep, with Bud looking down in tenderness on her pretty face, now showing signs of the terrible strain that they were undergoing. Bud thought of his position as her protector and gnashed his teeth in the bitterness of his soul as he contemplated his utter helplessness. Hot tears coursed down his cheeks and, dropping on Foresta's face, awakened her.

Foresta, who had been having troubled dreams, quickly lifted her head from Bud's lap and looked about in terror. Turning toward him she saw his eyes reddened from weeping. She threw herself on his shoulder and the two now gave way to their feelings for the first time.

"We have one consolation, Bud. They can't destroy our love for one another, can they?" said Foresta.

Bud was too full of sorrow at the plight of the wife of his bosom to reply. A deep groan of anguish escaped his lips. He leaned back against the log, Foresta still clinging to his neck. After a while both of them from sheer exhaustion fell asleep.

XX

The Blaze

Little Melville Brant stamped his foot on the floor, looked defiantly at his mother, and said, in the whining tone of a nine-year old child,

"Mother, I want to go."

"Melville, I have told you this dozen times that you cannot go," responded the mother with a positiveness that caused the boy to feel that his chances were slim.

"You are always telling me to keep ahead of the other boys, and I can't even get up to some of them," whined Melville plaintively.

"What do you mean?" asked the mother.

"Ben Stringer is always a crowing over me. Every time I tell anything big he jumps in and tells what he's seen, and that knocks me out. He has seen a whole lots of lynchings. His papa takes him. I bet if my papa was living he would take me," said Melville.

"My boy, listen to your mother," said Mrs. Brant. "Nothing but bad people take part in or go to see those things. I want mother's boy to scorn such things, to be way above them."

"Well, I ain't. I want to see it. Ben Stringer ain't got no business being ahead of me," Melville said with vigor.

The shrieking of the train whistle caused the fever of interest to rise in the little boy.

"There's the train now, mother. Do let me go. I ain't never seen a darky burned."

"Burned!" exclaimed Mrs. Brant in horror.

Melville looked up at his mother as if pitying her ignorance.

"They are going to burn them. Sed Lonly heard his papa and Mr. Corkle talking about it, and it's all fixed up."

"My Heavenly Father!" murmured Mrs. Brant, horror struck.

The cheering of the multitude borne upon the air was now heard.

"Mother, I must go. You can beat me as hard as you want to after I do it. I can't let Ben Stringer be crowing over me. He'll be there."

Looking intently at his mother, Melville backed toward the door. Mrs. Brant rushed forward and seized him.

"I shall put you in the attic. You shall not see that inhuman affair."

To her surprise Melville did not resist, but meekly submitted to being taken up stairs and locked in the attic.

Knowing how utterly opposed his mother was to lynchings he had calculated upon her refusal and had provided for such a contingency. He fastened the attic door on the inside and took from a corner a stout stick and a rope which he had secreted there. Fastening the rope to the stick and placing the stick across the small attic window he succeeded in lowering himself to the ground. He ran with all the speed at his command and arrived at the railway station just in time to see the mob begin its march with Bud and Foresta toward the scene of the killing of Sidney Fletcher.

Arriving at the spot where Fletcher's body had been found, the mob halted and the leaders instituted the trial of the accused.

"Did you kill Mr. Sidney Fletcher?" asked the mob's spokesman of Bud.

"Can I explain the matter to you, gentlemen," asked Bud.

"We want you to tell us just one thing; did you kill Mr. Sidney Fletcher?"

"He tried to kill me," replied Bud.

"And you therefore killed him, did you?"

"Yes, sir. That's how it happened."

"You killed him, then?" asked the spokesman.

"I shot him, and if he died I suppose I must have caused it. But it was in self-defense."

"You hear that, do you. He has confessed," said the spokesman to his son who was the reporter of the world-wide news agency that was to give to the reading public an account of the affair.

"Well, we are ready to act," shouted the spokesman to the crowd.

Two men now stepped forward and reached the spokesman at about the same time.

"I got a fine place, with everything ready. I knew what you would need and I arranged for you," said one of the men.

"My place is nearer than his, and everything is as ready as it can be. I think I am entitled to it," said the other.

"You want the earth, don't you?" indignantly asked the first applicant of the second.

Ignoring this thrust the second applicant said to the spokesman,

"You know I have done all the dirty work here. If you all wanted anybody to stuff the ballot box or swear to false returns, I have been your man. I've put out of the way every biggety nigger that you sent me after. You know all this."

"You've been paid for it, too. Ain't you been to the legislature? Ain't you been constable? Haven't you captured prisoners and held 'um in secret till the governor offered rewards and then you have brung 'em forward? You have been well paid. But me, I've had none of the good things. I've done dirty work, too, don't you forget it. And now I want these niggers hung in my watermelon patch, so as to keep darkies out of nights, being as they are feart of hants, and you are here to keep me out of that little favor."

The dispute waxed so hot that it was finally decided that it was best to accept neither place.

"We want this affair to serve as a warning to darkies to never lift their hands against a white man, and it won't hurt to perform this noble deed where they will never forget it. I am commander today and I order the administration of justice to take place near the Negro church."

"Good! Good!" was the universal comment.

The crowd dashed wildly in the direction of the church, all being eager to get places where they could see best. The smaller boys climbed the trees so that they might see well the whole transaction. Two of the trees were decided upon for stakes and the boys who had chosen them had to come down. Bud was tied to one tree and Foresta to the other in such a manner that they faced each other. Wood was brought and piled around them and oil was poured on very profusely.

The mob decided to torture their victims before killing them and began on Foresta first. A man with a pair of scissors stepped up and cut off her hair and threw it into the crowd. There was a great scramble for bits of hair for souvenirs of the occasion. One by one her fingers were cut off and tossed into the crowd to be scrambled for. A man with a cork screw came forward, ripped Foresta's clothing to her waist, bored into her breast with the corkscrew and pulled forth the live quivering flesh. Poor Bud her helpless husband closed his eyes and turned away his head to avoid the terrible sight. Men gathered about him and forced his eyelids open so that he could see all.

When it was thought that Foresta had been tortured sufficiently, attention was turned to Bud. His fingers were cut off one by one and the corkscrew was bored into his legs and arms. A man with a club struck him over the head, crushing his skull and forcing an eyeball to hang down from the socket by a thread. A rush was made toward Bud and a man who was a little ahead of his competitors snatched the eyeball as a souvenir.

After three full hours had been spent in torturing the two, the spokesman announced that they were now ready for the final act. The brother of Sidney Fletcher was called for and was given a match. He stood near his mutilated victims until the photographer present could take a picture of the scene. This being over the match was applied and the flames leaped up eagerly and encircled the writhing forms of Bud and Foresta.

When the flames had done their work and had subsided, a mad rush was made for the trees which were soon denuded of bark, each member of the mob being desirous, it seemed, of carrying away something that might testify to his proximity to so great a happening.

Little Melville Brant found a piece of the charred flesh in the ashes and bore it home.

"Ben Stringer aint got anything on me now," said he as he trudged along in triumph.

Entering by the rear he caught hold of the rope which he had left hanging, ascended to the attic window and crawled in.

The future ruler of the land!

ON THE AFTERNOON OF THE lynching Ramon Mansford alighted from the train at Maulville in search of Bud and Foresta. He noted the holiday appearance of the crowd as it swarmed around the depot awaiting the going of the special trains that had brought the people to Maulville to see the lynching, and, not knowing the occasion that had brought them together, said within himself:

"This crowd looks happy enough. The South is indeed sunny and sunny are the hearts of its people."

At length he approached a man, who like himself seemed to be an onlooker. Using the names under which Mrs. Harper told him that Bud and Foresta were passing, he made inquiry of them. The man looked at him in amazement.

"You have just got in, have you?" asked the man of Ramon.

"Yes," he replied.

"Haven't you been reading the papers?" further inquired the man.

"Not lately, I must confess; I have been so absorbed in unraveling a murder mystery (the victim being one very dear to me) that I have not read the papers for the last few days."

"We burned the people today that you are looking for."

"Burned them?" asked Ramon incredulously.

"Yes, burned them."

"The one crime!" gasped Ramon.

"I understand you," said the man. "You want to know how we square the burning of a woman with the statement that we lynch for one crime in the South, heh?"

The shocked Ramon nodded affirmatively.

"That's all rot about one crime. We lynch niggers down here for anything. We lynch them for being sassy and sometimes lynch them on general principles. The truth of the matter is the real 'one crime' that paves the way for a lynching whenever we have the notion, is the crime of being black."

"Burn them! The one crime!" murmured Ramon, scarcely knowing what he said. With bowed head and hands clasped behind him he walked away to meditate.

"After all, do not I see today a gleam of light thrown on the taking away of my Alene? With murder and lawnessness rampant in the Southland, this section's woes are to be many. Who can say what bloody orgies Alene has escaped? Who can tell the contents of the storm cloud that hangs low over this section where the tragedy of the ages is being enacted? Alene, O Alene, my spirit longs for thee!"

Ramon took the train that night—not for Almaville, for he had not the heart to bear the terrible tidings to those helpless, waiting, simple folks, the parents of Bud and Foresta. He went North feeling that some day somehow he might be called upon to revisit the South as its real friend, but seeming foe. And he shuddered at the thought.

XXI

Planning To Act

O n the morning following the Maulville tragedy, before Ensal was out of bed Earl was tugging viciously at his door bell. Recognizing the note of distress in the clang of the bell, Ensal arose, quickly attired himself and hurried to the door.

"Oh, it is my good friend, Earl. Glad—"

Ensal stopped short in the midst of his cordial greeting, so struck was he by that look on Earl's face that said plainly that some overmastering purpose had full charge of the man.

"Walk back," said Ensal, in a more subdued manner, leading the way to his room and steadying himself to meet some grave crisis which Earl's demeanor plainly told him was at hand.

"And what may I do for my friend?" asked Ensal soothingly, when the two had taken seats facing each other.

Earl placed an elbow on his knee, using his hand as a rest for his throbbing temples. Turning his eyes full in the direction of Ensal, as if searching for the very bottom of the latter's soul, he said,

"Have you read the morning paper?"

"No," replied Ensal.

"Read," said Earl, taking a paper from his pocket and handing it to Ensal.

"My God! This cannot be true!" exclaimed Ensal in tones of horror, as he read the detailed account of the Maulville burning. He arose and strode to and fro across the room.

"Never in all my wide range of reading have I ever come across a more reprehensible occurrence," muttered he.

"Listen," said Earl, in the tone of one having more to add.

Ensal paused in his walking and unconsciously lifted his hand as though to ward off a blow.

"The man and his wife who were burned at the stake were Bud and Foresta."

"What! Our Bud! Laughing, innocent, whole-souled Foresta!" almost shouted Ensal, the horror, through the personal element brought into the matter, now doubling its force.

"Poor Mrs. Crump! Poor Negro womanhood! Crucified at the stake, while we men play the part of women, for, what can we do?" said Ensal, looking at Earl, tears of pity for his people welling up in his eyes and stealing their way down his noble face.

"This is at once the saddest and the sweetest moment of all my life," said Earl, rising. Continuing, he said:

"The fact that a race that lashes itself into a fury and cries aloud for the sympathy of the outside world if a Negro casts a look of respectful admiration in the direction of a white woman, finds no limit to what it will do to the women of our race, fills my cup of humiliation to the brim. But I find a measure of compensation in the fact that you, dear Ensal, the arch-conservative, have at last been stirred to action."

Earl now paused to give emphasis to what he was to say next.

"Ensal, the Christ has bidden you, you say, to preach his Gospel to every creature. If the white people of the South permitted you to preach the Gospel to them, you would have some basis for the hope that you would be contributing your due share to the work of altering these untoward conditions. Since they deny you your way of reaching them, come and go our way," said Earl.

"Have you at last found a plan of escape from our awful condition that commends itself to your sober judgment, Earl?" asked Ensal, looking his friend earnestly in the face.

"I have" said Earl.

"Earl, come back tonight. My spirit is tired, tired. Give me the day for the finding of my truer self. I doubt whether the elements which this terrible shock has brought to the surface can be trusted to pass sanely upon matters of such vast importance."

Earl accepted the suggestion and departed.

During that day the two busiest brains in all the world, perhaps, were the brains of these two Negroes: Earl, arranging for the successful carrying out of his plans, and Ensal fortifying himself for events which he knew would largely affect the destiny of his people. He knew not the details nor even the direction of Earl's plans, but he knew that Earl was every inch a soldier and that the blood of some of the mightiest captains of the English speaking people was coursing through his veins.

XXII

The Two Pathways

The day wore on, and about dusk Earl returned to Ensal's home, and the two at once entered upon the consideration of the grave matter that was to be the subject of their conference.

"Before giving my plan, Ensal, I will present the course of reasoning that leads me up to the conclusion that it is the one path to pursue," began Earl.

"So do," said Ensal.

"The men and women," began Earl, "who moulded the sentiment that led to our emancipation and enfranchisement, who set in motion the influences that have tended toward our general uplift, are fast passing away. I am told that the younger generation now coming into power in the North is not as enthusiastic over the matter of helping us as were their fathers. As I see the matter, several influences are at work producing these changes.

"First: A very natural desire on the part of Northern people to be on more pleasant terms with their blood relations of the South.

"Second: The moving of whites from the South to the North, where, in social circles from which Negroes are debarred, they mould sentiment against the Negro. There are more than one million five hundred thousand Southern white people in the North.

"Third: Among the Negroes going North there is a shiftless, criminal element, whose tendency downward is aided by the prejudice against Negroes in labor circles of the North. This class of Negroes in some parts of the North almost monopolizes the attention of the criminal courts and the result is an erroneous opinion with regard to the race as a whole.

"Fourth: There is a decided drift of Northern capital to the South. The greater the holdings of the North in the South, the greater the indisposition of at least that element to have conditions down here disturbed, I think. I believe that by acting now we shall receive far more sympathy from the North than we would be likely to get a few years later."

"Suppose, for the sake of progress in the discussion we concede the validity of your conclusions. Granting that the present is the time to act, what would you do?" asked Ensal.

"Let me state first of all what I would not do. I would not attempt an exodus. The white people of the South would resort to force to prevent our leaving in a mass. I would not attempt a *general* uprising. They have absolute charge of the means of transportation and intercommunication as well as the control of the necessary equipments for waging war."

Earl now paused and looked steadily at Ensal, who awaited with almost breathless anxiety Earl's next words.

"When I was a lad I declaimed the address of Leonidas to his brave Spartan band, and the idea of a vicarious offering has ever since lain heavily on my heart.

"In Almaville here I have a picked band of five hundred men who are not afraid to die. Tonight we shall creep upon yonder hill and take charge of the state capitol. When the city awakes tomorrow morning it will find itself at our mercy. We also have a force of men which will take charge of the United States government building. This will serve to make it a national question.

"When called upon to surrender, we shall issue a proclamation setting forth our grievances as a race and demanding that they be righted. Of course, what we shall call for cannot be done at once, and our surrender will be called for.

"We shall not surrender. Each one of us has solemnly sworn not to come out of the affair alive, even if we have to commit suicide. Our act will open the eyes of the American people to the gravity of this question and they will act. Once in motion I am not afraid of what they will do. I am not fearful of America awake, but of America asleep.

"Such is my plan. In brief, it is the determination of desperate men to provoke intervention.

"Look at Cuba. A handful of men stayed in the field and kept up a show of resistance until our great nation intervened. It is within the power of the Negro race to bring about intervention at any time that it is willing to pay the price. I have found the men and recruited them from the ranks of the plain people who were already ripe for action for the following reasons:

"Labor circles here are just now very bitter toward the city government because of its course toward Negro roustabouts. The white men in charge of the boats that ply the river, fed their Negro hands poorly and made the whole crew eat with spoons out of one pan. They were afforded no sleeping accommodations, being forced to sleep on the bare floor. If a piece of freight was accidentally dropped overboard the Negro who did it was forced to jump into the water after it or be clubbed to death. Some roustabouts who were forced to jump overboard to recover freight lost their lives. These things have influenced the Negroes to abhor roustabout work. But the police force, in the interest of the boatmen, pounced down upon the Negroes and forced them to do the work, and this course is practically urged by one of our leading daily newspapers. In this condition of affairs, the laboring Negro sees a sign of a return to the conditions of slavery, and he is alarmed.

"If in a city of light such as is Almaville this spirit obtains, it won't be long, they feel, before the Negro laborers of the South will be firmly in the grasp of a new form of slavery. They are also alarmed at the clamor of leading newspapers for a vagrancy law which will be invoked in times when the Negroes refrain from labor in the hope of advancing their pay. The presence in our ranks of the labor element representing the Negro masses will give striking evidence of the effect things are having upon all classes of Negroes, welding them together.

"Now, Ensal, you have my whole story. This is to be the most sublime affair in the whole history of our race. Honor yourself, my friend, by joining our ranks."

Earl now ceased.

"Earl," began Ensal, slowly, earnestly, "do you know the Anglo-Saxon race and particularly that brand found in the South? Provoke the passions of that race, arouse the dormant but ever-present fear of secret plottings for a general uprising, and you will inaugurate the wholesale slaughter of innocent men, women and children. Satan hearing of what is going on, will resign his post as King of Hell, will broaden his title and move up to sit as Emperor of the South.

"No, no, no, Earl. Dark, dark is the night, but let us not mistake the glow of the 'jack-o'-lantern' leading to a bog for the gleam of the morning star ushering in the day."

Ensal ceased speaking and the two men looked at each other in silence.

"Do you regard yourself as having finished?" asked Earl after a few seconds of silence.

"Sir," he continued, "if in this hour when I am strangled with the ashes of Bud and Foresta you feed me with a negation—" He did not finish the sentence.

SUTTON E. GRIGGS

"I understand you, Earl. I must offset your proposition with a better one. Foreseeing that you would demand this of me, I have prepared myself," said Ensal.

Going to his desk he procured a rather bulky document. Ensal turned the manuscript over and over. In it he had cast all of his soul. Upon it he was relying for the amelioration of conditions to such an extent that his race might be saved from being goaded on to an unequal and disastrous conflict. He hoped that its efficacy would be so self-evident that Earl might stay the hand that threatened the South and the nation with another awful convulsion. No wonder that his voice was charged with deep emotion as he read as follows:

To the People of the United States of America
"The Anglo-Saxon race is a race of the colder regions and there evolved those qualities, physical, mental and temperamental, which constitute its greatness. A large section of the race has left the habitat and environments in which and because of which it grew to greatness, and in the southern part of the United States finds itself confronted with the problem of maintaining in warmer climes those elements of a greatness hitherto found only in the colder regions.

"The race in these warmer regions took firm hold of the doctrine of a foil, a something thrust between itself and the sapping influences of weather, sun and soil. The Negro was pressed into service as that foil. He was to stand in the open and bear the brunt of nature's hammering, while the Anglo-Saxon, under the shade of tree or on cool veranda, sought to keep pace with his brother of the more invigorating clime, counting immunity from the assaults of nature and superior opportunities for reflection as factors vital to him in the unequal race that he was to run.

"Not only was this foil deemed necessary to the maintenance of the intellectual life of the South, but to its commercial well being as well; for the white man was regarded as constitutionally unable to furnish the quality of physical service necessary to extract from the earth sufficient fruitage to have the South hold her own commercially.

"The wealth of the South, because of a deep seated conviction as to the absolute need of a foil for the white race in warmer climes, because of the hardiness of the Negro's frame, his docility, his habit of cheerfulness when at work, his largely uncomplaining nature, his conception that labor conditions are fixed, his individualism leading to ineptness in combining—these qualities the wealth of the South regards as ideal for the services of capital, and Negro labor is much preferred to that of chronically discontented, aspiring and combining whites.

"The capitalist influence would have the Negro treated humanely, would give him industrial, moral and religious training, and would have him enjoy the protection of the law that he might continue in the South, working in contentment and with efficiency in the lower forms of labor.

"But this element desires that the Negro play the part of the foil and accept this as mainly his mission in America. It has scant sympathy with the college professor and the political agitator that would set the race to dreaming very largely of higher things. The element, therefore, that is most desirous of retaining the Negro population and seeks to make the race satisfied with its present habitat is for the very reason leading to that course, thoroughly opposed to making a speciality of developing *all* there is in the Negro, so that the development that this element stands for is assuredly one sided.

"Opposed to the element that is half friendly to the Negro because of his superior qualities as a foil and commercial asset, are the white industrial rivals of the Negro, whose animosity is whetted by their conscious inferiority in matters physical to this son of the tropics, who is more nearly at home under southern sky than are the children of the colder regions.

"The industrial rivals of the Negro, led on by those who would exploit race prejudices for their profit and those who feel that grave danger lurks in a mixed civilization, keep the baser passions of the people so inflamed that such horrible outrages take a place that the future often seems overshadowed with a cloud dark, portentous and riftless.

"The two elements thus far mentioned, the half-friends of the capitalist class and the rancorous industrial rivals of the Negro, are opposed to each other on the question of the Negro's leaving the South, the former opposing and the latter favoring his elimination, but they are one in insisting that the Negro must be restricted in his aspirations. The question has another complication and a third element is to be reckoned with.

"There is a vein of idealism running through our country that would hold the American people to the thought that the United States has a world wide mission. It is the dream of this class that shackles, whether physical, political or spiritual, shall fall from every man the world around.

"This class says to the capitalist class of the South: 'Our ideals will suffer if we permit you to have political serfs, however well fed they may be.' To the class that would oppress the Negro it says, 'The patient suffering and material service of him whom you buffet entitles him in his own right to a home in this country, and here of all places justice shall be his portion.' This class has opened Northern institutions to them, and training has produced a large and aggressive army of able young Negroes enraptured with the expressed ideals of the republic.

"When it is sought by idealists to make the position of the American Negro square with the constitution, the capitalist class of the South, which fancies that it sees the sudden loss of the foil, and the rivals of the Negro in the labor world combine to oppose the programme looking to the political uplift of the Negro. As the Negro in the groove ('in his place') has the self-interest of the capitalist class on his side, while, aspiring to be as others are, he finds his erstwhile friends and chronic enemies forming a cordon to prevent his rise, it has been suggested that political advancement be made a secondary consideration.

"In view of the powerful forces which we find arrayed against a programme looking to the political advancement of the Negro we can understand the desire of the American people that it be made clear that the political needs of the Negro are vital to the improvement of present conditions. We shall therefore proceed to show how intimately the political question is inwrought in the whole situation.

"After the last word has been said in favor of the capitalist notion of race elevation, it is still found to contain the wonderfully fecund germ of repression. To sustain a notion from generation to generation that the Negro should be denied participation in the political life of his nation necessitates an atmosphere charged with the spirit of repression, a voracious guest, whose appetite calls for food other than the dainties set before him.

"The making of official life in the South independent of Negro sentiment was evidently intended to cause white men to feel free to act according to their own instincts, undeterred by calculations as to the possible effects of their course on the attitude of the Negro toward them.

"With repression the order of the day, and the process of the survival of the fittest operating along this plane, that man who best exemplifies the repressive faculty will survive in the political warfare and thus will be brought to the front the element out of touch with the broadening influences of the age, whose vision is yet bounded by the narrow horizon of race.

"The administration of the government, then, inevitably falls into the hands of the less refined and a contemned race of an alien blood is handed over to them to be governed absolutely. As might be expected under a system that picks its rougher spirits for rulership, the governing force is often worse in its attitude toward Negroes than are the great body of whites. Instead therefore of the government being the guide, piloting the people to broader conceptions, the governing power often sets in motion brutalizing tendencies that eventually sweep down and affect the people.

"Local sentiment has been invoked to hold in check the wrathful outpourings of United States senators, legislatures have held in check rampant governors, and cities have cried out against the acts of legislatures imposing repressive measures not warranted by local conditions, things that signify that repression sends to the front men whose tendency is to lower rather than advance civilization.

"It is generally conceded that the drift of the Negro population of the South toward the cities is due to the lack of police protection in the rural districts. In the city policeman, then, we have an opportunity to study the output of the system of repression at its highest level. Policemen are often the most unbearable of tyrants, arresting Negroes upon the most flimsy charges, and refusing to tolerate a word of explanation. It is actually a capital offense for a Negro to run from a policeman, however trivial the charge upon which he has been arrested.

"In Almaville, which represents the South at its highest point of civilization, policemen have wantonly shot to death Negro after Negro for seeking to elude arrest.

"The following article which we reproduce from one of America's most reputable journals, will speak for itself.

"'How lightly the wanton killing of a Negro has come to be regarded in some Southern communities is brought out by an incident of the week at Memphis, which hardly needs comment. An inoffensive Negro was hawking chickens about the street, when—, who was not in uniform at the time, jumped to the conclusion that the chickens had been stolen, and arrested the man. While he went to put on his uniform he left his prisoner in custody of a nearby grocer, rightly named—, to whom he handed his pistol, with the offhand injunction, 'If he tries to get away from you, kill him.' ——'s assertion that the Negro made a break for liberty is disputed by the testimony of bystanders, but at all events he fired on the Negro, wounding him so severely that he died the next morning. 'Well, you got him, didn't you?' said—on his return. 'If I didn't, I almost,' answered—with a smile. The policeman's only statement in palliation of the unprovoked killing was that the deputy to whom he delegated his authority had 'taken his instructions literally.' The most shocking feature of the affair is that—has not been arrested, and the policeman is apparently to continue on his beat. The 'Commercial-Appeal' may well exclaim in bitterness, 'Life in this community is cheap; the life of a Negro is so valueless that it is freely taken without fear of future punishment in this world.'

"The question may be asked as to whether there are provisions for redress against police outrages. There are courts and commissions that may be appealed to, but two considerations render these institutions of slight value to Negroes. In the first place the sentiment obtains that the evidence of a Negro is not to count as much as that of a white man. With this much the start the policeman has still another advantage. The policy of repression has fostered the idea that it is all right for a white man to commit perjury in cases where there is a contest between a white man and a Negro. Witness the manner in which election commissioners have often been chosen because of their known willingness to swear falsely as to the contents of ballot boxes.

"So, with little sentiment against perjury when a Negro is involved and the extra weight attached to the word of a white man as against that of a Negro, the wrongs of the Negro more often than otherwise go absolutely unavenged.

"Public utilities are likewise administered by white men who often maltreat Negroes. In Almaville a street car conductor was sentenced to two years in the penitentiary for the killing of an inoffensive Negro who was asking him for correct change and at whom, according to his own sworn statement, he shot 'to see him run.'

"In this same city a Negro woman was kicked off of a street car by the conductor for pulling through mistake the cord that registered fares instead of the one that signalled for the motorman to stop.

"For this same offense a Negro in Memphis was shot in the back four times and killed by the conductor, who was allowed to make his escape.

"Many good white people of the South will ask 'If this state of terror exists among our Negro population, how does it happen that it has not impressed itself more forcibly upon the public mind?' Largely because the affected people are voiceless and because they grow weary of invoking the aid of courts and commissions that somehow find their way clear to sustain the side holding membership in the race to which they belong. The Negroes, therefore, meet in groups and exchange accounts of outrages and bitterly sneer when they read in the white newspapers of the South accounts of the ideal relations of the two races.

"The claim of some of the white people of the South that the Negro needs no power in his own hands to insure a proper regard for his interests ought not to be tolerated for a moment in view of all that has happened since the whites have had exclusive charge of the southern governments.

"It has long been a contention of the Anglo-Saxon race that the people should retain power to protect themselves against possible indifference, incompetence or outright meanness on the part of public officials, and if Anglo-Saxons refuse to commit their welfare unreservedly into the hands of fellow Anglo-Saxons, it seems clear that it is placing too great a strain upon human nature to expect ideal results when an alien race is involved. Not only does repression bear such fruit as we have indicated, but it also bears heavily upon the repressed in other directions.

"All history shows that a race stands in need of great men, in need of the contributions of their superior powers, and the inspiration that their names will carry from generation to generation.

"Grappling with the affairs of state affords unique opportunities for growth, while the honor of having served the state operates as a magnifying glass enlarging the inspirational force of individuals so honored. Thus a race having the privilege of committing great trusts to its members draws as a dividend men of enlarged powers and names which will inspire. These influences reapplied to the needs of the state serve mightily to pull the people forward.

"Again, to fix a limit to the development of a race is to run counter to the forces of evolution which are indisposed to recognize barriers of any kind. The human mind revolts at a '*ne plus ultra*.' The Great Unknown has hid himself in the heart of things, and yet the fainting soul of man lingers forever at the barred door of His palace in a sort of rebellious worship, determined to learn of Deity even the forbidden things.

"The human mind is yet human when encased in a Negro body and if this mind chafes at limitations seemingly imposed by eternal forces, it will not submit to limitations arranged by finite creatures.

"We have no doubt arrived at the point in this discussion where it is in order to suggest a remedy for these ills. The offerings of the humane class of Southern white people who would like to settle the whole question upon the basis of the development of the Negro race along restricted lines, must, because of the danger that lurks in the principle of repression, be rejected as totally inadequate. Above all things, the government must go out of the business of repression, must cease tagging the Negro as an outcast among his fellows. The men who administer affairs must be made amenable to the sentiment of the whole body politic and not simply that portion represented by the white citizenship.

"One says: 'The nation felt all this and granted to the Negroes political power.' Explain to us those largely writ words 'Reconstruction Governments.'

"Right gladly do we respond to the task assigned.

"One whom the nation knows as perhaps the foremost living Southerner, who has acquired the art of speaking upon this whole matter in a way that seems to beget at least a respectful hearing everywhere, says: 'Few reasonable men now charge the Negroes at large with more than ignorance and an invincible faculty for being worked on.'

"To this we make reply, the overturning of slavery in the South was revolutionary and not evolutionary. There was no spiritual cataclysm to correspond with the political one. He who on one day ruled *over* the Negro was found spiritually unprepared to rule *with* him on the succeeding day.

"When, therefore, the Negroes were approached by two sets of men, the one set, composed of the former ruling class of the South, equipped morally and intellectually for good government, but wrong at heart upon the great question of human rights, the other composed largely of carpet baggers, scalawags and bad administrators, but true to the principle of equality before the law, it ought not to be surprising that a race fresh from the galling yoke of slavery should choose the set that would look after their liberties.

"This, we feel, fully explains the ills of reconstruction, and those that lament that they were thrust aside from leadership, should further lament that they were evidently not far enough away from the ruling of a race by a race to have charge of the momentous experiment of the joint rulership of races. The real blame for the unfortunate state of affairs falls, perhaps, upon those crushers of free speech in the South who, prior to the Civil War, allowed not the preaching of the doctrine of human rights which would have furnished men of the right temper and proper vision to take charge of the new order of things.

"But we gained much from those times that must not be lost sight of. We gained our racial awakening, the upward impulse. This was a supreme need of our country. For, what pen can set forth what would have been the outcome of a festering carcass of a dead race within our borders.

"The ballot put into the hands of the gloom enshrouded Negro sent a thrill of hope into his very bone and marrow, and the sense of responsibility and the beckoning of the high destiny of citizenship in a great republic begot such a fever of progress in the race that the problem is now that of dealing with the aspirations of the race rather than the more awful problem of trying to avoid the contaminating odor of a race dead to higher appeals, sinking and pulling the nation with it.

"And finally upon the question of reconstruction we find that perpetual disbarment is not visited upon the people of the mightiest city of the new world, because it has from time to time made mistakes and put bad men to the fore.

"Moreover, be it remembered that the Negro of today is not restricted to the choice of yesterday. Good men and true abound in both races in the South, who are now fully equipped to operate a truly democratic government.

"People of America: We were wrested by you from the savage wilds and thrown into your mould. Our bodies have been fitted to your climes, our spirits have been put in tune with yours. We love your institutions, and if your flag could speak, it would tell you that it has no fear of the dust when entrusted to our sable hands.

"The great burdens of your future need the cheer that we can bring, and your labors in the tropics now dimly foreshadowed, may put a premium on what we can yield. By the token of our patriotism and in sight of our willingness to yield all the blood or brawn or brain necessary for the advancement of our common country, we simply beg that you cast not away your ideals, that you do not unsettle the foundations of your democracy when you come to deal with us.

"Grant unto us equality of citizenship. Fix your standard for a man! If you choose, plant the foot of the ladder in a fiery test and engirdle each round with a forest of thorns. Do this and more, if your civilization and the highest needs of the unborn world require it. But when, through the fire and up the path of thorns, we climb where others climb, hurl us not back because of a color given us from above. Let one test be unto all men. Let the strong arm of the nation for its own good and for the ultimate good of humanity insist upon the observance of this principle wherever Old Glory floats. Let this be the guiding star of your policy toward us. This grave question settled, the vast army of Negro leaders absorbed in the momentous work of adjusting this external problem, will be free to turn undivided attention to the curing of those ills that are gnawing at the vitals of the race.

"Those most interested in the internal development of the race can render the cause so dear to their hearts no greater service than by facilitating the adjustment of the outer relation.

"The campaign, then, is one that concerns not only the political forces of the nation, but the moral forces as well, since the pressing of this great wrong upon the hearts of an inoffensive, patient and aspiring people tends to their moral undoing, not only by the evil passions engendered, but also, as has been pointed out, by the withdrawing of so much of the attention of the race from internal development to the absorbing, exacting and, in some respects, narrowing task of battling against an alien aggression.

"From the depths of our dark night we cry unto you to save us from the oppression inherent in the present situation and clear the way for our higher aspirations.

"In behalf of the Negroes of the United States of America,

ENSAL ELLWOOD

Ensal finished the document, folded it carefully and laid it upon his desk.

"Now Earl," he said, "let us print millions of this address and see to it that a copy thereof gets into every American home. Furthermore, let us see to it that it is translated into the various languages of the civilized world that the whole thought of the human race may be influenced in our direction. Earl, our cause is just and we must learn to plead it acceptably. That is our problem. Eschew your plan and join hands with me."

Earl was silent for a few moments and then said:

"This is all very good, Ensal, but it needs a supplement. Charles Sumner's oratory and Mrs. Stowe's affecting portraiture of poor old Uncle Tom were not sufficient of themselves to move the nation. There had to be a John Brown and a Harper's Ferry. Preserve that paper and send it forth. The blood of Earl Bluefield and his followers shed upon the hill crowning Almaville will serve as an exclamation point to what you have said in that paper," was Earl's comment.

Earl now arose to go. Ensal stood up facing him.

"Ensal, clasp my hand in farewell," said Earl feelingly.

"Earl, knowing the mission upon which you go tonight, criminal in its utter folly, I would not for my life put my hand in yours," responded Ensal.

A flush of anger overspread Earl's face, his lip quivered and he was upon the eve of uttering some biting remark. He suppressed his anger, however, and departed, determined upon making his offering of blood. True American that he was, Ensal was determined that the offering should be the output of brains, rather than of veins.

XXIII

They Grapple

Almaville is asleep, watched by the quiet moon, now about to disappear, and the far off silent stars.

Upon the bridge from which hundreds had seen little Henry Crump driven to his death; where the majesty of the law had been trampled under foot in the murder and mutilation of Dave Harper—upon this bridge now stood Ensal awaiting the coming of Earl who had to pass that way to reach the place of rendezvous agreed upon by himself and followers.

At about one o'clock Ensal, standing in the shadow of the framework of the bridge, saw Earl walking rapidly in his direction. As the latter was about to pass, Ensal laid a hand firmly upon his shoulder.

Earl looked around quickly to learn the meaning of the firm grasp and recognized him. There was a look of determination in Ensal's eye that caused Earl to feel that important developments were sure to follow.

"Earl, my friend, you shall not commit this blunder," said Ensal.

"Blood must be shed at some time and it might as well be shed now as at any other time," said Earl, staring Ensal in the face as though he might have reference to his (Ensal's) blood.

Ensal's grasp tightened, and he said, "I tell you frankly, Earl, you will have to disable me before you get to that crowd tonight."

"Turn me loose," said Earl, in a quiet, determined, yet kindly tone. "Ensal, you and I have been friends all of our lives. We sat in school together and hunted birds' nests in the woods side by side. I have sought your counsel from time to time and you have served as a check to me in many instances. But my mind is fully made up now, and it will not pay for even such a friend as you are to stand in my way. I warn you, beware!"

Ensal decided that it was time to act. He quickly pinioned Earl and backed him up against the iron railing. He had just heard the city clock strike one and felt that he could hold Earl in his grasp for one hour, at which time a policeman would come along, whereupon he could deliver Earl over to the officer. With Earl out of the way he felt that he could get around and dissipate the forces that he had organized.

Earl remembered that in Ensal's earlier days, he had suffered a fracture of his left arm, and in his struggling Earl now weighed heavily on that arm which began to weaken. Ensal soon saw that he was not going to be able to pinion Earl for the hour to intervene before the coming of the officer. So deciding, he concluded to stake all on a fall. He felt that if he could get Earl down and get the famous neck hold, which they had practiced so much in their youth, he could succeed in holding him in that way.

To and fro the two men swayed, each man feeling that the welfare of millions depended upon the outcome of this duel of the muscles.

At last Ensal gained an advantage and Earl was thrown. Earl pretended to be making violent efforts to hurl Ensal off of himself, but this was merely a feint. By skillful maneuvering unknown to Ensal he got hold of his pistol and sought to so aim it that he could shoot Ensal through the heart. Concluding that he now had the pistol at the right angle, he pulled the trigger. The trembling condition of his hand could not insure a steady aim and the pistol falling down sent the bullet crashing into his own side. Ensal leaped up, but Earl lay motionless upon the bridge.

It was now only a few moments before the policeman was due at that point and Ensal was in a quandary as to what to do. He was not long in doubt, however. Lifting the wounded man, he half dragged and half carried him to one end of the bridge where there were steps leading down to the river. He disappeared down the steps and hid under the bridge just in time to escape the eyes of the officer.

Ensal did what he could to staunch the flow of blood. He then tried to think. He did not care to expose Earl to the fury of a white mob by revealing the conspiracy. He preferred to heal the racial sore himself without calling a doctor, whose remedy might be worse than the disease. But if he kept Earl's illness secret and Earl died, he was himself liable to be arrested on the charge of murder. He concluded, however, to take the risk of handling the matter himself. He would have Earl nursed back to health and then demand that he leave Almaville on the ground that he was an unsafe leader for the people under existing conditions. He now felt the need of a confederate and his mind ran to Tiara, who was yet living in practical seclusion.

"By the way," said he to himself, "she lives near the river."

Taking possession of a boat which he found moored near by, Ensal put Earl into it and rowed until he was opposite Tiara's house. After considerable effort he succeeded in arousing the inmates.

Tiara attired herself and came out upon the back porch and listened to Ensal's story. She dared not look him in the face too often. Her eyes told too plainly of her suppressed love.

As humble as was Ensal's opinion of himself he was compelled to admit that the net result of this short interview was a decided conviction that Tiara was not altogether indifferent to him, that he held no mean place in her regard. But he was the more mystified as to why she had so persistently refused to allow him to call.

But all this is aside. Tiara accepted charge of Earl and in her faithful hands we leave him for the present.

XXIV

Out of Joint With His Times

J edge, I'd lack to mek' er few dimes. Ken I peddle limonade nigh de co't 'ouse do', sah, yer honah?"

The judge looked with a kindly eye upon the rather small, aged Negro, who made the above request. The look of the man was so appealing and his voice so sad of tone that the judge was moved to grant the request.

"Thank 'ee, jedge, thank 'ee," said the Negro, bowing low, his face and whole frame testifying to his immense joy at being allowed to sell lemonade at the court house door.

"His family must be starving," thought the judge, as he resumed his walk to the court house, haunted by the pleading look in the Negro's eye.

"He asked for that insignificant favor with as much soul as a man could put in a plea for his life," mused the judge, as he continued to think of that haunting look.

"That Negro would hardly tell me, but I would like to know what dark cloud it is that so patently casts its shadow over him," thought the judge, turning to cast a look in the Negro's direction. The Negro saw him turn and greeted him with another profound bow and humble laying off of his hands.

The judge entered the court room, which was now crowded with people from far and near. That day was to be a great day with them. The lynchers of Bud and Foresta were to be tried, but that was not what excited their interest.

The Congressman from the district in which Maulville was located had just died, and his successor was soon to be chosen. There was but little free discussion of political matters in that district, the white population generally rendering unswerving allegiance to the Democratic party, while the Negroes were equally as ardent in the support of the Republican party, each race claiming that so far as it was concerned the exigencies of the situation permitted no other course. In the absence of a political arena in which young statesmen might display their prowess, the court house became the nursery of statesmen in the South.

Thither then the people were flocking today, ostensibly to witness the trial of the slayers of Bud and Foresta, but in reality to pass final judgment upon the claims of the young prosecuting attorney who had announced himself a candidate to succeed the deceased Congressman. The ability of the young man was unquestioned and his exposition of the fundamental principles of the Democratic party was all that could be desired, they felt, but they wanted to hear him on the one question that was the final test of his acceptability, his attitude on the race question.

The court assembled and the crowds poured in. The prosecuting attorney, H. Clay Maul, son of Gen. Maul, after whom the town was named, arrived early and took his seat, his earnest face wearing the look of a determined man sure of his course. Well did he know how much was involved for himself personally in what was to transpire that day, but he had vowed on the previous night, which he had spent at his mother's grave, that he would do his duty regardless of its effect upon his own future.

The first case to be called was that of the man designated by the mob to apply the torch. The chief concern of the defense was in the matter of securing a jury. They expected the judge to do his duty, and the prosecuting attorney to put forth his best efforts to convict. But their reliance was in a jury in whom the race instinct would triumph over every other consideration and cause it to bring in a verdict of not guilty.

It was at last young Maul's time to speak and he arose, slightly nervous. He hesitated an instant before beginning. All the hopes of his deceased father concerning him, all the dreams of his boyhood, all the blandishments of fame and power came surging to his mind and his Ego said, "Spare thyself. Thy sacrifice will be in vain."

Overcome by conflicting emotions that gathered in his bosom at this moment, he waved his hand to the audience as if to say, "Wait," and sat down. His eyes were directed to the floor and his hand still outstretched to the audience, giving the people to understand that he was yet to be heard from.

Every eye in the room was now upon him, and all were conscious that a supreme struggle was going on in his bosom. At last he stood up, a smile of triumph upon his face. And thus it was that a son of the New South came into his spiritual inheritance.

The audience was more eager now than ever to hear every word of the forthcoming speech, and as it forever fixed the status of the young man with his fellows, we give enough of it to our readers to warrant them in passing judgment on the judgment of the people of Maulville, Miss. Said he:

"Upon an occasion such as this, in order that we may the better get our bearings, it might pertinently be asked as to why, in the evolution of things, you, honorable Judge, you, esteemed gentlemen of the jury, and myself, your humble servant, are here today addressing our attention to a crime which was in no wise directed against us personally.

"We are here to take care of the interests of society, to guard it against the influence of a savage deed whose foul breath blown upon our civilization threatens it with utter decay. Availing myself of the latitude accorded one in your court, honored Judge, I shall seek to point out all the involvements in the case which we have before us.

"God has given unto us, or, to be more exact, has permitted us to wrest from the Indian and from creeping snake and prowling beast, a goodly land. Here we raise a product that supplies a need of the world that cannot be so acceptably filled up to the present time by any other quarter of the globe.

"The world at large, therefore, has a vital material interest in the manner in which we conduct ourselves on this spot. We have in our midst Negroes who have a superior adaptation to the labor of the fields, and it is to our interest and to the interests of mankind generally, that they be treated properly, as in their humble way they do this their share of the world's work.

"Crown Murder king here today, if you will, and his bloody sceptre waved over our fields will drive the Negroes therefrom, keep us poor, and sadly disturb economic conditions in the most remote corners of the earth. The material interests of civilization at large, therefore, appeal to you for the administration of justice in our part of the world.

"But civilization has even higher interests involved. We must bear in mind that these are no longer days of isolation, that the deeds of Maulville have been canvassed throughout the earth. Man has been battling upward through the ages, and his savage instincts have sought to mount the ladder with him as he climbed. It has been one of the hardest of man's battles to leave behind him these depraved parts of his nature, and evidence that you carry your savagery with you will make the battle harder for the whole of the human family. And so the moral health of the world demands that every community have a pest house where the isolation and treatment of the morally diseased may forestall an epidemic.

"Coming nearer home, I would call your attention to our sister states to the north of us. These states are bound up with us in a political system. Destiny has made us one people, and by the outside world we must be reckoned with as a unit. Under these circumstances, the thought must unavoidably develop that *that* for which all are to be held responsible must, when the need arises, be made the subject of inquiry and action on the part of all.

"For the honor, then, of the other members of our political compact who form a part of our shield against the outside world, and to enable them in view of the attached responsibility, to accord, with a clear conscience, full deference to our claim to the right of local self-government, it is incumbent upon us to act worthily here.

"Gentlemen, our own larger interests are involved in this matter. It is our privilege, and our duty as well, to contribute our best heart and brain to the care of the interests of our nation and to the guidance of the world. But if our statesmen walk through the halls of Congress emitting from their garments the scent of burning human flesh, when they would put forth their souls as great magnets for mankind, the tender, sensitive world-heart will recede from their touch, and leave their hollow, resounding voices reverberating through space. Thus shall we lose our share of great world leaders.

"Gentlemen, the lives of white men will be placed in jeopardy by a miscarriage of justice here today. The jury that refused first to hang a white man for killing a Negro, seared its conscience, lowered its estimate of the value of human life, and now, without due process of law, the white man who kills any one is almost uniformly exempt from the death penalty. The maltreatment of Negroes according to immutable laws precedes but by one day the like maltreatment of whites.

"Need I to tell you of the patient dark faces that sit in their humble cabins today and quietly await your verdict which will make their lives secure, or subject to the caprice of the man with murderous instinct.

"Gentlemen of the jury, remember that the interests of your children are involved in this case. The capital on which they are

SUTTON E. GRIGGS

to begin life is necessarily that which they draw from your social manifestations. They saw that holiday crowd that gathered here on the day of the burning and some of those hot human ashes fell in their innocent faces. What happened here that day will be talked over by them in their childish sports. Let us give to them a fitting conclusion to the recital. We have made it possible for them to say that the deed was done. Let us avoid contributing to their hardness of heart, by causing them to say that the deed was spurned.

"Having at length put before you the claims of society whose mouthpiece I am this day, I am now ready to deal more specifically with the case before us.

"I have no hesitancy in asserting that the evidence before you, gentlemen, is of a sufficient character to justify the conviction of the defendant. The case is so plain that it seems like arguing an axiom to discuss it. I will not impugn the intelligence of this jury by a review of the evidence in so plain a case. But knowing the deadening miasma of race prejudice that hangs over, envelops and stifles us so often, I shall dwell briefly upon the nature of the crime committed by the defendant.

"A Negro, acting upon that instinct of self-preservation that ramifies all nature, shot down his would-be murderer, no other course save the surrender of his life being open to him. Have we gone back to the days of the cannibal kings, when it was deemed a virtue for a subject to lay down his life to satisfy a whim of his master? Have we, the proud Anglo-Saxon race, fallen so low that we are to ask that the Negro meekly lay down in our pathway, while we enjoy the pleasant sport of boring holes through his body? If this is not what we mean, how do you account for that writhing form, the form of that Negro, whose only offense was that he sought to preserve from the violence of man a life granted unto him by his Maker?

"And now I come to the crowning horror of the ages. Our poets have sung in loftiest strains of the devotion of woman.

"A Negro wife, true to that impulse of the woman's heart that has made this old world worth living in, that has taught men that the fireside is worth dying for, that impulse—devotion to a loved one in distress, led that girl to journey by her husband's side through bog and swamp, bearing up bravely under the scorching heat of the sun and wilting not in the dead of night amid the gloom of the beast infested forest.

"Ah! gentlemen, that girl deserved better of us than what we gave her. And I declare unto you that as the ages roll by, the people of the earth are going to make of those cruel flames that wrapped themselves about her nude body a fiery chariot of glory to carry the blessed memory of her devotion from age to age.

"Such will be the verdict of the future; but, gentlemen of the jury, you are this moment the mouthpiece of your age and we are concerned about your verdict.

"Gentlemen of the jury, the evidence in this case, the revolting nature of the crime and every consideration of society demands a verdict of guilty. We have reached the apex of infamy in the crime which lies unavenged at our doors.

"Let us retrace our steps beginning here today. Seeing whither our present policy as a people toward the Negro has led us, let us adopt another course.

"Is it a crime for me, one of your sons to invoke loyalty to our national constitution? If so I commit that crime. Let us accept the Negro as a partner in our government, and acts such as these will not occur. Nor in so saying do I abate one inch of my stand for white supremacy. As long as there are distinct races there will be racial aspirations for first place. But I crave not the first place born of the prestige of sitting upon a throne whose base is forever lapped by the waves of the blood of the innocent and the helpless. I stand for white supremacy in intellect, in soul power, in grasp upon the esteem of others through sheer force of character. But all this aside. Justice whom you cannot afford to banish from your borders calls upon you to pronounce over this defendant's head the verdict of guilty."

Young Maul's speech was now over, but he did not sit down. Having declared himself in the manner that he did, he knew that he was henceforth to be a political outcast, a pariah. He had not stood up for the extension of the caste idea to the political system and knew that its ban would henceforth be upon him. Yet in spite of the dreary future which his speech had carved out for him his soul was at ease, for he was conscious of having advocated that which was best for his people.

Grasping his hat he strode out of the room, not waiting for the verdict of the jury.

"It is a pity that our section can find no place for so true a soul presided over by so bright a mind," thought the judge, his eyes following young Maul, as the latter passed out of the court room, and through the court house yard, looking neither to the right nor to the left. The people understood his going. He was saying that he had done his duty and personally could be absolved from concern as to results.

The lawyers for the defense, feeling sure of the jury, saw no necessity for the making of speeches on their part. They waived their rights in this particular, and the jury, after being solemnly charged by the judge, was handed the case.

The Negro at the door selling lemonade had been an eager listener to all that was said in the case. He had now totally suspended his sales and, standing in the door was eagerly scanning the faces of the jurymen, who had announced that they did not need to retire, but could return a verdict on the spot.

"Come here, darkey, with your lemonade," called a white man on the outside to the Negro.

The Negro obeyed, though his heart for some cause was in the court room. Suddenly there was a tumult in the court room and the Negro dropped his lemonade bucket and ran to the door. He saw a crowd surging about the lyncher that had been on trial, and he cried out in startling tones:

"Gemmen, don't do dat. Don't kill de man. De boy whut wuz burnt, I'm his daddy. I jes' wanted yer ter 'nounce de man guilty so as ter tek de stain off'n de dead; but fur Gawd's sake, don' lynch de man."

The judge saw through it all at once and hastened to Silas Harper's side, for it was he, Bud's father. In sorrowful tones the judge said, "You are mistaken, friend. They are congratulating the man. They are not trying to hurt him. The jury has said that he was not guilty. You had better come and go with me. They might become enraged against you and have another lynching."

Silas Harper's jaws fell apart in amazement and his eyes took on the look of a terror-stricken, hunted animal. He meekly slunk along after the judge, and to an outsider would have appeared to be a criminal doomed to die.

XXV

A Joyful Farewell

Mr. Seabright sat upright in bed and rubbed his eyes. The gas was burning and there sat a man in one corner of his bedroom, turning a rifle over and over, in a cool manner, a keen look of satisfaction in his eyes.

"Am I dreaming? O, I am dreaming!" said Mr. Seabright, trying to thus reassure himself; but a man was sitting in a chair in the corner, all as plain as day.

"But I have had dreams that appeared as real," thought Mr. Seabright.

He pinched himself so as to further determine the fact as to whether he was awake or asleep. Being thoroughly convinced that he was awake, he quickly fell back in the bed and pulled the cover over his head. Remembering, however, the man's rifle, he pulled the covering far enough down to allow one terrified eye to keep track of the weapon.

"Mr. Seabright!" called the intruder.

"Sir," responded Mr. Seabright, in sepulchral tones.

"I think your wife belongs to that man Marshall's church," remarked the man.

Mr. Seabright nodded assent.

"Tell her that her pastor will hardly live till morning and that he would like to see her," said the man.

Mr. Seabright had now found courage to pull the cover down from over the other eye, and it now rested on his nose.

"Did you hear me," said the man, rather sharply.

"You will please excuse my boldness," said Mr. Seabright, tremblingly, "but you have a totally wrong conception of my disposition I fear, Mr. Stranger. You can get the full benefit of my services with only the butt end of that thing pointing my way, instead of the occasional shifting of the muzzle in my direction."

The stranger smiled coldly and said, "Tell her what I said."

Mr. Seabright now got out of bed and proceeded to the door opening from his room into that of his wife.

"Arabelle!" called Mr. Seabright through the partly opened door.

Mrs. Seabright, who was in the midst of a horrible dream, sprang out of bed.

"Arabelle, Percy G. Marshall is dying and would like to see you."

"O my God! Can I save him?" she cried, wringing her hands.

Excited though she was, it was not long before she was attired and rushing to the study of the church where she was told that she would find the dying man. The door of the study was slightly ajar so that she had no trouble in entering. There upon the sofa lay the dying man, his hand pressed to his side, evidently in an effort to staunch the flow of blood. It is the young man whom we saw repeating his childhood prayer after Mrs. Seabright in the Domain Hotel.

"I knew that it would come to this, mother. I wanted to live to tell you that," said the dying preacher.

"O my boy, my darling! O what has lain hold of me?" cried Mrs. Seabright, as she knelt by the bedside of the dying one and kissed his lips fervently.

A gasp and the spirit of the young man was gone. A loud scream rang out on the night air when Mrs. Seabright realized that it was all over with him.

"Wait, my boy, mother is coming."

Taking from her bosom a small vial she swallowed the contents, fell across the breast of the dead and joined him in the spirit land.

When Mr. Seabright had delivered to Mrs. Seabright the message of the intruder, he turned and looked at the man in a helpless sort of way. When Mrs. Seabright was gone the man remarked to Mr. Seabright:

"I been had my eye on your house for sevul years. It makes a good fort to shoot frum. It'll be turned to that use today. You'd better clean out, for a mob 'll be here soon."

"O my God! Have they found me out? O my God! my God!" said Mr. Seabright, wringing his hands.

"You may git now, I say," said the man.

Mr. Seabright sought to put on his clothes, but trembled so that he did not make much headway. His visitor, to expedite matters, assisted him in dressing.

"Take your money and the like. I won't need it where I'll be 'fore night," said the intruder.

Mr. Seabright took advantage of this offer to pile into a small valise all the money, valuable papers and jewels in the house that he could find. He went out of the rear door and passed back to his stable, and out into the alley.

Casting a look back at his house, he said: "Farewell, Hades!" Looking up into the heavens, he whispered as he ran: "In case, O stars, any inquiry is made of you as to my whereabouts, please let it be known, of course without specifying the exact spot, that I have gone to the land of the Eskimo. My face will soon be overgrown with a beard which I shall so dye that the keenest scented mob in all the world can not discern any difference between my humble self and the anatomy of the regulation Eskimo. So, farewell!"

XXVI

Gus Martin

Gus Martin, for it was he who was Mr. Seabright's visitor, saw to it that every window and door of the house was properly barred, and then repaired to the tower which commanded every approach to the house. To his very great surprise he found the tower a veritable arsenal with ammunition in abundance and death dealing devices of the most improved types. He perceived that the tower was protected by armor plate and was so constructed that one might fire upon others with practically no danger of being hit himself.

"Beyond doubt I shall go to judgment today, but I shall take along with me a putty good body guard," said Martin, as he settled himself back.

The day dawned beautifully, and Martin put a hand to his lips and threw a kiss at the sun. "Tomorrow I'll know more about you than I do now," said he. "And some others will, too," he added.

At about eleven o'clock he saw leaping the front gate a tall raw boned bloodhound.

"It's a pity a pore dum' brute has got to lead this pursession; but if it mus' be, it mus' be."

So saying, he lifted his rifle to his shoulder and a shot rang out on the air. The beast leaped high up in the air, twisted his head to one side and plunged forward lifeless. Within a few more moments a second hound appeared, and he met a like fate. Soon there was a clatter of a horse's feet and an officer of the law came dashing down the street. As he got opposite the Seabright home a rifle shot rang out and his horse fell, throwing the rider against an electric light post, and stunning him for the time being. Martin aimed his rifle at the officer as he lay, then lowered it.

"Not yet. Ain't had the confab yet."

The people in the vicinity perceived that there was something unusual going on and began to crowd in front of the space facing the Seabright residence. It soon became known that Rev. Percy G. Marshall had been murdered and the murderer had been tracked to the Seabright residence. It was also surmised that the offender was a Negro, as the hounds had traced him from the place of the killing to a Negro dwelling, thence on to the Seabright house. The city of Almaville was soon in a ferment and the white people poured out to that section of the town. Several thousand people were soon massed in the neighborhood of the Seabright residence.

Martin had provided himself with a speaking trumpet and through it he now shouted, "You people are permitted to stand in front uv these premises, but you mustn't 'tempt to git over my front yard fence."

Some one suggested the getting of a trumpet to induce whoever the party was to allow officers of the law to come in unmolested. The trumpet was procured and the following dialogue took place.

The trumpeteer of the crowd shouted, "Whoever you are, we call upon you in the name of the State to surrender."

Martin replied, "I'm a nigger. Martin is my name. I have killed a white man fur a good cause. Before I give up I would like to have a little talk with the sheriff. Tell him to step to the neares' tellerphone place and call up Seabright."

The sheriff did as requested and Gus went to the telephone.

"Say, Mistah Sheriff, this is Gus Martin that saw Dave Harper lynched. If I give up to you will you perteck me?"

"I'll do what I can, Martin. Of course, you know what you have done."

"Will you lose your life trying to perteck me?" asked Martin.

"Well, uh—well, Martin, that's pretty hard to say, considering you murdered one of my race, you know."

"Ring off," said Martin.

Gus now called up the Governor's office.

"Governor, this is Gus Martin. Will you perteck my life if I surrender to this heah sheriff? I am 'cused uv killin' a white preacher."

"I can do nothing unless called upon by the sheriff of your county," said the Governor, and put up the telephone receiver.

The Seabright residence had 'long distance' telephone connections and Gus called up the White House at Washington. He stated his case and the secretary to the President replied:

"We are powerless to act. The most that we can at present do is to create a healthy public sentiment against lynching."

"Ha! ha! ha!" laughed Gus through the telephone. "Is that all you can say to a man that risked his life fur your flag?"

Gus now called up the British legation to sound it on the question of proposing intervention on the part of the leading nations of the world. He was told that the problem was a domestic one and that foreign countries could not intervene. Gus returned to his trumpet and said,

"I have tellerphoned 'round the world and there ain't no justice nowhere fur a black man. We'll fight it out right here."

In the meantime five young men had formed an agreement that they would make the dash to the building. They had figured that Gus could not shoot all five before one of them could reach the lower door and be sheltered from the fire. They made the dash, but Gus was quicker than they fancied, and one by one they went down before his deadly aim. The city was in a frenzy.

We must leave the scene of combat for a while in order to be prepared for the dramatic turn events were about to take.

XXVII

Tiara Mystifies Us

Tiara was sitting on the front porch of her home gazing pensively out upon the blue hills that fringed the distant horizon.

On the day previous she had been able to pronounce the wounded Earl well and he had gone forth solemnly pledged to no longer rebel against the overwhelming desire of the Negro race to pursue steadily the policy of moral suasion, as exemplified by Ensal.

That morning Eunice had taken her departure and had for some reason or other refused to let Tiara know her destination.

Tiara missed Eunice, but there was a countervailing joy in her soul. Eunice gone, her period of exile was over, and Ensal—O, well, well; he could call to see her sometimes. That was as much as she would admit to herself, but there was an enlivening sparkle to those beautiful dark eyes whenever that individual came before her mind. She was intending that night to write him a note suggesting that he ought to call and receive an account of her stewardship in the matter of preserving Earl's life. That was a non-committal piece of territory on which a renewal of friendly relations might begin, she felt. The newsboy came riding along and tossed the afternoon paper upon her porch. She picked up the paper, opened it and glanced at the various headings. In an instant her interest in the paper was more than perfunctory.

She saw an account of the murder of Rev. Percy G. Marshall, and of the besieging of the supposed murderer that was still in progress when the paper went to press.

At that moment a white man was passing in a buggy. Tiara hailed him, grasped a hat and was soon in the buggy by his side begging him to speed her to the city, which the wondering man kindly did.

Directed by Tiara, the man drove to the edge of the crowd of besiegers. By brave struggling, her hat gone, her long hair down her back, her dress torn, she made her way to the front of the swaying, surging mass of frenzied humanity.

"Gentlemen," said she, "Let us stop this frightful slaughter. Suspend hostilities! Give me a chance and I will bring things out all right. All I ask is that you respect my prisoner."

Tiara's sweet, strong voice carried conviction and the crowd in silence awaited her action. Snatching a walking stick from a bystander and tearing a sleeve from her dress she made a flag of truce and mounted the steps of the gate.

Through his trumpet Martin shouted, "Flag uv truce held by the lady won't be shot at, purvided no one else comes with her."

The crowd now awaited with feverish anxiety the outcome of this new turn of affairs. Tragic as were the surroundings, the great throng found time to admire the great beauty, the magnificent form, the queenly carriage of Tiara, as bareheaded and with flag aloft she marched up to the citadel of the outlaw.

Martin met her at the door, let her in and ran back to the tower to see that no one took advantage of his absence to attempt to approach the building. But his precaution was unnecessary. It was a matter of honor with the great throng and none thought of violating the flag of truce.

Tiara followed Martin to the tower and spoke to him a few words in a low, earnest voice.

"Woman, is that true? And all this havoc to be laid at my door?"

"My God!" said Martin humbly. "My God," he murmured again. Steadily down the stairway he walked and flung the door wide open, saying to Tiara, who followed, "Well, I'm done. They may have me." Tossing his rifle in midair, he said, "I give up, gentlemen." Taking the white flag he marched down the sidewalk, stepped outside the gate and stretched forth his hand for the sheriff to handcuff him. No sooner was he thus fastened than the mob surged in upon him. A blow from a stick knocked him down. As he lay upon the ground the muzzle of a pistol was seen protruding from each of the side pockets of his pants. Leroy Crutcher, whose testimony had helped to stimulate the mob that lynched Dave Harper, was again on hand. Eager for a souvenir that would enable him to boast to the white people as to how he stood by them, he stooped down to snatch one of the protruding pistols. Martin had the pistols so set in his pocket that to snatch them would pull the triggers and cause them to fire. A shot rang out and ploughed into Leroy Crutcher's body and he fell a corpse.

The crowd swayed back from Gus in superstitious fear, taking him to be a remarkable personage to be able to keep up a bombardment in his condition. As no more shots came the mob felt reassured and drew near the prostrate form of Gus. His eyes looked up into scores of pistols now leveled at him, and as they rang out their death song Gus Martin smiled and died.

XXVIII

Poor Fellow

The whole of the night following the Gus Martin tragedy was spent by Ensal in sorrowful meditation, as he restlessly walked to and fro in his room.

The Rev. Percy G. Marshall had been an outspoken friend of the Negro. The white South, Ensal felt, had at one time seemed to fetter its pulpit, not allowing it much latitude in dealing with great moral questions that chanced to have an accompanying political aspect. Ensal had looked on with profound admiration as the young Rev. Mr. Marshall, by precept and by example, boldly led the way for an enlarged scope for the white clergy of the South.

Had the pulpit in question done its full duty in preaching against the institution of Slavery, it might have been eradicated by peaceful means, and the Civil War averted, was Ensal's firm conviction, and he further felt that the future well-being of the South and the happy adjustment of the relations of the races was largely dependent upon the extent to which the white preachers taught the brotherhood of man and invoked the application of the Golden Rule to all pending problems.

In all this work the Rev. Percy G. Marshall was a pioneer spirit, and by degrees the white pulpit of the South was growing more and more aggressive and emphatic. And now it was the irony of fate that this young minister should be slain by a member of the race for which he had imperilled his own standing among the whites.

In addition to his grief over the tragic death of the Rev. Mr. Marshall, there was another phase of the Gus Martin affair that gave Ensal deep concern. Gus was the child of the new philosophy that was taking hold of the race, which was as follows:

Faith in the general government was at a low ebb. Concerted action of a warlike nature on the part of the race was regarded as being out of the question, if for no other reason than that the Negro leaders were practically a unit in pronouncing such a course one of stupendous folly under the existing unequal conditions. Word was therefore being passed down the line that every man was to act for himself, that each individual was himself to resent the injustices and indignities perpetrated upon him, and that each man whose life was threatened in a lawless way could help the cause of the race by killing as many as possible of the lawless band, it being contended that the adding of the element of danger to mob life would make many less inclined to lawlessness.

Ensal saw where such a course would lead the race. Negroes were ordinarily approached in the name of the law and in that name disarmed. When the law had thus rendered them helpless, the mob would form and be presented with the object of its wrath bound hand and foot.

Resistance, then, to be effective would have to be offered to the officers of the law. The utter pitiableness of the lone Negro being sent by this philosophy to fight the organized power of modern society went home to Ensal's heart.

The night passed and dawn found him yet pacing his room. His mother summoned him to breakfast, but the all-night agony of his spirit had robbed him of an appetite. The mail man's whistle blew, announcing the morning's mail.

"I hope I will get a letter that will turn my thoughts into another channel."

Such was Ensal's solemn soliloquy. How little did he dream of what was in store for him. Going to his front gate he received the mail. To his great surprise, the handwriting on one envelope seemed to be that of Gus Martin. He quickly tore this letter open and read its contents. He looked around and about cautiously, as if to see if any one was observing him. He crumbled the letter tightly in his hand and started toward the house, when he began to sway to and fro. His head grew dizzy, he tottered and fell. His mother, who had been observing him through the window, suppressed an incipient scream that almost escaped her lips, and rushed to her son's side. She had seen the effects of the letter, and her first act was to attempt to gain possession of it for the possible protection of her boy. But even in his swooning condition he clutched the letter with so powerful a grasp that she could not wrest it from him. She now cried aloud for help, and neighbors came to her rescue.

Ensal was borne into the house, his mother keeping in close touch with the hand that held the letter. After some effort he was restored to consciousness, and his first words were,

"The letter! The letter! O my God! the letter!"

"You have it, my boy. It has never left your hand," said his mother.

"Thank heaven!" uttered Ensal fervently.

When Ensal seemed to be nearly restored to his normal state the neighbors retired.

"Mother, ask me not why, but prepare my things. I must leave America," said Ensal, in a tone so forlorn as to deeply touch the mother's heart. Drawing near to Ensal she threw her arms around his neck and looked into his eyes as if to read his soul.

Upon this holy scene where troubled son and anxious mother meet we will not obtrude, and so step lightly out of the room.

XXIX

A Revelation

The fact that Ensal was to resign his church and leave the country was soon known throughout Almaville and filled the hearts of the good people of both races with sore regret. Tiara was amazed.

"Am I no more to him than that," she asked herself.

Choosing an hour when she knew Ensal would not be in, Tiara called at his home to see his mother. Mrs. Ellwood received her in her bedroom. She dropped on her knees by Mrs. Ellwood's side, and said in tones that told of a sadly torn heart:

"Mrs. Ellwood, don't let your boy leave. We need him. I—, don't, don't let him go."

"I have plead with him, my dear, but his mind is made up, it seems," said Mrs. Ellwood sorrowfully.

"Perhaps he thinks that—that—that I am not—as good a friend to him as—ah! but he ought to—."

Tiara arose, clasped her hands tightly and bent her beautiful face toward the floor thinking, thinking. Tears began to gather as she thought of this culminating sorrow of a life so full of sorrows.

"Mrs. Ellwood," said Tiara, "when your son comes home, for my— well—please, oh please, beseech him to stay. Think me not immodest because I plead with you thus. I feel so sure; I know—somehow I know that if all were known between your boy and myself he would not leave the country, at least would not leave it—." Tiara paused and looked up at Mrs. Ellwood as she finished her sentence with the word, "alone."

"May heaven pardon my boldness," said Tiara, with clasped hands, lifted face and eyes straining for the light that would not come to her soul.

"I understand you, dear child. I must confess that I do not know what has come over Ensal."

The two women now sat down upon the bed, and, clasped in each other's arms, silently awaited Ensal's coming.

"Wait, dear," said Mrs. Ellwood. "I will bring you a copy of the farewell address which he has prepared. Girl, my heart is drawn to you and I love you, have loved you, and I always thought that Ensal loved you with all the ardor of his soul. But I don't understand. I will get the address. It might give us some light."

Mrs. Ellwood soon returned bringing with her the document, which was addressed to a Negro organization devoted to the general uplift of the race, a body that had been founded, and was now presided over by Ensal.

The paper ran as follows:

FELLOW MEMBERS

"I believe in the existence of one great superior Intelligence whom the Christians know as the God of heaven. I believe that this great being accords to men free moral agency, but gathers up all that we do and shapes it to his 'one far off divine event.'

"The Dutch slave trader that landed his cargo of slaves upon the banks of the James River was moved thereto by his greed for gain, we know. The Southerners who wrought upon their slaves and gave them the rudiments of civilization, wrought, we know, for the purpose of gain.

"The war which brought emancipation was not in itself a deliberately planned altruistic movement, but was precipitated upon the country, and waged primarily in the interest of the solidarity of the white race in America.

"In order that the Negroes might preserve their estate of freedom and thus obviate another martial conflict they were given the ballot, and, that the national life might not be corrupted by the putrid exudations from ignorant aliens to its civilization and its ideals, culture was provided for the liberated millions.

"The medley of motives working through all the past has at last produced in America the strongest aggregation of Negro life that has at any time manifested itself upon the earth.

"To say the least it is a striking coincidence that simultaneous with the turning of the thought of the world toward Africa and the recognition of the need therein of an easily acclimated civilizing force, that the American Negro, soul wise through suffering, should come forth as a strong man to run a race.

"In America we are confronted with a grave problem, the adjustment of our relations with a strong race. Some have suggested that our social absorption by this race is the only real solution of our difficulties.

"Fellow Negroes, for the sake of world interests, it is my hope that you will maintain your ambition for racial purity. So long as your blood relationship to Africa is apparent to you the world has a redeeming force specially equipped for the work of the uplift of that continent.

"Again, a seer linked to us by ties of blood, foreshadows that the paramount problem of our century will be the problem of the adjustment of the white to the darker races. If we disappear as a dark race this world problem must look elsewhere for special advocates. It seems to me that our situation is from every point of view eloquent with the voice of destiny.

"I go to introduce a working force into the life of the Africans that will make for their uplift. May it continue your ambition to abide Negroes, to force the American civilization to accord you your place in your own right, to the end that the world may have an example of *alien* races living side by side administering the general government together and meting out justice and fair play to all. If through the process of being made white you attain your rights, the battle of the dark man will remain to be fought.

"As I enter therefore upon the larger mission of the American Negro, it is with the confident hope that my base of supplies shall remain intact that our struggling kinsmen everywhere may ever find men of their blood piloting the whole strength of America into channels that make for the good of the whole human race.

Yours in perpetual bonds of brotherhood,
Ensal Ellwood

The two had just finished the reading of the paper when the door bell rang.

"Ensal's ring," whispered Mrs. Ellwood, who now closed Tiara in the room and went to meet her son.

Armed with the knowledge of the fact that Ensal was strong in Tiara's regard, Mrs. Ellwood was ready for a determined attack. Mother and son entered the study, Ensal perceived at once that his mother had something of importance to say to him.

"My boy," she began, "I know of the noble purpose that moves in your bosom and have ever been proud of it. I shall not chide you now that it turns your face to the fatherland. But I would have you marry."

"No! no! no! mother. O no! never," said Ensal, losing all his wonted calmness, but kissing his mother to let her know that his displeasure over the subject did not extend to her for mentioning it.

"My son, I shall hold you in utter disfavor unto the day of my death if you, without just cause, declare war upon womankind. How can you, my son!" said Mrs. Ellwood reproachfully.

Ensal grew calm and looked long and lovingly at his mother. He saw that for some reason or other his mother had taken up the battle against him and that he was under the necessity of exonerating himself. Said Ensal:

"Mother, I am going to divulge to you a secret which I had firmly resolved to carry to the grave with me. I have withheld it from you, not because I mistrusted you, my dear, dear mother, but for the sake of another. In all my life, mother, I have seen but the one girl whom I have loved, Tiara Merlow—and she loved another!"

The mother shook her head and smiled knowingly.

"Ah, but I know, mother. The object of her love was a white man. Gus Martin saw him kiss her and killed him, killed the Rev. Percy G. Marshall. The letter which gave me so much trouble told me all, told me all! O my God! She loved another."

Mrs. Ellwood sat and looked at Ensal utterly dazed. She arose and, thoroughly weakened physically by the shock of Ensal's information, crept out of the room to Tiara.

"Darling," she gasped, "he says that you loved another—a white man—a preacher—Percy Marshall. Daughter, darling, deny it! Deny it!"

"O! God of Heaven, what shall I do! What shall I do," groaned the unhappy Tiara.

With one hand pressed upon her throbbing heart and the other laid upon her fevered brow the beautiful girl left the Ellwood home.

XXX

Mr. A. Hostility

It will be recalled that in a very early chapter we saw a cadaverous looking white man, wearing a much worn suit of clothes, making a sketch of Ensal's home, as the latter was going out to make arrangements with Mrs. Crawford for the introduction of Tiara into the best circles of Negro life in Almaville.

And now in the crisis of the relations of Ensal and Tiara he comes forward to inject his peculiar virus into the awful wound made in Ensal's heart by the disclosures of the Gus Martin letter. Tiara, burdened creature, was hardly out of sight of Ensal's home when this man made his appearance and was ushered into the study. When he had taken the seat proffered him, he said:

"Gus Martin wrote me a letter, enclosing a copy of a letter which he had sent to you."

"O heaven, be merciful. Let it not come to that!" said the agonizing Ensal, shocked that Gus had let another know of the matter that had so disturbed him.

"Your prayer is not directed to me, but I hear, understand, and will answer it. You do not wish the public to know of the contents of your letter. You would shield the good name of the girl. As I shall very shortly trust you with one of the gravest of secrets you will have a hostage which will of itself insure silence on my part. You and I, I am sure are the only two persons to whom Gus communicated the affair and between us we can take care of the secret."

Ensal stepped across the room and clasped the man's hand fervently and the two regarded themselves as mutually pledged to secrecy concerning that matter and whatever was now about to be canvassed.

"It is not necessary for you to know my name, nationality or anything that pertains to me. I am the incarnation of an idea. You may know me as Mr. A. Hostility," said the man.

"Is there any significance attached to your choice of an initial to represent your rather significant given name?" asked Ensal.

"Decidedly," said Mr. Hostility. "The A stands for Anglo-Saxon, the God-commissioned or self-appointed world conqueror. I am the incarnation of hostility to that race, or to that branch of the human family claiming the dominance of that strain of blood."

The man drew his seat up to the table and, motioning for Ensal to take a seat on the other side, said "Come near me, friend."

Ensal did as bidden and sitting thus close to the man noted the almost maniacal look of intensity in his eye.

Keeping his eyes steadily on Ensal's face, Mr. Hostility lifted his hand to his inside pocket and drew out a leathern case. Laying it on the table he crossed his hands upon it and said:

"Will you hear me patiently? Gus Martin told me over and over again that you were a Negro who had dedicated your all to the welfare of your race. I began watching you years ago and I have carefully noted the trend of events waiting for the moment that would make our spirits congenial to each other, and I do believe that the dark shadow under which you stand will sober you into fellowship with my sombre soul."

"You seem to be bitter. I am more crushed than bitter," said Ensal.

"Yes, but bitterness is the next stage, and I am sure that consideration of a few things which I shall put before you will bring you to the next stage," said Mr. Hostility.

Opening the leathern case he said, "Look at this map."

Ensal bent forward and looked at a map of the world spread out before him.

"The world, you see, will soon contain but two colossal figures, the Anglo-Saxon and the Slav. The inevitable battle for world supremacy will be between these giants. Without going into the question as to why I am a Pro-Slav in this matter, I hereby declare unto you that it is the one dream of my life to so weaken the Anglo-Saxon that he will be easy prey for the Slav in the coming momentous world struggle."

"Do I understand that you are to talk treason to me today; for of course you know my people are tied up in a political system with the Anglo-Saxons," asked Ensal, with some warmth.

"Ah! That is the question? Are you a part of the American nation or a thing apart? I can prove that you are a thing apart—a fly in the stomach for whose ejection an emetic is being diligently sought. Now, hear me," said Mr. Hostility.

Always eager to hear what thoughtful men had to say with regard to his race, Ensal leaned back in his chair, determined to give earnest attention to this observer of American life, whose very hostility assured the acuteness of his observations.

Just at this moment Ensal's mother informed him that a committee was in their parlor, having come for the purpose of pleading with Ensal to reconsider his determination to leave America.

"Madam," said Mr. Hostility, "tell the gentlemen that there is a party closeted with your son, who has the one key to the Southern situation long needed by your race, and that I am sure your son will abide in America."

Mrs. Ellwood cast a look of warning at her son as she withdrew from the room. She was not at all favorably impressed with Mr. Hostility, and had been ill at ease ever since he entered the house.

Ensal said, "Excuse me a few moments, Mr. Hostility," and stepped out of the room.

Mrs. Ellwood, knowing that her son would follow her, stopped in the hallway, and when he came dropped a pistol into his coat pocket, saying in a whisper, "My dear boy, do be careful."

Ensal smiled sadly and kissed his mother.

"Tell the committee, mother, that my mind is fully made up and a discussion of my going would be utterly useless. Take the name of each, assure them all that I appreciate their interest and will call on them to have a social chat before I leave, provided, however, they agree not to seek to disturb my purpose in this regard."

Ensal's mother went to the parlor with his final word, and Ensal returned to Mr. A. Hostility.

Tiara was now at home praying that Ensal might not leave America yet awhile. Mr. A. Hostility was also praying to his evil genius for a like result.

Monstrous incongruity! How often do diverse spirits from widely differing motives work toward a common end!

XXXI

Two of a Kind

While Ensal was absent from the room Mr. Hostility had caught sight of a book which he perceived was the work of a rather conspicuous Southern man, who had set for himself the task of turning the entire Negro population out of America. He clutched the book eagerly and said to himself:

"I will further inflame the fellow with this venomous assault on his race. I will further ripen his heart for my purposes."

Upon Ensal's return to the room, Mr. Hostility called his attention to the book written for the express purpose of thoroughly discrediting the Negro race in America. The militant look that came into Ensal's eye pleased Mr. Hostility immensely. "I will get him! I will get him!" thought he.

Ensal did not speak for some time, allowing his weary mind to go forth upon excursions of thought begotten by the mention of the book. The movement for which this book stood, constituted what Ensal regarded as one of the most menacing phases of the problem of the relation of the races. He knew that in the very nature of things a policy of misrepresentation was the necessary concomitant of a policy of repression. Now that the repressionists were invading the realm of literature to ply their trade, he saw how that the Negro was to be attacked in the quiet of the AMERICAN HOME, the final arbiter of so many of earth's most momentous questions, and he trembled at the havoc vile misrepresentations would play before the truth could get a hearing.

Ensal thought of the odds against the Negro in this literary battle: how that Southern white people, being more extensive purchasers of books than the Negroes, would have the natural bias of great publishing agencies on their side; how that Northern white people, resident in the South, for social and business reasons, might hesitate to father books not in keeping with the prevailing sentiment of Southern white people; how that residents of the North, who essayed to write in defense of the Negro, were laughed out of school as mere theorists ignorant of actual conditions; and, finally, how that a lack of leisure and the absence of general culture handicapped the Negro in fighting his own battle in this species of warfare.

At last Ensal discussed the book with such warmth that Mr. Hostility greatly rejoiced. Leaning across the table, his fiery eyes glowing more fiercely than ever, he almost shrieked:

"Friend, aside from that book, knowest thou not unto what the content of the Southern policy is leading? Extinction, sir, extinction! Listen to me awhile."

"One could hardly be more absorbed than I am at this moment," said Ensal, rather glad of the warmth of the discussion that took his mind somewhat away from his personal grief.

"The Southern white man, when it comes to you, is a believer in caste. He believes or professes to believe that God, who created the worm and the bird, also created the Negro and the white man, and that the gulf between these respective orders of creations is just as wide in the one case as in the other. Follow this caste idea to its last analysis. The lower orders must give way to the higher. The mineral is absorbed into the vegetable and we get the herb, the cow comes along and crops the herb, the man comes along and eats the cow. The higher order is given the power of life and death over the lower. Can't you see that your race is simply preserved because it is not yet in the way of the white race?" said Mr. Hostility.

"Proceed," said Ensal.

"Even now, when have you heard of a white man's being hanged for the murder of a Negro, however cold-blooded the murder? Can't you see the awful significance of that fact? Over seventy-five thousand Negroes have been murdered in the South since your Civil War and I know of just one hanging of a white as a result. Again, the worst houses to live in are assigned to your people; the lower forms of labor, involving the most exposure and danger to life, are reserved for your folks. Phosphate mines and guano factories shorten human life wofully and your people are sought for these 'life shortening' jobs. Mark my words," said Mr. Hostility, rising and bending across the table, "when the Anglo-Saxon feels the need of it, he is going to exterminate you folks. Theories to the wind! When has a theory or sentiment of any kind been allowed to stand in the way of his interests?"

"Well, what are we to do?" asked Ensal, anxious to draw the man out.

The man dropped back to his seat. "Now that's right," said he; "'Where there is a will there is a way,' you Americans say." Reaching into his vest pocket he pulled out a bottle which was hermetically sealed. "There, there, lies your salvation," said he, tapping the bottle.

"How so?" enquired Ensal.

"This thing came to me like a revelation," said the man. "The way to attack an enemy is to get at him where you can do him the most harm at the least risk to yourself." A sinister smile now played upon the man's face. "Your color is the thing that operates against you Negroes. You can take what is your curse and make it your salvation."

The man was delighted with the interest that was plainly evident on Ensal's face.

"Listen!" said he, bending forward and speaking in low tones. "The pigment which abides in your skin and gives you your color and the peculiar Negro odor renders you immune from yellow fever. This bottle here is full of yellow fever germs. Organize you a band of trusted Negroes, send them through the South, let them empty these germs into the various reservoirs of the white people of the South and pollute the water. The greatest scourge that the world has ever known will rage in the South. The whites will die by the millions and those that do not die will flee from the stricken land and leave the country to your people.

"The desolation wrought will for a time disorganize this whole nation and the Pan-Slavists will have the more time to plan for the coming struggle.

"My scheme helps you and helps the Pan-Slavist cause and disposes of a common foe, a section of the white race. Of course, we will have you Negroes to fight in the last contest. But you would prefer being the ones living to make the fight, would you not?" asked the man, now nervously awaiting Ensal's next words.

Ensal was silent for a few seconds. Then he asked slowly:

"Do you make that proposition to me, a follower of the Christ?"

"I have anticipated you there. Did not God use plagues and a wholesale slaughter to solve the Egyptian race problem? Shall you be more righteous than God?"

"Really would you, a civilized being, propose to me a course that involves the wholesale destruction of women and innocent babes?" asked Ensal with mounting wrath.

"Did not your God tell the Hebrews to wage a war of extermination on the Canaanites?" asked the man.

Ensal arose and pointing his index finger at the man, said with a voice vibrant with deep feeling:

"Now hear me a while. During the Civil War my race met the requirements of honor where-ever the test was applied—whether it was in the test of the soldier on the field of battle or the slave guarding the women and children at home.

"Nor has freedom altered this trait of Negro character," continued Ensal. "When discussion rages fiercest, Negro servants continue to abide in white families, with no thought of leaving or of being dismissed. Negro men sit in carriages by the side of the fairest daughters of the Southland and take them in safety from place to place. The Negroes do the cooking for the whites, nurse their babies, and our mothers hover about the bedside of their dying. This they do while their hearts are yearning for a better day for themselves and their kind. But the racial honor is above being tainted. Let the Anglo-Saxon crush us if he will and if there is no God! But I say to you, the Negro can never be provoked to stoop to the perfidy and infamy which you suggest.

"And as for you, sir, I pronounce you the true yoke fellow of him about whose book we have been talking, who, wearing the livery of the unifier of the human race, smites the bridge of sympathy which the ages have builded between man and man, who, inflamed racial egotist that he is, would burn humanity at the stake for the sake of the glare that it would cast upon the pathway of the one race. Is the issue clearly enough drawn between us?"

Mr. Hostility nervously folded his map of the world, restored his bottle of germs to his pocket, and stood facing Ensal in silence for a few seconds, his keen disappointment adding to the uncanny look of his face.

"Remember, we have each other's secrets," said Mr. Hostility meaningly in tones that showed his keen regret at the failure in this instance of his long cherished scheme. This somewhat recalled Ensal to himself.

"Yes! Yes! Fear me not. I do not need to impose anything whatever between your suggestion and our racial honor. That is simply unapproachable from that quarter. For that reason I am not tempted to repeat to others what you have said to me."

Thus reassured, Mr. Hostility made a bow of mock humility, directed at Ensal a look of utter contempt, and disappeared.

Ensal dropped upon his knees and prayed thus:

"O Spirit eternal, God of our fathers, move thou upon the hearts of the American people and bid them to lift thy children of the darker hue from their 'low ground of sorrow,' where all the evil influences of the world feel free to tempt them. In all the dark night that may yet await them, when men shall so beset them as to threaten the sustaining influence of patriotism, grant from the dawn eternal the lighted taper of hope that shall throw its beams athwart the darkness, and furnish a cheering glimpse of the fair end of all things. Watch with thine all seeing eye and nail with thine omnipotent hand the machinations of those who would poison human hearts and destroy the humane instincts that are the graces of our faulty world. Abide thou here forever and grant that the post of pilot of our planet be given unto this land unto which, though I depart, my heart is moored by the sweat of brow, flowing blood and anguish of spirit contributed by my ancestors. Grant unto this prayer the full measure of consideration that can be bestowed by divine will upon the heart pleadings of an earnest humble soul."

XXXII

WORKING AND WAITING

Tiara had gone home from her painful interview with Mrs. Ellwood, and sought the seclusion of her room for the purpose of trying to think out a course of action. She was able, she felt, to make all things plain to Ensal, but in order to do this it would be necessary to make disclosures, which, if given publicity, would very materially affect the welfare of others. She felt that Ensal would sacredly guard her revelations, but her disclosures would be of little service to him if he could not use them to protect himself in case the charge against her became public.

Not desiring to put him in a possibly embarrassing position, Tiara concluded to bear her sorrow until such a time as she would be free to defend herself openly, if such a course became necessary. As to when she would be in a position to do this, Tiara was utterly unable to tell and, to add to the horror of the situation, there was absolutely nothing that she could do to advance her interests. Chance, blind chance, so far as she could see, had her fate in hand, and to all the pleadings of her heart as to what was to become of her, no answer came.

The time came for Ensal to depart, and the lips of Tiara were yet sealed by circumstances and did not utter the word that would have set all matters right with her, but wofully wrong with some others, perhaps. It soon became evident to Tiara that she could not stand the strain of a life of hopeless brooding and Ensal had not long been out of America before she began to cast around for a line of endeavor.

Before leaving America, Ensal had published the address which he had prepared in his contest with Earl, and Tiara chose as her mission the placing of a copy thereof in every American home, feeling that it would draw to conditions in the South a greater degree of interest on the part of the nation as a whole.

Not only did Tiara thus appeal to outside influences for an amelioration of conditions, but she also addressed herself to matters that depended upon forces operating within the race. She looked upon the dead line in the business world as being as baneful as that in the political world.

This spirit of caste in the upper grades of employment in the South forbade Negroes from working side by side with the whites. She felt that the most practicable manner of banishing this dead line was for Negroes to combine their capital and launch enterprises that would make it possible for their people to rise in keeping with the claims of merit, unhampered by the fact of their color. She felt that the infusion of hope in the industrial world, the breaking of the bands that hopelessly chained the Negroes to the lower forms of labor was a question of far reaching consequence, and in every way possible she brought the question home to the hearts of the people.

To do this work the more successfully, Tiara took the lecture platform and traveled from city to city, pleading her cause. She also took an active interest in the question of local option, seeking to suppress the liquor traffic wherever local sentiment could be educated to the point that made such a course possible. This work of temperance brought her very often before audiences in which there were white people and Negroes, and sometimes she spoke to audiences in which there were white people only.

It may be said with truth that Tiara was deeply concerned in all these matters and sometimes felt that it was perhaps destiny's way of forcing her out of a reserve that had hitherto denied the world the benefit of some of her powers. But while her heart was in this work, it must also be confessed that she never faced an audience but that her beautiful eyes surveyed it with eagerness, ever in search of some one woman face.

Her correspondence grew to be very large, and each batch of letters, before being opened, was looked over hurriedly in the hope of finding a certain woman's handwriting. A close student of countenances could have discerned over and over the signs of disappointment that her weary heart would often register upon her beautiful face. Days and months and then years dragged their way slowly along.

At last one day Tiara's patient waiting seemed about to be rewarded. An exclamation of joy, a happy little laugh, a beautiful face that told of a weary heart at last made glad, indicated that the letter which Tiara had long hoped for had come.

Tiara took the next train for Goldsboro, Mississippi, a small town in the interior of the state. It was not until the next morning that her train pulled up to her stopping place.

"Can you tell me where the Hon. Q. A. Johnson lives?"

"To be shuah, ma'am," said the Negro lad to whom Tiara had spoken. "Ef you'll git right in heah, you'll be dah befoh yer know it, ma'am," said he giving a Chesterfieldian bow.

As Tiara took the back seat of the double seated buggy, a young Negro man clambered upon the front seat by the side of the driver whom Tiara had accosted. He had a somewhat intelligent looking face and was evidently accustomed to good society, although his clothes on this occasion were ragged and dirty. This Negro had been on the train with Tiara since leaving Almaville, but she had been so absorbed in the object of her mission that she was oblivious to all that was passing around her.

"Whar you gwine?" asked the driver of his Negro companion.

"Scuse me, but beins you don't seem to be over prosp'rous, I specks you had kinder bettah pay in advance," said the driver, with a diplomatic smile that said, "Now, don't get mad. This is a business matter."

Without a word the stranger pulled out a bill and handed it to the driver, who took out his fare.

Tiara reached the Johnson residence, which was a large building, built on the colonial style and surrounded by as fine a set of trees as one could wish to see. Tiara went around to the kitchen and was taken into the dining room by the Negro woman cook.

"You will please withdraw as I desire to be alone when I meet Mrs. Johnson," said Tiara to the cook, with a pleasant smile.

Mrs. Johnson pulled aside the sliding door leading into the dining room and, catching sight of Tiara, uttered a scream of joyous surprise and rushed into her arms. Tiara gently disentangled herself in order to close the door which Mrs. Johnson had left open. Sitting down by Mrs. Johnson's side, Tiara took hold of her hand and talked in low, earnest tones for a few moments, watching her countenance the while.

"No, no, no, I could not think of that for a moment. No, no, no," said Mrs. Johnson, and in her heart there grew a great coldness toward Tiara for even suggesting such a thing.

As for Tiara her hopes fell to the ground, and with despair written upon every feature she arose to go. The two went to the back door through which Tiara had entered, Mrs. Johnson in an excited manner saying over and over again: "O no, no! Such a thing is not to be thought of for a moment!" words that pierced Tiara like a dagger each time they were uttered.

Sitting on a bench in the back yard waiting, as he said, for an opportunity to ask Mrs. Johnson for a job, sat the Negro who had ridden on the train with Tiara and had come to the Johnson residence as she came. Mrs. Johnson looked at him, felt herself grow weak, and swooned away. The Negro had looked scrutinizingly at Mrs. Johnson, and now arose hurriedly, evidently satisfied with his inspection. When Mrs. Johnson recovered consciousness, she asked wildly,

"Where is he? The Negro, where is he? Ah, he will—"

Mr. Johnson, who had been summoned from the library to assist in caring for his wife, placed his hand over her mouth and prevented her from talking further.

Tiara, who had become somewhat dazed by Mrs. Johnson's treatment, had not stopped to help care for the swooning woman, but had walked away as one in a trance. How she made her way back to Almaville, she never knew.

XXXIII

Back in Almaville

The Hon. H. G. Volrees sat in his office room looking moodily out of the window. Since the desertion of his young bride his life had been one long day of misery to him. His mystification and anger increased with the years, and he had kept a standing offer of a large reward for information leading to the discovery of his wife. He had vowed vengeance upon the author or authors of his ruin.

"Come in," said he in a response to a knock on his door.

A young Negro man walked in and Mr. Volrees turned around slowly to look at his caller.

"This is Mr. Volrees?" asked the Negro.

Mr. Volrees nodded assent, surveying the Negro from head to foot, noting the flush of excitement on his swarthy face.

"I understand that you have offered a reward for information leading to the discovery of the whereabouts of your wife," said the Negro.

An angry flush appeared on Mr. Volrees' face and he cast a look of withering contempt in the Negro's direction, who read at once Mr. Volrees' disgust over the fact that he, a Negro, dared to broach the question of his family trouble.

"Pardon me," said the Negro, turning to leave.

"Come back! Are you a fool?" said Mr. Volrees angrily, his desire for information concerning his wife overcoming his scruples.

"My wife took me to be one and left me," said the Negro in a tone of mock humility.

Mr. Volrees looked up quickly to see whether he meant what he was saying or was making a thrust at him. The solemn face of the Negro was non-committal.

"Now, what do you know?" asked Mr. Volrees gruffly.

"I know where your wife is," said the Negro.

"How do you know that she is my wife?"

"I was the porter on the train that you and she began your bridal tour on," replied the Negro.

"How have you been able to trace her?"

"I was the porter on the train on which she first came to Almaville. She came into the section of the coach for Negroes, and she and a Negro girl created a scene."

"Go on!" almost shouted Volrees, now thoroughly aroused.

"The reward?" timidly suggested the Negro.

"Of course you get that. Go on!" said Volrees, with increasing impatience.

"The affair was so sad-like that I always remembered the looks of the two women," resumed the Negro. "One night not long ago I saw the Negro girl buy a ticket to Goldsboro, Mississippi. It came to me like a flash that she was going to see your wife. She had the same sad look on her face that she had the night I saw them together. I followed this girl to Mississippi and sure enough I came upon your wife."

Volrees had now arisen and was restlessly moving about the room, his brain in a whirl.

"Was she living with some family, or how was she situated?" he asked.

"She and her husband live—"

"Her husband!" thundered Volrees, grabbing the Negro in the collar, fancying that he was grabbing the other husband.

"The people there say that she is married," said the Negro timidly.

"I will choke the liver out of the miscreant," said Volrees, tightening his hold in the Negro's collar as if in practice.

"I am not the man," said the Negro, with growing determination in his voice. Volrees was thus recalled to himself and resumed his restless tramping.

"No, you are not the man. You are only a—nigger."

Grasping his hat, Volrees strode rapidly out of the room. At the door he bawled back,

"You will get your reward."

The Negro followed Volrees at a distance and noted that he went to the office of an exceedingly shrewd detective.

In the course of a few days the city of Almaville was shocked with the news that a Mrs. Johnson, wife of a leading Mississippi planter had been arrested and brought to Almaville on a charge of bigamy. The prosecutor in the case was the Hon. H. G. Volrees, who claimed that the alleged Mrs. Johnson was none other than Eunice Seabright, who had married him. Mrs. Johnson denied being the former Miss Seabright, and employed able counsel to conduct her defense.

The stir in the highest social circles of Almaville was indeed great, and for days very little was talked of save the forthcoming Volrees-Johnson bigamy trial.

SUTTON E. GRIGGS

XXXIV

A Great Day in Court

Long before the hour set for the trial of the alleged Eunice Volrees on the charge of bigamy the court house yard and the corridors were full of people, but, strange to say, the *court room* in which the trial was to take place, though open, was not occupied. The crowds thus far were composed of Negroes and white people in the middle walks of life, who looked upon the forthcoming trial as a 'big folks" affair and, as if by agreement, the court room was spared for the occupancy of the elite. As the hour for the trial drew near the carriages and automobiles of the upper classes began to arrive. Each arrival would come in for a share of the attention of the middle classes and the distinguishing feature of each personage was told in whispers from one to another.

When the carriage of the Hon. H. G. Volrees rolled up to the court house gate silence fell upon the multitude and those on the walk leading to the court house door fell back and let him pass. His face wore a solemn, determined look and the common verdict was, "No mercy there. A fight to a finish."

The court room was now fairly well filled with Almaville notables, and the plain people now crowded in to get seats as best they could or to occupy standing room. Almost the last carriage to arrive was that containing Eunice. The curtains to the carriage were drawn so that no one in it could be seen until the door was opened. Eunice and her lawyers stepped out and quickly closed the door behind them. Contrary to the expectations of many, she wore no veil and each person in the great throng was highly gratified at an opportunity to scrutinize her features thoroughly. A way was made for her through the great throng and she walked to the prisoner's seat holding to the arm of her lawyer.

The case was called, a jury secured, and the examination of witnesses entered into. The first witness on the part of the State was the Hon. H. G. Volrees himself. As he took the witness chair a bustle was heard in the room. The people in the aisle were trying to squeeze themselves together more tightly to allow a man to pass who was leading a little six-year-old boy, who had just been taken from the carriage which had brought Eunice to the trial. "Make room, please. I am taking her son to her," the man would say, and the crowd would fall away as best it could.

The Hon. H. G. Volrees had opened his mouth to begin his testimony when he noticed that his attorney, the opposing counsel, the judge and the officers of the court had turned their eyes toward the prisoner's seat. As nobody seemed to be listening to him he halted in the midst of his first sentence and turned to see what was attracting the attention of the others. As he looked, a peculiar sensation passed over him. Perspiration broke out in beads and his veins stood out like whip cords. He clutched his chair tightly and cleared his throat.

There sat beside Eunice her child, having all of Mr. Volrees' features. There were his dark chestnut hair, his large dark eyes, his nose, his lips, his poise and a dark brown stain beneath the left ear which had been a recurrence in the Volrees family for generations. The public was mystified as it was commonly understood that the marital relations had extended no farther than the marriage ceremony. The presence of this child looked therefore to be an impeachment of the integrity of Mr. Volrees and of Eunice. The wonder was as to why nothing about the child had been mentioned before. Mr. Volrees sat in his chair, his eyes fixed on the boy.

The lawyer at length resumed the examination of Mr. Volrees, but the latter made a sorry witness. It was evident that the coming in of this child had thoroughly upset him in some way. He was mystified, and his mind, grappling with the problem of his likeness sitting there before him, could not address itself to the functions of a witness in the case at issue. He was finally excused from the witness chair.

The other witnesses, who, out of sympathy for H. G. Volrees had come to identify Eunice as his bride, seeing his collapse, did not feel inclined to take the prosecution of the case upon themselves and their testimony did not have the positiveness necessary to carry conviction. It was very evident that the state had not made out a case and an acquittal seemed assured.

The Negro porter was in the court room eagerly watching the progress of the trial, knowing that the obtaining of his reward hinged upon the outcome of the case. He saw the trend of affairs and felt that something had to be done to stem the tide. He saw Tiara sitting in the court room, and said to the prosecuting attorney in a whisper, "Yonder is a colored girl who knows her thoroughly and can tell all about her."

To her great surprise Tiara was called as a witness. She was a striking, beautiful figure, as she stood to take the oath that she would tell the truth, the whole truth and nothing but the truth.

"Mr. Judge," said Tiara, in a sweet, sad voice, "can it go on record that I am not a volunteer witness in this case?"

The judge looked a little puzzled and Tiara said, "At any rate, judge, if in after time it be said that I did not on this occasion stand up for those connected with me by ties of blood, I want it understood that I did not seek this chair—did not know that I was to be called; but since I am here, I shall fulfil my oath and tell the truth, the whole truth and nothing but the truth."

Tiara now took her seat in the witness chair.

Eunice leaned forward and gazed at Tiara, her thin beautiful lips quivering, her eyes trying to read the intent of Tiara's soul.

Tiara looked at the recording clerk and appeared to address her testimony to him. Now that she was forced to speak she desired the whole truth to come out. Her poor tired soul now clutched at proffered surcease through the unburdening of itself. She began:

"In revolutionary times one of your most illustrious men, whose fame has found lodgment in all quarters of the globe, was clandestinely married to a Negro woman. My mother was a direct descendant of this man. My mother's ancestors, descendants of this man, made a practice of intermarrying with mulattoes, until in her case all trace of Negro blood, so far as personal appearance was concerned, had disappeared. She married my father, he thinking that she was wholly white, and she thinking the same of him. Two children, a boy and a girl, having all the characteristics of whites, were born to them. Then I was born and my complexion showed plainly the traces of Negro blood. The community in which we lived, Shirleyville, Indiana, in a quiet way, was much disturbed over the Negro blood manifested in me, and my mother's good name was imperilled.

"My mother confessed to my father the fact that she was a descendant of Negroes and he made a like confession to my mother as to his ancestry. When Shirleyville found out that my parents had Negro blood in their veins, I was regarded as a 'reversion to type,' and the storm blew over. My father became Mayor of the town, and great ambitions began to form in my mother's heart.

"A notable social event was to take place at Indianapolis and my mother aspired to be a guest. She met with a rebuff because she had Negro blood in her veins. This rebuff corrupted my mother's whole nature, and hardened her heart. She had my father to resign as Mayor. Our home was burned and we were all supposed to have perished in the flames. This was my mother's way of having us born into the world again.

"My mother, father and the other two children began life over as whites, and I began it over as a lone Negro girl without family connection, and we all had this second start in life here in your city.

"Most all people in America have theories as to the best solution of the race problem, but my mother fancied that she had the one solution. She felt that the mixed bloods who could pass for whites ought to organize and cultivate unswerving devotion to the Negro race. According to her plan the mixed bloods thus taught should be sent into the life of the white people to work quietly year after year to break down the Southern white man's idea of the Negro's rights. She felt that the mixed bloods should lay hold of every center of power that could be reached. She set for herself the task of controlling the pulpit, the social circle and the politics of Almaville and eventually of the whole South and the nation. O she had grand, wild dreams! If she had succeeded in her efforts to utilize members of her own family, she had planned to organize the mixed bloods of the nation and effect an organization composed of cultured men and women that could readily pass for white, who were to shake the Southern system to its very foundation. With this general end in view, she had her son trained for the ministry. This son became an eloquent preacher. My mother through a forged recommendation, which, however, the son did not know to be forged, had him chosen as pastor of a leading church in this city.

"My mother had a strange power over most people and a peculiar power over my brother. He did not at all relish his peculiar situation, but my mother insisted that he was but obeying the scriptural injunction to preach the gospel to every creature. The minister in question was none other than the universally esteemed Rev. Percy G. Marshall, who now rests in a highly honored grave in your most exclusive cemetery, from which Negroes are barred as visitors."

There was a marked sensation in the court room at this announcement concerning the racial affinity of the Rev. Percy G. Marshall.

"I visited my brother clandestinely; often he and I sorrowed together. On the night of the murder, which you all remember, and preceding that sad event, closely veiled I visited him at his study. When we were through talking I arose to go and opened the door. 'Kiss your brother.

We may not meet again,' said he sadly. Neglecting to close the door I stepped up to him and kissed him. When I turned to go out I saw that Gus Martin, whom Leroy Crutcher, as I afterwards found out, had set to watching me, had seen us kiss each other. I hurried on home embarrassed that I could not explain the situation to him. When on the next day I read of my brother's death, I immediately guessed all. That is how I had the key to bringing Gus Martin to terms. When he found out his awful mistake he was willing to surrender.

"So resulted my mother's plans for the mastery of your Southern pulpit."

Turning to Eunice, she said, "There is her daughter. Through her my mother hoped to lay hold on the political power of the state. But that girl loved a Negro, the son of the prosecutor, the Hon. H. G. Volrees (sensation in the court).

"After leaving her husband, Eunice came to live with me. Earl Bluefield, who is Mr. Volrees' son (decided sensation) was wounded in a scuffle that was not so much to his credit, and he was brought to my house to recover. Eunice waited on him. They fell in love, left my home and married. This explains how that boy favors the Hon. Mr. Volrees. It is his grandson."

Tiara now stood up and said, "Mr. Judge, it may not be regular, but permit me to say a few words."

The whole court seemed under a spell and nobody stirred as Tiara spoke.

"My mother is dead and paid dearly for her unnatural course. But do not judge her too harshly. You people who are white do not know what an awful burden it is to be black in these days of the world. If some break down beneath the awful load of caste which you thrust upon them, mingle pity with your blame."

Tiara paused an instant and then resumed:

"One word to you all. I am aware of the fact that the construction of a social fabric, such as your Anglo-Saxondom, has been one of the marvelous works of nature, and I realize that the maintenance of its efficiency for the stupendous world duties that lie before it demand that you have strict regard to the physical, mental and moral characteristics that go to constitute your aggregation. But I warn you to beware of the dehumanizing influence of caste. It will cause your great race to be warped, to be narrow. Oratory will decay in your midst; poetry will disappear or dwell in mediocrity, taking on a mocking sound and a metallic ring; art will become formal, lacking in spirit; huge soulless machines will grow up that will crush the life out of humanity; conditions will become fixed and there will be no way for those who are down to rise. Hope will depart from the bosoms of the masses. You will be a great but a soulless race. This will come upon you when your heart is cankered with caste. You will devour the Negro today, the humbler white tomorrow, and you who remain will then turn upon yourselves."

Tiara paused and glanced around the court room as if to see how much sympathy she could read in the countenances of her hearers. The rapt attention, the kindly look in their eyes gave her courage to take up a question which the situation in the South made exceedingly delicate, when one's audience was composed of Southern white people.

"One thing, Mr. Judge, wells up in me at this time, and I suppose I will have to say it, unless you stop me," said Tiara, in the tone of one asking a question.

The judge made no reply and Tiara interpreted his silence to mean that she was permitted to proceed.

Said she: "You white people have seen fit to make the Negro a stranger to your social life and you further decree that he shall ever be thus. You know that this weakens his position in the governmental fabric. The fact that he is thus excluded puts a perennial question mark after him. Furthermore the social influence is a tremendous force in the affairs of men, as all history teaches. To all that goes to constitute this powerful factor in your life as a people, you have seen fit to pronounce the Negro a stranger. The pride of the Negro race has risen to the occasion and there is a thorough sentiment in that race in favor of racial integrity.

"So, by your decree and the cordial acceptance thereof by the Negro, he is to be a stranger to your social system. That is settled. The very fact that the Negro occupies an inherently weak position in your communal life makes it incumbent upon you to provide safeguards for him.

"Instead, therefore, of the Negro's absence from the social circle being a warrant for his exclusion from political functions, it is an argument in favor of granting full political opportunity to him. When a man loses one eye, nature strengthens the other for its added responsibility. Just so, logically, it seems absurd to hold that the Negro should suffer the loss of a second power because he is shut out from the use of a first.

"Your Bible says: 'And if a stranger sojourn with thee in your land, ye shall not vex him.' White friends of the South! Let me beseech you

SUTTON E. GRIGGS

to vex not this social stranger within your borders; the stranger who invades your swamps and drains them into his system for your comfort; who creeps through the slime of your sewers; who wrestles with the heat in your ditches and fields; who has borne your onerous burdens and cheered you with his song as he toiled; who has never heard the war whoop but that he has prepared for battle; whose one hope is to be allowed to live in peace by your side and develop his powers and those of his children that they may be factors in making of this land, the greatest in goodness in all this world. Don't circumscribe the able, noble souls among the Negroes. Give them the world as a playground for their talents and let Negro men dream of stars as do your men. They need that as much as you do. As for me, I shall leave your land."

Turning to Eunice, Tiara stretched forth her hands, appealingly and said, "Sister, come let us leave this country! Come."

"Ha! ha!" laughed Eunice, with almost maniacal intensity, as she waved her hand in disdain at Tiara, who now slowly left the witness stand.

All eyes were now turned toward Eunice, who had arisen and stood trying to drive away the passions of rage that seemed to clutch her vocal cords so that she could not speak. At last getting sufficient strength to begin, she said:

"Honorable Judge and you jurymen: I declare to you all today that I am a white woman. My blood is the blood of the whites, my instincts, my feelings, my culture, my spirit, my all is cast in the same mould as yours. That woman who talked to you a few moments ago is a Negro. Don't honor her word above mine, the word of a white woman. I invoke your law of caste. Look at me! Look at my boy! In what respect do we differ from you?"

She paused and drawing her small frame to its full height, with her hands outstretched across the railing, with hot scalding tears coursing down her cheeks, she said in tremulous tones:

"And now, gentlemen, I came here hoping to be acquitted, but in view of the statements made I want no acquittal. Your law prescribes, so I am told, that there can be no such thing as a marriage between whites and Negroes. To acquit me will be to say that I am a Negro woman and could not have married a white man. I implore you to convict me! Send me to prison! Let me wear a felon's garb! Let my son know that his mother is a convict, but in the name of heaven I ask you, send not my child and me into Negro life. Send us not to a race cursed with petty jealousies, the burden bearers of the world. My God! the thought of being called a Negro is awful, awful!"

Eunice's words were coming fast and she was now all but out of breath. After an instant's pause, she began:

"One word more. For argument's sake, grant that I have some Negro blood in me. You already make a mistake in making a gift of your blood to the African. Remember what your blood has done. It hammered out on fields of blood the Magna Charta; it took the head of Charles I; it shattered the sceptre of George III; it now circles the globe in an iron grasp. Think you not that this Anglo-Saxon blood loses its virility because of mixture with Negro blood. Ah! remember Frederick Douglass, he who as much as any other mortal brought armies to your doors that sacked your home. I plead with you, even if you accept that girl's malicious slanders as being true, not to send your blood back to join forces with the Negro blood."

Eunice threw an arm around her boy, who had arisen and was clutching her skirts. She parted her lips as if to speak farther, then settled back in her seat and closed her pretty blue eyes. Her tangled locks fell over her forehead and the audience looked in pity at the tired pretty girl.

Eunice's attorneys waived their rights to speak and the attorney for the prosecution stated that he, too, would now submit the case without argument.

"Without further formality the jury will take this case under advisement. You need no charge from me. You are all Anglo-Saxons," said the judge solemnly in a low tone of voice.

The jury filed into the jury room and began its deliberations. A tall, white haired man, foreman of the jury, arose and spoke as follows:

"Gentlemen: We have a sad case before us today. That girl has the white person's feelings and it seems cruel to crush her and drive her from those for whom she has the most affinity to those whom she is least like. Then, I pity the boy. He carries in his veins some of our proudest blood, and it seems awful to cast away our own. But we must stand by our rule. One drop of Negro blood makes its possessor a Negro.

"Our great race stands in juxtaposition with overwhelming millions of darker people throughout the earth, and we must cling to the caste idea if we would prevent a lapse that would taint our blood and eventually undermine our greatness. It is hard, but it is civilization. We cannot find this girl guilty. It would be declaring that marriage between a white man and a Negro woman is a possibility."

A vote was taken and the jury returned to the court room to render the verdict. "The prisoner at the bar will stand up," said the judge. Eunice stood up and her little boy stood up as well. There was the element of pathos in the standing up of that little boy, for the audience knew that his destiny was involved in the case.

"Has the jury reached a verdict?" asked the judge.

"We have," replied the foreman.

"Please announce it."

The audience held its breath in painful suspense. Eunice directed her burning gaze to the lips of the foreman, that she might, if possible, catch his fateful words even before they were fully formed.

"We, the jury, find the prisoner not guilty."

"Murder!" wildly shrieked Eunice. "Doomed! Doomed! They call us Negroes, my son, and everybody knows what that means!" Her tones of despair moved every hearer.

The judge quietly shed a few tears and many another person in the audience wept. The crowd filed out, leaving Eunice clasping her boy to her bosom, mother and son mingling their tears together. Tiara lingered in the corridor to greet Eunice when the latter should come out of the room. She had thought to speak to her on this wise:

"Eunice, we have each other left. Let us be sisters as we were in the days of our childhood."

But when Tiara confronted Eunice, the latter looked at her scornfully and passed on. When Tiara somewhat timidly caught hold of her dress as if to detain her, Eunice spat in her face and tore herself loose.

XXXV

EUNICE! EUNICE!

With slow, uncertain step, a wild haunted look in her eye, Eunice, clutching her little boy's hand until it pained him, moved down the corridor toward the door leading out of the court house. She was about to face the world in the South as a member of the Negro race, and the very thought thereof spread riot within her soul. The nearer she drew to the door the greater was the anguish of her spirit. More than once she turned and retraced her steps in the corridor, trying to muster the courage to face the outer world in her new racial alignment. At last she stood near the door, her whole frame trembling as a result of the sweeping over her spirit of storm after storm of emotions. Her little boy, unable to grasp the import of his mother's behavior was eagerly scanning her face and weeping silently in instinctive sympathy.

With a sudden burst of courage Eunice stepped out of the court house door and a young white man, who had been awaiting her, stepped up to speak to her. His hat was tilted back on his head, a lighted cigar was in his mouth, and his hands were thrust deep in his trousers pockets.

Eunice looked up at him, saw the wicked leer in his eyes, and recoiled.

"Don't be scared, Eunice. I stayed here to tell you that the hackman who brought you here got a chance to make a little extra by taking some white ladies home and said for you to stay here until he got back. He won't be gone but a few minutes."

The suggestive look, the patronizing tone, the failure to use "Mrs.," on the part of the man that addressed her, and the action of the hackman in leaving her to take some white woman home, served as a tonic to brace up the quailing spirit of Eunice.

Her first brush with the world as a member of the Negro race had aroused her fighting spirit.

"How dare you address me in that manner, you boorish wretch!" exclaimed Eunice, her small frame shaking with indignation.

The young man seemed rather to enjoy Eunice's rage and coolly replied, "Well, Eunice, you know, Eunice, that you are a Negress now and there are no misses and mistresses in that race. If you were a little older I would call you 'aunty;' if you were a little older still I would call you 'mammy;' if very old, 'grandma Eunice.' But as it is, I have to call you plain 'Eunice.' My race would disrespect me if I didn't follow the rule, you know."

"You wretched cur! You yap!" screamed Eunice.

"As this is your first day in the 'nigger' race I won't bother you for calling me out of my name. But let me give you a piece of advice. We white folks like a 'nigger' in his place only, and you find yours quick. And remember that you 'nigger' women don't come in for all that stepping back which we do for white women. We go so far as to burn your kind down here sometimes. As for that brat there, bring him up as a 'nigger' and teach him his place, if you don't want him to see trouble." So saying the young white man turned and walked away, leaving Eunice enraged and amazed at his effrontery.

The refined classes among the whites who would not under any circumstance have wantonly wounded Eunice's sensibilities, had nevertheless issued the decree of caste and the grosser ones among them were to execute it, and Eunice was tasting the gall that the unrefined pour out daily for a whole race to drink.

Typical of that class that enjoyed seeing the Negroes writhing under their wounded sensibilities, this young man had craved the honor of being the first to make Eunice taste the bitterness of her new lot in life.

Eunice and her son now proceeded to the street car. A number of white women boarded the car just in front of her and the conductor politely helped them on. When her time came to step up, he caught hold of her arm to assist her. When a glance at her face told him who she was, he (having seen her picture in the newspapers, and learned the result of the trial) quickly turned her loose so that she fell off the car, badly spraining her ankle.

Eunice did not understand his action and looked up at him inquiringly. The contemptuous look upon his face explained it all. With her sprained ankle she hobbled on the car and took a seat near the rear door. A number of half-grown white boys were on the rear platform and felt inclined to contribute their share of discomfort to the newly discovered Negro woman. They hummed over and over again the "rag time" song. "Coon, coon, coon, I wish my color would fade!"

When Eunice and her son arrived at her hotel she alighted from the car unaided, and painfully journeyed to her room, which was being thoroughly overhauled by an employee.

"Where—where—is my room?" asked Eunice, haltingly, fearing that she had somehow made a mistake.

"You haven't any in this hotel," was the gruff response.

"But I have; I am in the wrong room, perhaps," said Eunice.

"No, you have been in the wrong race. You are a 'nigger' and we don't run a 'nigger' hotel. Your things are piled up in the alley, and you will please get out of the building as quickly as you can."

Eunice's mind now ran back to the occasion of her first stay in that hotel, recalled how royally she was treated then and contrasted it with the treatment she was now receiving. Stepping to the mirror she gazed at herself saying:

"What leprosy, what loathsome disease has befallen me that everybody now spurns me. One cruel little word—Negro—has converted fawning into frowning and a paradise into hell."

Taking her boy by the hand she started out of the building as hurriedly as her sprained ankle would permit.

"Back doors for 'niggers,'" shouted the employee, as he saw that Eunice had started toward the front entrance.

Rage mounted the throne in Eunice's heart and she turned towards her tormentor. She parted her lips and the oaths of stern men were upon the eve of bursting forth, but she repressed them and was soon out of the hotel. The railroad station was not far away and she preferred walking to submitting to the indignities that might attend riding on the cars. Appearing at the railroad ticket office she applied for a berth in a sleeper. Her face was known there, too, and she was told that all the berths were taken. A white woman going on the same train was the next to apply for a berth and was given her choice of a number. Eunice noticed the discrimination and returned to the clerk.

"You must have been mistaken as to the train I am to travel on, for the lady that has just left secured a berth on that train after I had failed," said Eunice pleadingly, for she desired the seclusion of a sleeping car for her mournful journey home.

"You belong to a voteless race and I can't give you a berth," said the ticket agent.

"What has voting to do with my getting a suitable place to ride on a train?" said Eunice, tears of vexation coming into her eyes.

"Everything," said the young man more sympathetically.

"You see it is this way," he continued. "The Governor of this state, who sprang from a class of whites, who never had much love for the Negro, happened to take a sleeper that was occupied by a few Negroes who did not conduct themselves properly. Though the great body of Negroes who were able and disposed to occupy berths were genteel and well-behaved, this governor, to properly bolster his dignity resolved upon a course that would work discomfort for thousands. He threatened to recommend to the legislature that a law be passed demanding separate sleeping cars for the two races unless Negroes were kept out of sleepers. We lose less by keeping Negroes out than we would by being compelled to operate two sets of cars. If you people had voting power and could stand by us we could stand by you. It is a matter of business with us."

"You are discriminating against me without the warrant of law and are subject to a suit," said Eunice.

"The case will be tried by a white jury and a verdict will be rendered against us. We will be required to pay the cost of the court and to hand over to you one cent!"

Taking her little boy by the hand, Eunice slowly turned and walked away while the tears rolled down her cheeks. She did so much crave the darkness and seclusion of a berth, where she could take an inventory of the new world into which she had come, but there was no escape from the lighted coach occupied by Negroes. Getting on the train she took a seat in the section of the coach set apart for Negroes. The Negro porter thinking she had made a mistake took her into a coach for whites.

"Take that woman back. She is no white woman," bawled out one of the passengers, who had in his hands an afternoon paper containing a likeness of Eunice and an account of the trial.

The puzzled porter turned to Eunice and said, "Are you a—are you a—" He was afraid to ask the woman as to whether she was a Negro fearing she might be a white woman and would have him killed for the insult; and he was equally afraid to ask her as to whether she was a white woman, fearing that if she was white she would resent a question that seemed to imply any sort of resemblance to a Negro. It occurred to him to say:

"This coach is for whites and the one you came out of is for Negroes."

Saying this he left hurriedly, leaving her to select the coach in which she was to ride. Eunice groped her way back to the section of the coach set apart for Negroes.

Earl had heard by means of the long distance telephone of the outcome of the trial, and desiring that the first meeting with Eunice after the sad experience should be private, he had preferred sending to the railway station for her, to going himself. He was now in his library when Eunice and her son reached the house. As Eunice pushed open the library door and stood facing her husband she stretched forth her hands and said in tones that pierced Earl's heart:

"Doomed! Doomed! Assigned to membership in the Negro race! Made heir to all the contempt of the world. Doomed! Doomed!"

Earl stood with folded arms and a heart whose emotions cannot be portrayed, and looked at the picture of woe before him, his beautiful wife frantic and despairing and his little son already feeling in his youthful spirit the all pervading gloom that creeps through the Negro world.

"Be not dismayed, Eunice, dear! I am not at the end of my resources. I shall yet burst a bomb in this Southland," said Earl.

Eunice rushed to Earl clutched his arms and looked up wildly into his eyes. "Earl, dear Earl! Tell me! Tell me quickly and tell the truth! Is there, can there be any hope for the Negro here or elsewhere?"

Earl did not answer at once. He looked steadily into her eyes and realized that he was in the immediate presence of a soul about to make a final plunge into the dark, dark abyss of despair. It was to him a holy presence and he could not lie!

"Eunice, dear, there is hope. Slowly, but surely the world is working its way to a basis of justice for all," said Earl.

"My boy! Is there hope for him?"

"The hope of sublime battling, dear," said Earl.

"Is that all there is for my boy? No hope of reward. Only battle! battle!" asked Eunice.

"Grant me a favor, Eunice. I know what that look in your face means. I see that you are thinking of leaving me, and of taking my boy and your boy with you. You are planning suicide," said Earl.

"Ha! ha!" laughed Eunice, in the uncanny tones of madness. "You guess well. Come with us," she said, casting a look in the direction of a drawer where she knew the pistol to be.

"Grant me this favor, Eunice. Don't die. Spare my boy. Live and let my boy live a little while longer. I have several more lines of attack. If they fail then we can all go."

Eunice whirled around the room gayly and said with childish glee, "You will then die with us, will you? Ha! ha! ha!" A terrible fear stole over Earl as he watched her peculiar behavior.

"Live! Ha! ha! ha! 'Nigger,' 'darkey,' 'coon'—live! Yes, I'll live! I'll live!

Whee—poo—poo—wheep!" screamed Eunice, now dashing wildly about the room. She had gone mad.

At the earliest moment practicable Earl bore the raving Eunice out of the Southland, carried her to a sanitarium in a northern city. Giving the physician in charge a history of the case and allowing him time to study it, Earl awaited the verdict as to Eunice's chances of recovery.

"Mr. Bluefield, to be absolutely frank with you, I am compelled to say that, in my opinion, your wife's case is an incurable one. The one specific cause of her mental breakdown is the Southern situation which has borne tremendously upon her. That whole region of country is affected by a sort of sociological hysteria and we physicians are expecting more and more pathological manifestations as a result of the strain upon the people.

"Only one thing could cure your wife and that is the reversal of the conditions that have wrought upon her mind. She has lucid moments, but whenever her mind forcibly recurs to the Southern situation she again plunges into the gulf of despair. If in these lucid moments you could place before her a ladder of hope, I am of the opinion that a cure would be effected. That is equivalent to saying, I fear, that the case is incurable, for I can see no way out of the Southern tangle."

Such were the awful words addressed to Earl Bluefield by the physician in charge of the sanitarium when Earl called to learn of him his opinion concerning Eunice's case.

Earl walked forth from the sanitarium and journeyed hurriedly to the southern border of the city. When the houses of the city were well at his back and he had an unobstructed view to the south, he paused and, holding his right hand aloft, he said:

"Hear, O spirit world, if such there be, that, in the days to come, you may witness how faithfully Earl Bluefield, Humanity's Ishmaelite, kept his word. Non-existent was I until the whim of a Southern white man, trampling upon the alleged sacred canons of his race, called me into being and endowed me with the spirit of his kind. In the race into which I was thrust, I sought to manifest my martial spirit, but met with no adequate response from men grooved in the ways of peace. I found me a wife with spirit akin to mine, and like myself a victim of the bloods. The two of us withdrew from the active affairs of men, and from our own heath looked out upon the land of our birth, in the very which we had been made aliens. And now we have been dragged from our happy seclusion and gibbeted.

"And thinkest thou, O Southland, that the last has been heard of me? Ha! Ha! For fear that thou mayest deceive thyself thus, hear the oath of Earl the Ishmaelite:

"By the wrenched chords of the heart of a boy spurned by a contemning father; by the double shame of a mother wickedly wooed and despised in the one breath; by the patience and optimism of the blood of my black forbears; by the energy and persistence of my grant of blood from Europe—by all these mighty tokens, I make oath that this nation shall rest neither day nor night until this shadow is lifted from my soul. And I further make oath, O despisers of the offerings of my higher self, that I shall meet your every fresh wound with face the more uplifted because thereof, and to better meet all that you have to hand out to me, I shall keep company with the Spirit that makes nerve food of disasters and ascension chariots of whirlwinds."

XXXVI

Enthusiastic John Blue

In a room of a hotel in the city in which the sanitarium having charge of Eunice was located, Earl Bluefield sat upon a sofa, his hands, with the fingers tightly interlaced, resting between his knees, his head and shoulders bent forward. The intense, haggard look upon his face told plainly of the painful meditation in which he was engaged.

Owing to Earl's peculiar status in the world, Eunice, beloved as a wife, was far more to him than a wife. He looked upon himself as a sort of exotic in the non-resisting Negro race and considered himself a special object of scorn on the part of the white people of the South, who seemed to him to resent his near approach unto them in blood, and to mistrust *his* kind more than all other elements in Negro life. In the absence, therefore, of a perfect bond of racial sympathy anywhere, Eunice became to him his world as well as his wife, and no more horrible suggestion could be made than that he should go through life apart from her. Here indeed had been a marriage—the welding of two into one.

Earl was not brooding as one who had hopelessly lost his all, but was plotting as one who would save his all. The task of the knight of old upon whom was the burden of rescuing some lovely maiden from imprisonment in a seemingly impregnable fortress, was but child's play compared to the task before Earl, who must scale the walls of the castle of despair and batter down doors that laughed at the feebleness of steel if he would claim Eunice for his own again. He was face to face with the dreadful fact that nothing but the solution of the long standing race problem of America could release to him the one so dear to his heart, so essential to his existence.

As Earl sat canvassing the terrible plight in which he found himself, his mind ran the whole gamut of panaceas that had been proposed for a solution.

His own martial scheme of his earlier, unmarried days passed in review before his mind, but failed to appeal to him as it did in the days of yore. So far as he himself was concerned he would have welcomed a death in a glorious cause as an honorable release from the ranks of the advocates of universal justice, who, to his impatient spirit seemed to be marking time in the face of an aggressive foe. But death for himself would not rescue Eunice!

His mind recurred to the impression that seemed to prevail in some quarters that the solution of the problem mainly hinged upon giving industrial training to the Negro masses.

"That," said he to himself, "will solve a large part of the Negro's side of the problem, but how great an army of carpenters can hammer the spirit of repression out of those who hold that the eternal repression of the Negro is the nation's only safeguard? What worker in iron can fashion a key that will open the door to that world of higher activities, the world of moral and spiritual forces which alone woos Eunice's spirit and mine? What welder of steel can beat into one the discordant soul forces of willing Negroes and unwilling whites, the really pivotal point of the problem? Really pressing is the need of industrial training for our people, but my peculiar case calls for something that must come from Lincoln the emancipator rather than from Lincoln the rail-splitter."

Earl next thought of Ensal's proposed campaign of education which had been vigorously carried on by Tiara and he said: "It is one thing to produce a Niagara and another thing to harness it. O for a means of harnessing all the righteous sentiment in America in favor of the ideals of the Constitution." Thus, on and on Earl soliloquized, groping for the light.

He stretched out upon the sofa and sought to refresh his tired brain with a few moments of sleep, but sleep refused to visit him. Suddenly he leaped from the sofa and said:

"I have it! I have it! Eunice shall be free."

He now began to make hurried preparations for a trip South. While he is thus engaged we shall divulge to the reader the process of reasoning that at last led him to what he conceived to be daylight.

"Two things must be done," argued Earl within himself. "Repression in the South must die and men with broader visions in that section must take charge of affairs. This is an age of freedom and an age of local self-government. Freedom must obtain in the South, and largely through some agency found or developed therein. The most effective way of killing repression is to make it kill itself and out of the soil nurtured by its carcass will spring a just order of things.

"I will lure repression to its death and then find my force within the South that will lead the South into nobler ways."

Understanding this much of Earl's new plan we are now prepared to follow him and intelligently watch developments.

The scene now shifts from the North to the South.

FULLY CONSCIOUS OF THE STUPENDOUS character of his undertaking, Earl walked slowly up the walk leading to the office of the Governor of M——, a Southern state. He was steadying himself for the coming effort.

When shown to the governor's office he said:

"This is the governor of the state of M——, I believe."

"They say that such is the case," responded the governor, smilingly.

"I am just from the North and am making a tour of the South. I am traveling *incognito* and would like to be known to you as John Blue. As I shall broach only matters of common public interest in case you honor me with an interview, I shall be pleased to have you excuse me from making myself further known to you in a personal way," said Earl, with great affability.

The governor was captured at once by Earl's suave manner and actually fancied that some Northerner of exceeding great note was paying him a visit.

"Well, I am glad to see you—glad to see you. The more you men of the North see our Southern 'niggers' the more you will sympathize with us," said the governor.

"Do you think that either we Northerners or you Southerners get anything like an adequate view of the Negro?" asked Earl Bluefield, alias John Blue.

"Why not?" asked the governor.

"Well, you Southern people don't mix with them socially, practically never enter their best homes, and would be amazed, I am told, if you really knew of the high order of their development socially. It is said that you call them 'niggers,' that your children speak of them as such, that you often speak harshly of them in your home circles, that many of your men are not as refined as they might be when they are dealing with Negro women, and that for these reasons the better grade of Negroes are leaving your domestic service, so that your observation of the Negro is more and more centered upon the type that does not represent the race at its best."

"I had never thought of that. We do call them 'niggers.' I have a lot of trouble in keeping a cook. I wonder if that is the reason. Well,

well, who would have thought that there was anything about a 'nigger' that Southerners would have to be told by a Northerner," remarked the governor, winding up with a loud guffaw.

"As for the tourist class of Northerners," resumed John Blue, "and Northerners residing in the South, they see only the rougher side of Negro life, much as do you Southerners. The Northern missionaries whose duties place them in touch with the best and worst that there is in Negro life have the real rounded view of the situation."

The governor's affability now disappeared. Said he:

"Don't praise those mawkish missionaries to me. They are down here educating the heads of 'niggers.' We white folks have got enough heads to run this country."

"Your irritation," said Earl, "paves the way for me to say what I came to say. We Northerners are tired of being estranged from you Southerners. We are becoming a world power and should have a thoroughly united country. Why don't you Southern people begin a campaign of education and let the North know your real mind, so that we won't tread on your corns so often, to use a homely phrase."

"Ha, ha! the North knows my views. They were heralded abroad everywhere and gave me the governorship. I had five planks in my platform and, to match your homely phrase with another one, they took like hot cakes," said the governor.

"Would you object to outlining your platform to me," asked Earl.

"Object? Why I am the boldest man in the South. I don't bite my tongue. Surely you have heard of me," said the governor.

"Yes, I have heard of you," said Earl, "but I did not know but what you had been misrepresented by political enemies."

"Well, you can judge for yourself as to whether I have been misrepresented or not. The five planks of my 'nigger' platform are these," said he.

"First, this is a white man's country.

"Second, one drop of Negro blood in a man's veins makes him a 'nigger.'

"Third, public office, neither federal nor state, was gotten up for a 'nigger' to hold.

"Fourth, all money spent on educating a 'nigger,' except to teach him to work, is a squandering of the public funds.

"Fifth, the outside world be d——d. We will deal with the 'nigger' to suit ourselves.

"I will also tell you confidentially that I am one that don't want the 'nigger' question out of politics. We are living side by side with these 'niggers,' and public agitation helps our people to keep in mind that there is an impassable gulf between the races. Such men as I am would be perfect fools for trying to solve this 'nigger' problem. A crazy man can see that the solving of this problem puts my kind out of business. Thousands of Southern men can whip me out of my boots on any issue outside of abusing the 'nigger.' That's where I can go them one better. Haven't you observed the universal lament that we are not up to the standard in point of statesmanship. The trouble is we ride into our kingdoms so easily. It don't take a genius to persuade a people that you can beat a more tender-hearted man keeping a 'nigger' in his place. We machine men in the South don't want this 'nigger' bugaboo put down. It's our war whoop."

"Aside from the political use to which you put your announced views on the race question, you really believe them, don't you?" asked Earl.

"O yes. I think the good of the world demands that the 'nigger' be kept in his place," replied the governor.

"Now, I am getting to the point," said Earl. "Lincoln once said our country could not always exist half slave and half free. You see he was right. Now a lesser light than Lincoln tells you that the policy of repression must obtain in all our country or none, for the nationalizing spirit is at work, and is sure in time to produce a national unity of some sort. Shall this unity, so far as touches the question of the races, be upon the Northern or Southern basis, is a very live question for you Southerners. Now I suggest that you Southern people make this question a national one."

"How can we raise the issue," asked the governor.

"Easily. You people have been tolerating Negroes in federal positions down here for years. Collectorships of ports, marshalships and numerous positions of honor have all along been held by Negroes. Become tired of this and demand that they be withdrawn. That will be an invitation to the nation to join with you in your policy of repression."

"Good! Good!" said the governor, clapping his hands.

"You can go further. The presidency of our nation is where the copartnership of the states finds conspicuous concrete expression. Demand that none but a repressionist or a man silent on that question be allowed to occupy that chair."

"Good! Good! Good!" exclaimed the governor.

"Now as to your chances. The race instinct is in the North, but is not cultivated as much as it is in the South. Send your men to the North who are most adroit in their appeals to prejudice and you will find a force there to join you. Then remember you Southerners sprang to arms so gallantly in that skirmish with Spain that you made a fine impression. It was discovered that you had been brave enough not to allow defeat to rankle in your hearts, a really good quality. A more opportune time for you Southern people to take a stand would be hard to conceive," said Earl.

Down came the governor's hand upon his desk with a thud.

"Don't you know I have been thinking that very thing. I have great influence in the councils of my party and I shall see to it that the 'nigger' question is the next national issue," said the governor.

"You will have one little backset," said Earl.

"The man whom you will have to oppose has made fewer Negro appointments than any of his more immediate predecessors and those made have been of a very high order—a thing that could not always be said. Again, he has made it a point to have no Southern adviser save a known friend of the best element of the Southern people."

The governor looked wrothy again. "Best element," said he, sneeringly. "He is losing his time fooling with that crowd. All we radicals have to do is to crack our whips and they run to cover."

"That brings us to another point of considerable importance. When the campaign is launched, whose views on the race question shall be in the foreground—the views of the radicals or conservatives in the South," asked Earl.

"The radicals shall occupy the center of the stage, sir. We are tired of these half-way policies!" thundered the governor.

Earl now arose to go.

"You will certainly hear from us radicals as never before in the history of the nation—that is, since we jumped in the saddle and brought on the war," said the governor.

"By jinks, you don't think another war will come on, do you, Mr. Blue?" asked the governor.

"Oh, no; we have had our last war with lead and steel. All of our internal conflicts for the future must be intellectual, it seems," answered John Blue.

"I am glad to hear you say that, for if we got into another tangle I do believe to my soul that these 'niggers' would be a little less quiet than they were before. But for our political alliance with the North we of the South would have to be one of the most truckling of nations. For, what could we do to a foreign foe with all these discontented 'niggers' squirming in the fires of race prejudice, like so many worms in hot ashes. You are sure there won't be any physical fighting?" remarked the governor.

"The North would hardly hit you, for you are blood of their blood and they know how utterly helpless you are with an awakened race in your borders thoroughly of the opinion that you are not giving them a semblance of fair treatment," said John Blue.

"I gad, we must bring the North our way. I see that whoever, in this fight of the races, gets the outsider is going to carry the day. We are coming in the next campaign. Look out for us."

The two men bade each other adieu and Earl walked out of the office.

Earl invaded state after state in the South and conferred with the radical leaders wherever he went and found the sentiment everywhere prevailing that the time was ripe for the radical South to pull off its mask and let the world see its real heart.

With an anxious heart Earl watched the forming of the lines of the campaign. Men in all parts of the country, whose only hope of success lay in obtaining the political power in the hands of the radicals, besought them to forego making the Negro question an issue, but they were deaf to all appeals.

The convention dominated by the radicals met, and John Blue, alias Earl Bluefield, was there. When the Anti-Negro plank was read, from his seat in the gallery a mighty cheer rang out that started a wave of enthusiasm unsurpassed in the history of political conventions.

As John Blue stood waving a flag and cheering, his eye swept over that great throng, and he said to himself:

"O bonnie Southland: if you had developed real statesmen among you, men who knew their age, they would be here to tell all these people save myself to be quiet, on the ground that it is indelicate for a corpse to cheer at its own funeral. But your really great men are at home sorrowing over your coming humiliation. This day's work is the beginning of the end. Eunice, the sky brightens!

"Heaven of heavens, I thank thee that thou hast so arranged it that the American people must now say as to whether or not the caste spirit shall be allowed to lay his bloody tentacles on the political life of the whole nation."

XXXVII

Postponing His Shout of Triumph

With ceaseless, tireless energy Earl Bluefield went everywhere in the North during the campaign that followed, assailing the political power in control of the South. The heat of his heart warmed his words and his eloquence thrilled the nation.

"How has it happened that an orator of such power has remained so long hidden from the nation's gaze?" was the question everywhere asked.

In an address to Northern labor, which was heralded far and wide, Earl said:

> "To those of you who in the sweat of your brow earn your bread, I bring the message that your earning of a livelihood, a very grave matter with you, is affected by the Southern situation.
>
> "It has been said that the South is freer from labor strikes than any other equal area of territory within the borders of civilization. The weakness of the Negro in the body politic, his lack of means to insure his protection, gives timidity to Negro labor and causes it to be little inclined to organize.
>
> "The enforced cheapness of Negro labor brings down the price of all labor, just as a house sinks with its foundation. Lo, the word has already gone forth that the South is the place for capital, that labor is cheap, that there is an absence of social unrest found elsewhere.
>
> "Read your commercial journals and note how many of the institutions upon which you have depended for a livelihood have been transferred to this land of cheapness and peace, ominous peace. Note how your captains of industry are asseverating that factories in the North must cut wages in order to compete with those that have gone South.
>
> "Your economists saw in the days preceding civil strife that the workingman of the North could ill afford to compete with slave labor at the South. Permit me to say to you that the half-slave, the political slave, made timid by an environment that tends to crush his spirit and dwarf his energies, is a menace to

you, holding the white labor of the South down and affecting you of the North.

"Again, adverse conditions at the South will drive the Negro to your very door. Some day when you desire to remain away from work to allow your employers leisure to ponder a condition which you desire improved, you will find the Negro there to take your place.

"Men of the North, mark well my words: You must lend your aid to an adjustment of relations in the South upon an equitable basis or be confronted with the question of the disorganization and readjustment of your own affairs. Stand out against the repressionists of the South, make the whole nation a field of fair play and then we will not have this one disturbing center distributing trouble to all other parts of the nation."

Addressing the business interests of the country, he said:

"Work is the one American word, and as a result great is the monument erected to our industry. Our accumulations are enormous.

"From time to time questions affecting the whole wealth of the nation must be passed upon by the people. These repressionists have shown that there is no interest so vital but that they will smite it hip and thigh if by so doing they may advance the policy of repression. You are confronted therefore with a power that bids you to become repressionists or stand subject to onslaughts whenever the fancy obtains that a lick at your interests will do their cause good.

"You cannot commit yourselves to the cause of repression. It taints character. You are great employers of labor. In the mighty problems that are to confront you your spirit will be your most valuable asset. You must keep it pure at all hazards. Nor can your business interests long endure these constant jars from the repressionists. You cannot afford to accept either horn of the dilemma offered you by the repressionists. Your only remedy lies in smiting repression."

To the statesmen whose anxious eyes were upon the future of the nation, he said:

"In the days that are now upon us and in the years that are to come there can be no escape, perhaps, from some ills of which the fathers never dreamed, unless a larger grant of power be given unto our national government. However pressing the situation, rely upon it, the repressionists will seek to keep the nation in swaddling clothes for fear that added power might some day turn its attention to the question of repression."

In an address to the whole people, he said:

"A power that would wrong a race, that would in any way restrict human growth, that would not have the nation a fair and open field, is out of tune with heaven, is working at cross purposes with the whole universe, and will carry into an abyss all whom it can mislead."

The Negroes are a people capable of great enthusiasm and ardent attachments. All their fervor was thrown into the campaign. Any vast body of people with deep convictions have the power to greatly impress others. The settled conviction of the Negroes that their very destiny in America hinged, it seemed, upon the outcome of this election, was not without its psychological effect upon the public mind.

The cause championed by Earl marched to a glorious triumph at the polls, but he took no part in the jollification that followed.

"My work is only half done," was the reflection that kept him calm in the presence of the victory for which he had made the full offering of his soul.

XXXVIII

He Cannot, But He Does!

Ensal Ellwood entered his room in his home in Monrovia, Liberia, West Coast Africa, a thoroughly dejected man. He had just returned from an extended trip in which he took a survey of his work and contemplated the outlook. His investigations had served to increase his hopes as to the possibilities of the African race, but he was nevertheless depressed.

Nor was this the first time during his stay in Africa that this gloomy atmosphere seemed to envelop him. In fact, he was the subject of frequent attacks of melancholia which the many friends that he had made had found inexplicable.

This depression was not due to the African fever, because science had been able to prepare his system to resist that debilitating agency.

It was not due to a want of encouragement in his plans. He had met this on every hand. A number of Southern men in sympathy with the higher aspirations of the Negro race, hopeless of seeing those aspirations realized in the Southland, had placed at his disposal a large sum of money with which to draw off the Negro population from unfriendly points in the South and establish them in Africa.

Far sighted capitalists of America seeing in an awakened Africa a possible market for American goods, thought it wise to keep in touch with this young man who was to be so largely the great awakening agency.

England, France and Germany vied with each other in offering inducements for him to devote his energies to their respective holdings. The Republic of Liberia was wild with joy over his interest in her welfare. The King of Abyssinia had made urgent requests for him to come to his borders.

Thousands of cultured young men and women had caught Ensal's zeal for the world-wide awakening of the race and were only awaiting his signal to flock to his standard.

And yet his heart was heavy. Ensal took his seat at his desk and rested his throbbing brow thereon. He mused to himself, saying:

"Here I am with the mightiest work of the ages on my hands, and the door of opportunity before me, and yet, terrible, terrible thought, I see failure written upon my skies. For my spirit lags; there is no quickening battery at my life's center. Ah! it is awful to be dead alive. That which would quicken my spirit and give me the needed zest to face the work of an Atlas, the bearing of a world upon my shoulders—that influence is far removed from me, farther than those stretches of thousands of miles tell of."

During Ensal's absence of many months his mail had accumulated until now he found himself face to face with a huge pile of unopened letters and newspapers. Lifting his head from his desk, he wearily turned to his mail.

In the pile of letters he came across one from Earl Bluefield which ran as follows:

My Dear Ensal

There is great need of you in America at this hour, and a golden opportunity for winning an enduring place in the history of the world awaits you.

The repressionists of the South made their policy an issue in the presidential campaign which has just come to a close, and they have been most badly beaten.

As you know, statesmanship is a great passion with the South and she is not going to remain contented in the position of impotent isolation to which her repressionist element has consigned her. A new order of leaders will now be put forward as the spokesmen of the South and the fairness of their words is going to be seized upon by the nation as offering hope for a new order of things.

Since the liberal element among the whites of the South are to be given a day in court, there is great need of that type of Negroes that has standing with them. I, as you know, am *persona non grata*. I have added to my unpopularity by the manner in which I lambasted the repressionist element in the campaign just closed.

Come to America and help the nation to reap the fruits of its victory over repression.

Apart from my interest in the Negro race, which you of course have never doubted, I have grave personal interests at stake, and know not what I shall do if you fail the nation in this hour of its need. A sorrow as great as the world has ever known hangs over me and over the Negro race. Come and lift it.

Earl Bluefield

"No, I cannot go. I cannot be that near to Tiara. Heaven knows that I would be driven mad to see, to be near that girl, and be conscious that her love lies buried with another. No, I cannot go. America may need me, but so does Africa, so does Africa." Such were Ensal's thoughts upon the reading of Earl's letter.

Now all of you who believe in altruism; who believe in the giving of one's self for others; who believe in fixedness of purpose; who have in any wise pinned your faith to that man Ensal—let all such prepare yourselves for evidence of the utter frailty of man. Bear in mind that Ensal claims to seek the highest good of his race, that he has chosen Africa as the field for the greatest service, and that he has just rejected a proposition to return to America from an ultra-radical, who of all men has come to regard him as the man of the hour.

Picking up a package of newspapers, he tore the wrappers off and noticed that they were Almaville papers.

"I have seen that face before," said he, looking at the likeness of Eunice Seabright Volrees-Bluefield reproduced in one of the papers.

He now turned to the reading matter, taking note of a column that had blue marks calling attention thereto. This was an account of Eunice's trial and contained in full the words of Tiara in court on that occasion.

"O my God!" exclaimed Ensal when he came to that part of Tiara's testimony which disclosed the fact that the Rev. Percy G. Marshall was her brother. Now observe him, you who have faith in man.

"Landlady! landlady!" Ensal exclaimed, rushing out of his room in search of that personage. Finding her, he said excitedly, "Put everybody in Monrovia at work packing up my possessions, please. I must leave."

"What can this mean, pray tell. *I understood that you were to devote your life to this work*," said the landlady, much amazed at the sudden turn of affairs.

"What work? Life?" asked Ensal, absent-mindedly.

"The uplift of Africa, the redemption of your race," replied the landlady.

"My *race*, dear madam, is to catch the first steamer returning to America. Just now the whole world with me converges to that one point. Let us be in a hurry, please."

As Ensal stepped off the gangplank and again touched American soil, Earl was there to greet him. Arm in arm the two men wended their way through the crowded streets until they reached the hotel at which Earl was stopping.

Earl told Ensal the story of Eunice's derangement and of his quest for a message of hope with which to effect her cure. Ensal readily grasped the situation. At times in the past friends had hinted that the problem would derange him.

"Let us serve each other," said Ensal. "I will go South and see what message I can bring back for you to carry to Eunice. I will serve you thus. While I am thus engaged there is something you can do for me. The kissing of the Rev. Percy G. Marshall by Tiara, made known to me by poor Gus Martin, caused me to abandon my purpose of seeking the hand of Tiara. I wish you to go to her, and pave the way for a visit from me. Tell her that I have always known that she was the noblest girl in all this wide, wide world; that I looked upon the kissing incident as a pure love affair, not knowing but that she was one who held that of one blood God had made all the sons of men to dwell upon the face of earth; and that I felt that death alone prevented her and the Rev. Mr. Marshall from becoming man and wife in some other part of the world.

"Now, Earl, tell her all this. You are her brother-in-law and can find a nice way of talking freely with her concerning the matter. May I depend upon you?"

"To the utmost," replied Earl earnestly.

The two men now parted, each in search of hope for the other. Earl's task was comparatively easy, for Tiara had all along fully understood Ensal and felt no need of the assurances which Earl sought to bring. Earl was more than happy at the outcome of his mission, happy that he could inform Ensal that the way was now clear for him to declare himself to Tiara.

We shall now follow Ensal to find out what measure of success attended his mission.

　　　　　　　　　　SUTTON E. GRIGGS

XXXIX

A Son of the New South

I understand that a few years ago a Negro man and woman were burned at the stake in this neighborhood. Would you kindly show me the place?"

This request came from Ensal Ellwood and was addressed to young Maul, the attorney who had plead so earnestly for the conviction of the lynchers of Bud and Foresta. A sad look stole over young Maul's face.

"I never go that way if I can avoid it easily. That was indeed a horrible affair and our section, according to the law of retribution, will have it to pay for," replied young Maul, won by Ensal's kindly tone and look. "There is the kindly Negro of the past revised and brought down to date," thought young Maul, as he looked at Ensal and further studied him.

"It has already paid for it, perhaps," said Ensal. "It may be that some one of this place was marked by nature to shed unfading lustre upon your state, and could have made these rivers and hills and plains revered in all the earth, but the light of his genius was extinguished by that smoke, perhaps, perhaps," said Ensal sadly.

The two men now walked in the direction of the scene of the burning. They soon arrived at the spot, and Ensal looked long at the charred trunks of the trees that had served as stakes. He scanned the trees from the parched roots to the forlorn tree tops, took note of the fact that the bark was missing and reflected that the absent bark was no doubt yet serving as souvenirs in many Maulville homes.

"They are dead—the trees I mean—and perhaps it is well. Time will now eat away their vitals and they shall no longer stand as monuments to the shame of our land," said Young Maul.

"Suppose we sit down. I have much to say to you, Mr. Maul," said Ensal, who felt himself the ambassador of millions and of Tiara's demented sister. Anxious indeed was he that he should succeed in the object of his visit.

The men walked over to the Negro church near the scene, and took seats upon the steps thereof.

"Quite a fitting place for my talk," began Ensal. "My name is Ensal Ellwood. Looking at the spot where the South is seen at its worst is but a prelude to what I have made a long journey to say to you," said Ensal.

"I shall be glad to hear what you have to say, Mr. Ellwood," said young Maul.

"I notice that you say 'Mister,'" said Ensal, in kindly tone.

"I am not one of those that believe that my manhood is compromised by the use of the term 'Mister' to a Negro. I remember that the greatest of all Southerners and the greatest of all world heroes, the immortal Washington, once lifted his hat to a Negro man. When asked about his action he replied that he could not let that Negro be more polite than he was. I take the same position. I think a man's manhood is exceedingly feeble when it has to have an army of sentinels to be always on the alert, to keep somebody from kidnapping it," said young Maul.

"To come at once to the point, Mr. Maul, I have come to you to make overtures for a treaty of peace between the Negroes of the United States and the white people of the South," said Ensal.

"I shall hear you gladly," said young Maul.

"George Washington, Thomas Jefferson and Robert E. Lee are to the people of the South stars of the first magnitude, and you would like to send other stars to keep them company. But, changing the figure, an actor must have a stage that places him in the full view of his audience, if he would do his best work. Our nation is the stage upon which your sons are to strive for immortality.

"To labor to the best advantage they must have the chance to be vested with the authority of the nation, the power of the whole people. Given that power, the scroll of immortality will at least be laid before them that they may make effort to write their names thereon," said Ensal.

"Now, Mr. Maul," he continued, "the Negro population is so distributed that it now holds the balance of power in the nation. We have it in our power to keep the South out of its larger glory.

"However unpalatable it may be to a Southern white man, he must reckon with the fact, that between himself and the coveted favor of the nation stands the will of the Negro."

"That is very apparent," said young Maul.

"While we can hamper," resumed Ensal, "the white people of the South nationally, they can trouble us considerably locally. Now, we are not enemies of the South, and take no delight in the crippling of her influence *per se*, and we would like to see this unarmed strife come to a close. Nothing would give the Negroes greater joy than to see the right kind of a white man from the South made President of the nation.

"And the right kind of men exist in the South! There were perhaps as many white men from the South in the Union army as there were Negroes.

"Only one thing is now needed to gladden the hearts of the Negroes of the United States and cause them to turn enthusiastically to the making of the South the grandest section of the Union," said Ensal.

"What can that be, pray?" said young Maul.

"Mr. Maul, excuse me for not stating at once. Cast your eye back over the history of our country and take note of the woes that have been heaped upon the South and upon the nation by the radicals among you.

"There was a strong anti-war party in the South prior to the breaking out of the civil war, but the radicals overwhelmed them and brought on that disastrous conflict.

"Immediately after the war the radicals got control of some of your state legislatures and began to pass laws that would have practically re-enslaved the Negroes. The radical policy of the nation, as revealed in reconstruction measures was the child of radicalism in the South, so charge the burdens and woes of that period to your radicals.

"'Carpet-baggers' and 'scalawags' mismanaged affairs in the South, and some of your good people, you state, resorted to lawless methods to displace them. The radicals took charge of this lawless organization, you claim, prostituted it, and made a record of crime and villainy in the South so great that eleven large volumes in the records of Congress are required to merely hint at the atrocities. The nation grew quiet for a period, to catch your point of view and reason with you, and your radicals misread its attitude and thought that it had undergone a change of heart. They led the South to its recent crushing defeat.

"The radicals who have oppressed the Negroes of the South and sent them North, sent them forth with heart burnings, and through the pivotal states of the North they are ever on guard to turn the tide of battle against your section. Radicalism, then, is building up a political power in the North that will be a potent factor in continuing the isolation and impotence of your section, and will render the wish of a Negro ward politician of the North of more consequence than the combined pleadings of all your congressional delegation from the South.

"In the South today radicalism is widening the breach between the races and that old kindly feeling is fast disappearing, being succeeded by suspicion and hate.

"The bonds of personal friendship which have served to keep things quiet in the South when circumstances seemed most forbidding are being snapped asunder. The sullen hatred of the Negroes engendered by the rabid utterances and violent conduct of the radicals among the whites is pregnant with harm to the South, and tends to summon to a resurrection the entombed savagery of some members of the race, and to dishearten others in their upward strivings. On and on I could go, showing the awful wreckage in the pathway of the Southern radical.

"If the nation would ever heal this sore the radicals must be suppressed. If the Negroes attempt their undoing a feeling of racial solidarity among the whites greets them. If the North attempts it a sectional feeling is stimulated.

"I come now to the one thing that will gladden the hearts of the Negroes and the nation and make secure the glory of the South. *We would have you good white people of the South to assert yourselves*—that class of you who have not been carried away with that false doctrine that the problem can be solved with the Negro shorn of political power. In short, the one missing factor now needed is *aggressiveness* on the part of the right thinking white people of the South," said Ensal, who now ceased and awaited with anxious heart young Maul's reply.

"As to the matter of our aggressiveness, Mr. Ellwood," responded young Maul, "have no doubt on that score. The South has been so unmercifully carved in the slaughter pen into which her radicals led her, that she is now willing to hear from men of saner moods. Many a true Southerner, silent through force of circumstances, has been waiting for just this hour. Watch us. We are going to suppress lynching, enforce laws impartially, allow Negroes all their rights as citizens, make no discriminations because of race, color or previous condition of servitude, and encourage them to develop their God-given powers fully. Nor shall we be afraid of them. They did not strike us in the back in the time of civil strife and they have never lost a kindly feeling for us in spite of what the radicals have done to them. Quite well has Professor Shaler said that if the two races do not live in amity it will not be the fault of the Negroes."

"Mr. Maul," said Ensal, grasping the young man's hand, "well might the struggling world, writhing up from its low estate, rejoice that your type is now to assume charge of the destiny of the white race in the South."

"Now, Mr. Maul," continued Ensal soberly, "one thing for which we Negroes are to labor might be construed as an evidence of distrust of the better element of Southern people, and I would have you to understand us. The radicals of the South, as I have stated, invited radicalism from the North as the only sure antidote. To correct some evils, numbers of your good people condoned a departure from accepted standards of ethics. Men whom you knew to be perjurers, ballot box stuffers and violaters of law were, because of those very qualities, allowed to occupy high station among you. Many of you felt that your ills could only have been cured in that way. We Negroes have felt that a moral revolution could have been effected, and would have left no residue of evil in its wake. But other methods prevailed and you now have among you a class of men who feel no compunctions of conscience at cheating. Having blunted their consciences cheating us, they will now seek to cheat the better element of whites in the era of promised agressiveness. We Negroes are going to ask one favor of the nation, and that is that it enforce its constitution, which provides one test for all American citizens. If we win it will not only free us from the repressionists, but will free the better element of Southern whites as well. Your type of men can then have a chance in the South."

Young Maul sat meditating a while and then said:

"Do you know that in a fair test of strength the better element of whites even now would triumph at the polls. But the spirit of fraud built up to dethrone the 'carpet bag' government yet lingers to haunt those who would now dispense with it, which shows how dangerous it is to do evil even that good may come.

"We of the South hear much of bribery and corruption in the North, and I stand ready to co-operate with the decent element to purify the suffrage of the entire nation."

"You favor then the enforcement by Congress of the Fifteenth Amendment to the Constitution," asked Ensal.

"I would not have our nation live a lie and pollute the whole stream of our people's life. If the nation is lawless it can hardly expect its citizens to be different. I stand for the enforcement of law, all law. The very life of the nation itself depends upon the purity of the electorate, and the ballot box is as sure to become sacred in America as our nation is to stand," said young Maul earnestly.

"Now that we understand each other on those matters, let me now say a few words to you concerning some needs of the Negro race," continued young Maul.

"Radicalism and aggression on the part of some of the whites constitute one phase of our problem, but the weakened condition of your race must also be reckoned with as a factor. Had Africa been in a position to make it uncomfortable for all who sought to hold her children in bondage, there would have been no traffic in slaves from that continent. While we are going to do what we can to hold in check those who would oppress or restrict you, we expect you to eliminate the weakness in your race that invites attack.

"You must become intellectually strong, so that you may always be in hailing distance of the world's thought power which determines the destiny of the human race.

"Take special note of what I am now going to say," continued young Maul. "When an air of genuine democracy pervades the South and the spirit of caste no longer obtains in the political and industrial world, forms of labor now regarded as beneath the dignity of white people will no longer be so regarded, and the Negro will find himself face to face with competition in fields now conceded to him. While political power is necessary to safety in the body politic, do not expect too much of it, and neglect not the industrial crisis.

"As to politics, it is clear that your political problem in the South is going to be a difficult one. You see, your race was freed by a political party which conducted the war of the sections. It is hard to get your people to do other than vote with that party, while the more substantial element of the whites in the South have for a hundred years been in the opposing party. The great misfortune of the political situation is that the Negroes and the better element of whites never pull together in the one political harness."

"We have given that matter much thought and feel that we have a solution," said Ensal.

"My friend, if you can solve that problem you have gone a long way toward solving the whole problem," said young Maul.

"Here is our plan," began Ensal. "The Negroes have discovered the utter impotence of the class of whites who joined them for the sake of office, and the federal pie-counter element of whites has utterly lost favor with the great body of Negroes. The situation within the Negro race is therefore ripe for a new alignment. We have come to the conclusion that the American people need an idealist class in their political life, and it would be a great gift to the nation for the Negro to point the way for such a party.

"The Negroes are going to organize in the South an Eclectic party that will serve as an antidote to to safety in the body politic, do not expect too much of it, and neglect not the industrial crisis.

"As to politics, it is clear that your political problem in the South is going to be a difficult one. You see, your race was freed by a political party which conducted the war of the sections. It is hard to get your people to do other than vote with that party, while the more substantial element of the whites in the South have for a hundred years been in the opposing party. The great misfortune of the political situation is that the Negroes and the better element of whites never pull together in the one political harness."

"We have given that matter much thought and feel that we have a solution," said Ensal.

"My friend, if you can solve that problem you have gone a long way toward solving the whole problem," said young Maul.

"Here is our plan," began Ensal. "The Negroes have discovered the utter impotence of the class of whites who joined them for the sake of office, and the federal pie-counter element of whites has utterly lost favor with the great body of Negroes. The situation within the Negro race is therefore ripe for a new alignment. We have come to the conclusion that the American people need an idealist class in their political life, and it would be a great gift to the nation for the Negro to point the way for such a party.

"The Negroes are going to organize in the South an Eclectic party that will serve as an antidote to the tendency toward party worship. We shall separate city from county politics, county from state, and state from national. We shall often, perhaps, be found supporting one party's candidate for governor and another party's candidate for president. The question of human rights and the civil and political equality of all men shall be a first consideration with us, and we shall go to the aid of the class of men of like faith on these points, it matters not in what political party they may be found. The best interests of the people, and not party loyalty, shall be our creed.

"In this way we shall be able to co-operate with the best element of Southern white people. Though not posing as the political leader of my people, I feel sure that I correctly forecast their policy," said Ensal.

"Great possibilities lie in that direction, and I firmly believe that we have at last found the way of peace and honor and justice to all," said young Maul.

The two young men now parted, and Ensal went to the telegraph station and sent the following message to Earl:

"Problem will now be solved. Aggressiveness on part of better element of whites assured. The whole machinery of the national government is in hands that will accord them support. Working basis in political matters agreed upon for better element of both races. Am writing you at length."

When in due course of mail Ensal's promised letter reached Earl and set forth the prospects of an adjustment of the questions at issue, Earl was exultant and felt that he had at last good news to carry to Eunice.

XL

Sorrow and Gladness

In the parlor of the sanitarium Earl sat awaiting the coming of Eunice, his face telling of the hopes now alive within his heart.

With an exclamation of joy Eunice ran and threw herself into his arms. During her whole stay in the sanitarium the Negro question had not been broached to her and her mind seemed almost normal. Earl now sought to complete the work by letting her know that things had at last been set right and that the color of a man's skin was to no longer be in his way. Standing over her he whispered:

"Eunice, the American people have decreed that the door of hope shall not be closed to any of their citizens because of the accident of birth."

A strange glow came into Eunice's eyes.

"When will the duly authorized power see to it that the states live according to this decree and apply one test to voters of both races," asked Eunice so quietly, so intelligently, that hopes sprang up in Earl's breast.

Stooping, he kissed his wife, saying:

"I can't say, my darling; but it will surely come in time."

"Time!" shrieked Eunice. "Same old thing! Time! Bah! We shall all die in 'time.' Earl, are you turning against me, coming to me with that old word 'time?' Ah! Earl, are you a Southerner? Time! Earl, can't you persuade the people to let justice do now what they are waiting for 'time' to do?"

Jumping up she whirled round and round until from sheer exhaustion she fell into her weeping husband's arms.

"O thou of little faith, counterpart of my own darker days, Eunice, awake! Awake! The currents are forming that will sweep the caste spirit out of the political life of the nation. Awake, my Eunice! Awake!" plaintively spoke the grief-stricken husband to the unheeding ears of his wife.

While hope thus wrestles with despair, we visit another parlor.

In the parlor of Tiara's home Ensal sat awaiting the coming of the girl that he had loved so long and so ardently, on whom he had now called for the purpose of asking her to link her destiny with his.

Ensal had delivered many speeches in the course of his lifetime, but he could hardly recall one that had given him as much trouble as the short speech which he had sought to prepare for Tiara. Form after form of approach came to him, but they were all rejected as being inadequate to the occasion, so that when the beautiful Tiara appeared in the parlor door Ensal was absolutely and literally speechless.

With love-lit eyes Tiara walked unfalteringly in his direction and, with a smile for which Ensal the great altruist, mark you, fancied he would have been willing to return from a thousand Africas, she extended her hand to him in greeting.

There is a saying among the Negroes to the effect that "If you give a Negro an inch he will take an ell." Whatever may be the meaning of that expression, this we do know, that when Tiara gave Ensal one hand, he *deliberately*—no, we won't make the offense one of premeditation—he, without deliberating the matter at all, hastily took not only more of the hand than what Tiara offered, but the other one as well.

For the sake of Ensal's reputation for poise, already a little shaken, we fear, we fain would draw the curtain just here; but as we have all along sought to tell the whole truth about matters herein discussed, we will have to allow our hero's reputation to take care of itself the best way it can. Without obtaining any more consent than that which was plainly written in Tiara's eyes, and without any pretense at delivering any one of the many thousand little preliminary speeches framed for the occasion, Ensal bent forward and kissed Tiara!

Now that he has by this act lost favor with you, dear reader, we shall expose him to the utmost!

Dropping one of Tiara's hands, an arm stole around her waist, and Ensal kissed her again and, sad to say, again, and, vexing thought, again. And to cap the climax, the two were joyfully married that night, and on the next day set out for Africa, to provide a home for the American Negro, should the demented Eunice prove to be a wiser prophet than the hopeful, irrepressible Earl; should the good people of America, North and South, grow busy, confused or irresolute and fail, to the subversion of their ideals, to firmly entrench the Negro in his political rights, the denial of which, and the blight incident thereto, more than all other factors, cause the Ethiopian in America to feel that his is indeed "The Hindered Hand."

Notes for the Serious

1. The author of THE HINDERED HAND was an eyewitness of the driving of "Little Henry" to his death by the officers of the law.

2. The details of the Maulville burning were given the author by an eyewitness of the tragedy, a man of national reputation among the Negroes. Some of the more revolting features of that occurrence have been suppressed for decency's sake. We would have been glad to eliminate all of the details, but they have entered into the thought-life of the Negroes, and their influence must be taken into account.

3. The experiences of Eunice upon being assigned to membership in the Negro race are by no means overdrawn. The refined, cultured and most highly respected young woman whose actual experiences form the groundwork of that part of the story was not only thus accosted and insulted by a white man of the order indicated, but was actually beaten in a most brutal manner and fined fifteen dollars in the police court.

4. The following statement of facts lends interest to the contention of one of the characters of THE HINDERED HAND, to the effect that the repressionist order of things brings forward, by its own force an undesirable type of officials.

During the recent presidential campaign the repression of the Negro was made an issue in the state of Tennessee.

The most representative audience that assembled during the whole campaign in the State was wrought to its highest pitch of enthusiasm by the following outburst of eloquence from the Junior Senator of that state: "The man that does not know the difference between a white man and a 'nigger' is not fit to be President." The kind of a state Legislature begotten by a campaign in which the foregoing remark marked the highest level of the discussion so far as the popular taste was concerned, may be judged from the following comments on that Legislature after it adjourned:

"There were many men in the last Legislature upon whose faces the mark of incompetency or worse was as plain as the noonday sun."

—*The Nashville American*

"It would be better for Tennessee to groan on under present laws and let the Legislature meet no more in ten years if it were possible under the Constitution."

—*Lebanon Banner*

"Mediocrity was in the saddle, and picayunish partisan politics held the center of the boards."

—*Franklin Review-Appeal*

"The Legislature has adjourned. Many praises unto the 'Great I Am.'"

—*Murfreesboro News-Banner*

"Throwing bricks at the Legislature is a favorite pastime, but really a brick is hardly big enough for the purpose.

—*Franklin County Truth*

"In our opinion the present Legislature will go down in history as the most incompetent body of lawmakers that ever sat in the capitol of Tennessee."

—*Tullahoma Guardian*

"The Tennessee Legislature has adjourned and perhaps done less to commend itself than any of its predecessors."

—*Obion Democrat*

"The people elect the legislators and the people are responsible for the character of men they elect and send to Nashville to make and unmake laws. We know the Legislature was bad, even miserable, but the members got their commissions from the people."

—*Gallatin News*

"The weekly press of the state is almost unanimous in its condemnation of the late Legislature. * * * As we have said before, the general littleness of the body, its petty conduct in many instances, its trades and combinations, the autocratic methods of self-seeking members, the quarrels, the cheap declamations and intemperate and undignified and unwarrantable public denunciations by members who should have shown a better sense of dignity and decency, the dishonesty in juggling with bills, the unreliability of promises—the general record and conduct of the body marked it as unworthy of the state or the approval of the people. What man of established reputation would care to be known as a member of such a Legislature as the one recently adjourned?"

—*The Nashville American*

These comments are from newspapers of the same political faith as the Legislature.

5. The question might be raised as to whether the conditions set forth in THE HINDERED HAND are true of some special locality or are general in character.

As to how general the conditions complained of are one may infer from the following editorial from a leading Southern newspaper, which never fails in defense of the South where defense is possible.

"In South Carolina, as we have noted, the safest crime is the crime of taking human life. The conditions are the same in almost every Southern State. Murder and violence are the distinguishing marks of our present-day civilization. We do not enforce the law. We say by statute that murder must be punished by death, and murder is rarely punished by death, or rarely punished in any other way in this State, and in any of the Southern States, except where the murderer is colored, or is poor and without influence. Now this state of affairs cannot last forever. We have grown so accustomed to the failure of justice in cases where human life is taken by violence that we excuse one failure and another until it will become a habit and the strong shall prevail over the weak, and the man who slays his brother shall be regarded as the incarnation of power."

—*The Charleston News and Courier*

6. Since the recent defeat of the ultra radical element in the national campaign, there has been a marked improvement as to the more violent manifestations of race prejudice, emphasizing the fact that actual political power can procure respect.

7. It must never be concluded by those interested in these matters that the mere suppression of mob violence approaches a solution of the race problem. The programme of the Negro race, that must be ever kept

in mind as a factor to be dealt with, is the obtaining of all the rights and privileges accorded by the State to other American citizens.

8. Acknowledgment is here made of the generous aid often extended the Negro race in its efforts to rise by the liberal element among the whites of the South. One of the most notable achievements of this element has been the manner in which they have fought off the attacks of the repressionists, directed against the education of the Negroes in the public school systems of the South, so amply provided for by the "Reconstruction" Governments.

9. The overwhelmingly predominant sentiment of the American Negroes is to fight out their battles on these shores. The assigning of the thoughts of the race to the uplift of Africa, as affecting the situation in America, must be taken more as the dream of the author rather than as representing any considerable responsible sentiment within the race, which, as has been stated, seems at present thoroughly and unqualifiedly American, a fact that must never be overlooked by those seeking to deal with this grave question in a practical manner.

THE AUTHOR

A HINDERING HAND

SUPPLEMENTARY TO THE HINDERED HAND

A Review of the Anti-Negro Crusade of Mr. Thomas Dixon, Jr.

A Hindering Hand

The Poor White and the Negro

FROM THE DOOR OF A squalid home, situated mayhaps upon a somewhat decent spot in a marsh or upon the very poorest of soil, the poor white man of the South, prior to his emancipation by the Civil War, looked out upon a world whose honors and emoluments cast no favoring glances in his direction.

Between the poor white and his every earthly hope stood the Negro slave. As his thoughts now and then stole upward toward the higher social circles, he realized that the absence of slave quarters from his home entailed his absence from those upper realms. If in the marts of toil he offered the labor of his hands, he felt his cheeks tingling from the consciousness that others regarded him as being upon a level with slaves; and at the best the market for his labor was very limited, for the fatted slave stood in his way.

So utterly forlorn was the condition of the poor white that the enslaved Negro felt justified in meeting his protruding claim of racial superiority with contemptuous scorn. In the very nature of things the strongest sort of repulsion developed between this class of whites and the Negro slaves. The work, therefore, of overseeing and driving the slaves on the plantations of the more wealthy whites, fitted the habitual mood of the poor white exactly. No form of service was more congenial to him than that of whipping intractable Negroes for their masters.

It thus came to pass that the poor white man registered it as his first duty to wreak vengeance upon this unbowing, scornful Negro standing between him and all that was dear to his heart. This feeling of hostility was handed over from father to son, from generation to generation, until the very social atmosphere was charged with this bitter feeling.

When the Civil War came this neglected and despised class suddenly became important and furnished its quota of soldiers and commanders. Nathan Bedford Forrest hailed from this class, and as a result the American people have on their annals Fort Pillow and its savage-like massacre. When the war was over, the poor white class began to bestir itself in civil life, and from that class the nation derived the Hon. Benjamin R. Tillman, of South Carolina.

And now literature is receiving its contribution from this class of whites, in the work being done by Mr. Thomas Dixon, Jr., of North Carolina, who does not hail from the more wealthy and more friendly element of Southern whites, but from mingling with the poorer classes, where hatred of the Negro was a part of the legacy handed down from parent to child. For, before Mr. Dixon's marriage he was a poor man and was viewed by the Negroes of Raleigh, N. C., as one belonging to the class of their hereditary enemies. It is with the outpourings of a man who has been steeped in all the traditions of this hostile atmosphere that we are now called upon to deal.

The goal toward which Mr. Dixon is striving is the ejection from America of nearly ten million of his fellow citizens, against the overwhelming majority of whom he can allege no unusual offense save that they are of African descent.

The work of their fathers and of themselves in wresting the fields of the South from the clutch of forest; in crimsoning American soil with their blood in every war that has been fought; in yielding of all of the best of their heart and mind for this country's good is, according to Mr. Dixon, to count for naught.

Harnessing Hatred

IT IS TO BE CONCEDED that the presence in large numbers of two distinct races in the same territory under a democratic form of government constitutes a grave problem, and profound is the wish of many of both races that a separation might be effected. Mr. Dixon is by no means a pioneer in desiring a separation. The great emancipator desired this result.

But Mr. Dixon is a pioneer in the matter of seeking to attain his end by an attempt to thoroughly discredit the Negroes, to stir up the baser passions of men against them and to send them forth with a load of obloquy and the withering scorn of their fellows the world over, sufficient to appall a nation of angels.

Mark the essentially *barbarous* character of Mr. Dixon's method of warfare.

There is the good and the bad in all men. The world has learned since the days of the Christ that by far the best means of obtaining the largest results of unalloyed good is by appealing to the best that there is in men rather than to the worst. In no respect is the reactionary character of Mr. Dixon's crusade more apparent than in his attempt to attain his ends through his appeals to the worst that there is in men.

Mankind has been grouping itself from time immemorial, according to certain physical likenesses, and each race or group has had more or less of prejudice against alien groups. It has been the one struggle of the higher human instincts to enable men, in spite of differences of form, of feature, to find a common bond of sympathy linking mankind together.

Uncle Tom's Cabin grappled in the mire of Southern slavery and lifted a despised and helpless race into living sympathy with the white race at the North. To cut these chords of sympathy and re-establish the old order of repulsion, based upon the primitive feeling of race hatred is the first item on Mr. Dixon's programme.

The adopting of a course so patently barbaric stamps Mr. Dixon as a spiritual reversion to type, violently out of accord with the best tendencies of his times.

The very opposite of Mr. Dixon is Professor Nathaniel F. Shaler, of Harvard, himself a Southerner, who approaches this same grave question of the relation of the races and seeks to prepare the American people for the consideration of the subject free from the distorting influence of prejudice.

A Serious Handicap

THE CULTIVATION OF RACE HATREDS on the part of Mr. Dixon and others who labor with him, if successful will react on the American people sadly to their detriment. The wonderful activity of American industries call loudly for the world as a market for their goods. The dark races of the world, now backward in the matter of manufacturing, must largely furnish these markets. The cloven foot of America's race prejudice will make itself manifest, and its owner will find it increasingly difficult to secure a ready purchaser for his goods.

We have a hint of what will happen in the awakened darker world in the boycott of American goods by the Chinese, because of the rude treatment by American custom officials, of unoffending Chinese, a treatment born of the spirit of race hatred.

Mr. Dixon is Shrewd

Let us now take note of the various artifices resorted to by Mr. Dixon to unhorse the Negro in the esteem of the North and bestow his place upon those who would repress him.

In his first Anti-Negro book, Mr. Dixon was shrewd enough not to make a Southerner who was *persona non grata* to the North the hero of the story. The poor old Ex-Confederate soldier, rank secessionist, the real hero and dominating figure of his times, in this book is tied out in the back yard, while the post of honor is given to a little boy whose father fought most unwillingly against the Union. Mr. Dixon's choosing for a hero this lad, whose father wore a confederate uniform over a union heart, forcibly reminds one of the reply of the whimpering soldier whom the captain was upbraiding for cowardice under fire.

"You act as though you were a baby," angrily shouted the captain to the frightened soldier.

"I wish I was a baby and a gal baby at that," whimpered the soldier, reasoning that "gal babies" were exempt not only from that battle, but from all others.

While Mr. Dixon was in search of a hero that would be far removed from what was regarded as treason in those days he might have made assurance doubly sure by doing further violence to the predominating sentiment of the day by making his hero—not his heroine—a "gal" baby.

Mr. Dixon Scoffs

One of the brightest pages in the history of this nation will be that which tells the story of those men and women of the North, who, over the protests of loved ones, faced the ostracism of their kind in the South that they might open the Negroes' eyes to the hitherto forbidden glories of modern civilization and take care that the spiritual was not lost sight of in the new maze of world wonders. Withered indeed must be the soul that could scoff at such moral heroism, and yet that is just what Mr. Dixon does. He suggests that the people who produced a Washington and a Jefferson hardly needed missionaries to perform work among the Negroes within their borders.

But it must be borne in mind that as a part of the propaganda in favor of retaining the Negro in slavery, the white people of the South thoroughly committed themselves to the doctrine of the *ineffaceable*, *inherent* inferiority of the Negro, and had no largeness of faith in his possibilities along lines of higher culture. It is evident, then, that if salvation was to come at all, it was to come from a source that deemed such an outcome possible.

The Earlier Church Life of the Negro

Mr. Dixon essays to portray Negro worship and makes of it a very grotesque affair.

Over against Mr. Dixon's representation of Negro worship as a heathenish affair, we place the old plantation melodies evolved in those and earlier days. Charged as these melodies are with true religious fervor, they stand as a bulwark against all who would assail these earlier gropings of the race after the unknown God. Equally misplaced are the sneers of Mr. Dixon at the Negro minister. The center of the whole social fabric erected by the Negro race in the South is the Negro church, and to the zeal and power of the untutored Negro pastor and his more favored successor is this success due. Subtract from the assets of the Negro race those things placed there through the instrumentality of the Negro minister and small will be the remnant.

Again, this religion and this minister at whom Mr. Dixon sneers, are really responsible for the pacific character of the Negro population of the South. The Negro race is a great fighting race. The native optimism of the individual soldier causing him to discount his own chances of being killed, coupled with his ability to be lost in his enthusiasms, make the Negro very effective as a soldier.

Africa has been one great battle field and the internecine strife of fighting Africans is in a measure responsible for the plight of the Negro race in the world, as a union of forces could have the better halted alien aggression. But in America the Negro was taught the Gospel of peace. The singing of the American Negro is said to lack the martial strain found in the fatherland. For the peace loving Negro, credit the church and the Negro minister, whom Mr. Dixon would have the world contemn.

Mr. Dixon Stabs to Kill

The late Hon. George F. Hoar, of Massachusetts, once remarked (we quote from memory), "Our population is composed of various races of mankind, but there are four great things upon which we are all united: Love of home, love of country, love of liberty and love of woman." The glory of the Anglo-Saxon race has come largely of the estimate it has placed on woman.

Mr. Dixon would break the accord of the American Negro with the rest of his fellows by picturing him as the savage enemy of womankind. In order to attain his end he picks up the degenerates within the Negro race and exploits them as the normal type. In one of his books Mr. Dixon makes a Negro school commissioner solicit a kiss from a white girl when she applies to him for a position. The man of this character in the Negro race is known of all men familiar with the Southern Negro to be an exotic, for nowhere in the world does woman get more instinctive deference from men than what Negro men render to the white women of the South. The very fact that degenerates sometimes make them the objects of assaults, invests them with a double measure of sympathy and deference on the part of the great body of Negro men.

Where Mr. Dixon's Power Fails

Mr. Dixon displays great power in depicting the emotions of the white people when the news was borne to them that a little white girl had been outraged and slain by a Negro.

Mr. Dixon, there were other hearts throbbing in that neighborhood! Oh, that you had the spirit and the power to give utterance to those heart throbs.

The Negroes, whose absence from the mob you would ascribe to sympathy with the criminal, were in their homes sorrowing over the death of the little one, sorrowing over the disgrace that was so undeservingly brought upon the race, and wondering whether your mob had the right man or was making a mistake that would leave the really guilty free to again bring death and grief and wrath to the white race and grief and shame unspeakable to the Negro race.

As To Intermarriage

Not content with picturing the Negro race, as a race prolific with the assaulters of women, Mr. Dixon would further have the world believe that the highest ambition of the cultured Negro man is to find for himself a white wife.

Perhaps it may not be out of place just here for the writer to disclose what he considers, from close observation, to be the attitude of the Negroes on the question of the intermarriage of the races. They do not hold with that group of writers who contend that the Negro is inherently inferior to the whites and that a mixture of the blood of the races produces an essentially inferior being. Dumas, holding his own among the French; Browning and S. Coleridge-Taylor among the English, and Douglass, among the Americans, to their minds belie that assertion. Nor yet do they hold that the races must needs depend upon this infusion for its greatness. The unmixed Toussaint L'Ouverture, Paul Laurence Dunbar and J. C. Price speak up for the innate powers of the race.

Accepting the race as it came to them from slavery, during which mulattoism was forced upon it, the Negroes have gone on developing race pride and visiting their supreme disfavor upon all who signify inability to find thorough contentment within the race. The marriage of Frederick Douglass to a white woman created a great gulf between himself and his people, and it is said that so great was the alienation that Mr. Douglass was never afterwards the orator that he had been. The delicate network of wires over which the inner soul conveys itself to the hearts of its hearers was totally disarranged by that marriage.

Pride of Race

IT WAS THIS FEELING OF race pride which the Negroes have and thoroughly understand, that Mr. Dixon was picturing in that Northern statesman who would not give his daughter in marriage to a Negro suitor who was his political ally. This pride of race Mr. Dixon confounds with the prejudice which he would glorify. How utterly absurd it is to infer that it is inconsistent in a father to apply a totally different test to a man aspiring to be his son-in-law to that applied to a man asking for political rights! The rejection of a man because he lacks generations of approved blood behind him is classed by Mr. Dixon as race discrimination, whereas such rejections are daily made for similar reasons within all civilized races.

Backward Africa

IN HIS EAGER GRASPING AFTER anything that would seem to serve his purpose of thoroughly discrediting the Negro, Mr. Dixon holds up the backwardness of Africa as an indication of the inherent inefficiency of the Negro race. The life of the great body of the Negro race has been cast for untold centuries in Africa. This one simple fact has meant and still means so much. The peculiar character of the African coast, lacking as it is in great indentations, the immense falls preventing entrance into its greatest river, the Congo—these things have caused Africans to be more nearly isolated from the rest of humanity than has been the case with any other large body of people. With isolation and lack of contact the Negroes have been compelled to rely upon their own narrow set of ideas, while the progress of other peoples has been the result of the union of what they begot with what strangers brought them.

The soil of Africa fed the Negroes so bountifully that they did not acquire the habit of industry, and with a plenty of time on their hands they warred incessantly. The hot, humid atmosphere made them black and sapped their energies. To save them from yellow fever, nature gave them pigment and lost them friends. Other peoples have hesitated to intermarry with them because of their rather unfavorable showing in personal appearance.

Some hold that a race is great in proportion to the distance it has wandered through intermarriage from the parent stock. The great races of the world, it is held, are the mixed races. When the Africans' environments robbed them of comeliness and attractive qualities, they were thrown off to their own one blood, no one courting alliance with them.

The merest tyro of a sociologist knows that these are the essential facts which account for the backwardness of the African people, and yet Mr. Dixon would fasten upon Negroes the charge of inherent inferiority because of the showing made under circumstances most adverse to the development of civilization.

Reconstruction Days

THE MOST PATHETIC PAGE IN the history of the Negro race in America is the story of reconstruction days. Kept in ignorance during the days of slavery his one great desire under freedom was for knowledge and self-improvement. Because the white South was spiritually unprepared to deal with the new order of things, and because the North did not desire to make one great military camp of the South, the Negroes en masse were summoned forthwith to the task of establishing governments in the Southern states in harmony with the Constitution of the United States. The men whom the Negroes supported accomplished that task well, but in other respects betrayed their trusts.

When corruption in office, a thing by no means confined to one era of the world's history, became manifest, in many quarters an appeal was made to the Negroes to help overturn the corruptionists. And be it said to the honor of the race, the cry for good government never failed to rally Negro support, even at a great sacrifice. When Wade Hampton was struggling for the dethronement of corrupt governments in South Carolina, six thousand Negroes took part in one of the parades during his canvass for the governorship.

But some states did not have leaders prepared to deal with the Negroes as political equals, leaders who were wise enough to appeal to the good within the race. In such places the unreasoning, undiscriminating, brutal, murderous mobs arose to do by violence what better and wiser men had done elsewhere through moral suasion. Had enlightened methods been employed the sky would not have been as portentous as it is today. As it is, we have the sickening record of the atrocities of the Ku Klux Klan and the heritage of evil and lawlessness left in its wake.

Over against Mr. Dixon's lurid and grossly misleading pictures of the conduct of the Negroes in reconstruction days, we offer the following tribute to the race, clipped from the columns of the Nashville *Banner*, perhaps the most widely read daily newspaper in the state of Tennessee, and a paper opposed to the reconstruction policy pursued by the federal government:

> "Let us do the negroes justice. There is no spirit of bloodthirsty and incendiary revolt prevailing among them. History and experience have shown that there never existed a more tractable people considering all the trying conditions and circumstances to which they have been subjected. In time of war and in the frightful reconstruction period, when they were urged and tempted by false friends and incentives and had opportunities of evil appalling to contemplate, they were restrained as perhaps no other people would have been restrained and were more sinned against than sinning. And today as a people they have no mind except to accept the best that may come to them."

Mr. Dixon Vs. Hon. James G. Blaine

MR. DIXON'S HOPE IS EVIDENTLY IN the young North. That the young people may not be wedded to the traditions of their section, he would impress the young North that what their fathers did in the way of bestowing equality of citizenship upon the Negro, was the result of a leadership blind with the spirit of revenge. As a complete rebuttal to this contention on his part, we quote from an article which appeared in the North American *Review* from the pen of the late Hon. James G. Blaine:

"It must be borne in mind that the Republicans were urged and hastened to measures of amelioration for the Negro by very dangerous developments in the Southern States looking to his re-enslavement in fact, if not in form. The year that followed the accession of Andrew Johnson to the presidency was full of anxiety and warning to all the lovers of justice, to all who hoped for 'a more perfect union' of the States. In nearly every one of the Confederate States the white inhabitants assumed that they were to be restored to the Union with their State governments precisely as they were when they seceded in 1861, and that the organic change created by the Thirteenth Amendment might be practically set aside by State legislation. In this belief they exhibited their policy towards the Negro. Considering all the circumstances, it would be hard to find in history a more causeless and cruel oppression of a whole race than was embodied in the legislation of those revived and reconstructed State governments. Their membership was composed wholly of the 'ruling class,' as they termed it, and, in no small degree, of Confederate officers below the rank of brigadier-general, who sat in the legislature in the very uniforms which had distinguished them as enemies of the Union upon the battlefield. Limited space forbids my transcribing the black code wherewith they loaded their statute books. In Mr. Lamar's State the Negroes were forbidden, under very severe penalties, to keep firearms of any kind; they were apprenticed, if minors, to labor, preference being given by the statute to their 'former owners;' grown men and women were compelled to let their labor by contract, the decision of whose terms was wholly in the hands of the whites; and those who failed to contract were to be seized as 'vagrants,' heavily fined, and their labor sold by the sheriff at public outcry to the highest bidder. The terms 'master' and 'mistress' continually recur in the statutes, and the slavery that was thus instituted was a far more degrading, merciless and mercenary than that which was blotted out by the Thirteenth Amendment.

"South Carolina, whose moderation and justice are so highly prized by Governor Hampton, enacted a code still more cruel than that I have quoted from Mississippi. Firearms were forbidden to the Negro, and any violation of the statute was punished by 'fine equal to twice the value of the weapon so unlawfully kept,' and 'if that be not immediately paid, by corporal punishment.' It was further provided that 'no person of color shall pursue or practice the art, trade, or business of an artisan, mechanic, or shopkeeper, or any other trade or employment (besides that of husbandry or that of a servant under contract for labor), until he shall have obtained a license from the judge of the district court, which license shall be good for one year only.' If the license was granted to the Negro to be a shopkeeper or peddler he was compelled to pay $100 per annum for it, and if he pursued the rudest mechanical calling he could do so only by the payment of a license fee of $10 per annum. No such fees were exacted of the whites, and no such fee of free blacks during the era of slavery. The Negro was thus hedged in on all sides; he was down, and he was to be kept down, and the chivalric race that denied him a fair and honest competition in the humblest mechanical pursuit was loud in its assertions of his inferiority and his incompetency.

"But it was reserved for Louisiana to outdo both South Carolina and Mississippi in this horrible legislation. In that State all agricultural laborers were compelled to make labor contracts during the first ten days of January for the next year. The contract was made, the laborer was not to be allowed to leave his place of employment during the year except upon conditions not likely to happen and easily prevented. The master was allowed to make deductions from the servants' wages for injuries done to 'animals and agricultural implements committed to his care,' thus making the Negro responsible for wear and tear. Deductions were to be made for 'bad or negligent work,' the master being the judge. For every act of 'disobedience' a fine of $1 was imposed on the offender, disobedience being a technical term made to include, besides 'neglect of duty' and 'leaving home without permission,' such fearful offenses as 'impudence,' 'swearing,' 'indecent language in the presence of the employer, his family, or agent,' or 'quarreling or fighting with one another.' The master or his agent might assail every ear with profaneness aimed at the Negro man and outrage every sentiment of decency in the foul language addressed to the Negro women; but if one of the helpless creatures, goaded to resistance and crazed under tyranny, should answer back with impudence, or should relieve his mind with an oath, or restore indecency, he did so at the cost to himself of $1 for every outburst. The 'agent' referred to in the statute is the well-known overseer of the cotton region, and the care with which the lawmaker of Louisiana provided that his delicate ears and sensitive nerves should not be offended with an oath or an indecent word from a Negro will be appreciated by all who have heard the crack of the whip on a southern plantation.

"It is impossible to quote all the hideous provisions of these statutes under whose operation the Negro would have been relapsed gradually and surely into actual and admitted slavery. Kindred legislation was attempted in a large majority of the Confederate States, and it is not uncharitable or illogical to assume that the ultimate re-enslavement of the race was the fixed design of those who framed the law and of those who attempted to enforce them.

"I am not speculating as to what would have been done or might have been done in the Southern States if the National Government had not intervened. I have quoted what actually was done by legislatures under the control of Southern Democrats, and I am only recalling history when I say that those outrages against human nature were upheld by the Democratic party of the country. All Democrats whose articles I am reviewing were in various degrees, active or passive, principal or endorser, parties to this legislation; and the fixed determination of the Republican party to thwart and destroy it called down upon its head all the anathemas of Democratic wrath. But it was just at this point in our history when the Republican party was compelled to decide whether the emancipated slave should be protected by national power or handed over to his late master to be dealt with in the spirit of the enactments I have quoted.

"To restore the Union on a safe foundation, and to re-establish law and promote order, to insure justice and equal rights to all, the Republican party was forced to its reconstruction policy. To hesitate in its adoption was to invite and confirm the statute of wrong and cruelty to which I have referred. The first step taken was to submit the Fourteenth Amendment, giving citizenship and civil rights to the Negro and forbidding that he be counted in the basis of representation unless he should be reckoned among the voters. The Southern States could have been readily readmitted to all their power and privileges in the Union by accepting the Fourteenth Amendment, and Negro suffrage would not have been forced upon them. The gradual and conservative method of training the Negro for franchise, as suggested and approved by Governor Hampton, had many advocates among the Republicans in the North; and though in my judgment it would have proved delusive and impracticable, it was quite within the power of the South to secure its adoption or at least its trial.

"But the States lately in insurrection rejected the Fourteenth Amendment with apparent scorn and defiance. In the legislatures of Louisiana, Mississippi, and Florida it did not receive a single vote; in South Carolina, only one vote; in Virginia, only one; in Texas, five votes; in Arkansas, two votes; in Alabama, ten; in North Carolina, eleven, and in Georgia, where Mr. Stephens boasts that they gave the Negro suffrage in advance of the Fifteenth Amendment, only two votes could be found in favor of making the Negro even a citizen. It would have been more candid in Mr. Stephens if he had stated that it was the legislature assembled under the reconstruction act that gave suffrage to the Negro in Georgia, and that the unreconstructed legislature, which has his endorsement and sympathies and which elected him to the United States Senate, not only refused suffrage to the Negro but loaded him with grievous disabilities and passed a criminal code of barbarous severity for his punishment.

"It is necessary to a clear apprehension of the needful facts in this discussion to remember events in the proper order of time. The Fourteenth Amendment was submitted to the States

June 13, 1866. In the autumn of that year, or very early in 1867, the legislatures of all the insurrectionary States, except Tennessee, had rejected it. Thus and then the question was forced upon us, whether the Congress of the United States, composed wholly of men who had been loyal to the Government, or the legislatures of the rebel states, composed wholly of men who had been disloyal to the Government, should determine the basis on which their relation to the Union should be resumed. In such a crisis the Republican party could not hesitate; to halt, indeed, would have been an abandonment of the principles on which the war had been fought; to surrender to the rebel legislatures would have been cowardly desertion of its loyal friends and a base betrayal of the Union cause.

"And thus, in March, 1867, after and because of the rejection of the Fourteenth Amendment by Southern legislatures, Congress passed the reconstruction act. This was the origin of Negro suffrage. The southern whites knowingly and willfully brought it upon themselves. The reconstruction act would have never been demanded had the Southern States accepted the Fourteenth Amendment in good faith. But that amendment contained so many provisions demanded by considerations of great national policy that its adoption became an absolute necessity. Those who controlled the Federal Government would have been recreant to their plainest duty had they permitted the power of these States to be wielded by disloyal hands against the measures deemed essential to the security of the Union. To have destroyed the rebellion on the battlefield and then permit it to seize the power of eleven States and put a check on all changes in the organic law necessary to prevent future rebellion would have been a weak and wicked conclusion to the grandest contest ever waged for human rights and for constitutional liberty.

"Negro suffrage being thus made a necessity by the obduracy of those who were in control of the South, it became a subsequent necessity to adopt the Fifteenth Amendment. Nothing could have been more despicable than to use the Negro to secure the adoption of the Fourteenth Amendment and then to leave them exposed to the hazard of losing suffrage whenever those who had attempted to re-enslave them should regain political power in their State. Hence the Fifteenth Amendment, which never pretended to guarantee universal suffrage, but simply forbade that any man should lose his vote because he had once been a slave, or because his face might be black, or because his remote ancestors came from Africa."

Thus is scattered to the four winds, we feel, Mr. Dixon's claim that the Negro suffrage was born of the spirit of revenge.

Mr. Dixon's Wide Hearing

IF MR. DIXON IS SO WHOLLY false as we have set forth in this paper, the question naturally arises as to how he could have obtained such a hearing as has been accorded him. Of the many factors which perhaps operated to secure this hearing we shall mention a few that commend themselves to us as possible causes.

In the first place, there is that great American spirit of fair play. The Negro through Uncle Tom's Cabin and the Tourgee novels had his day in court, and it was felt to be only just that the South be heard in all fullness.

Another factor in Mr. Dixon's success in obtaining his hearing we believe to be his choice of the hour in the world's history in which to demand a hearing. Queen Victoria, who had reigned so long and honorably, had just summoned by her death all of Anglo-Saxondom to her bier, where in a common sorrow over the departure of a great and good woman they learned anew how that, fundamentally, they were all about alike.

About this time, too, a poet had arisen, with voice to reach, for the time being, at least, the whole English speaking world, furnishing another scrap of evidence that differing forms of government, wide seas and varying problems had not affected their spiritual unity.

Anglo-Saxon lads, peacefully sleeping in the harbor of a Latin nation, had been treacherously blown up, and at the sight of that which was thicker than water in the hold of the Maine, the Anglo-Saxons of the world got still closer together.

In the war that followed, the South had its first opportunity of attesting with its blood its professions of love for the Union flag which it had sought to lower in four years of bloody strife. As a result of that war the Northern and controlling section of the country felt impelled by the logic of the situation to force an unaccepted relation upon an alien race, thereby providing the one outstanding section of the Anglo-Saxon race with some form of a race problem.

These various happenings brought the English speaking people wondrously close together and bridged the chasms made by internecine wars and conflicting ideas of government.

Listen now to the dream of Thomas Carlyle as set forth in his lecture on "The Hero" as a poet. Says he:

"England, before long, this island of ours, will hold but a small fraction of the English; in America, in New Holland, east and west to the very antipodes, there will be a great Saxondom covering great spaces of the globe. And now, what is it that can keep all these together in virtually one nation, so that they do not fall out and fight, but live at peace, in brother-like intercourse, helping one another? This is justly regarded as the greatest practical problem, the thing all manner of sovereignties and governments are here to accomplish: what is it that will accomplish this? Acts of parliament, administrative prime-ministers cannot. America is parted from us, so far as parliament could part it. Call it not fantastic, for there is much reality in it; here, I say, is an English king whom no time or chance, parliament or combination of parliaments, can dethrone! This King Shakespeare, does he not shine, in crowned sovereignty, over us all, as the noblest, gentlest, yet strongest of rallying signs; indestructible; really more valuable in that point of view than any other means or appliance whatsoever? We can fancy him as radiant aloft over all the nations of Englishmen, a thousand years hence. From Paramatta, from New York, wheresoever, under what sort of parish-constable soever, English men and women are, they will say to one another: 'Yes, this Shakespeare is ours, we produced him, and we speak and think by him; we are of one blood and kind with him.'"

As set forth here the travail of the English heart is toward a unified Saxondom, and, as indicated above, its hour had come. It was in the hour when the world paused in awe to see a fruition of this dream, that Mr. Dixon asked—*insisted* upon being heard. Anxious to know upon what terms the South would be a contented member of this new accord, Mr. Dixon, essaying to speak for the South, got his hearing.

What a terrible enemy to humanity does Mr. Dixon prove himself to be when, essaying to speak for the South, he would impart to this mighty force, with work before it worthy of the gods, a larger measure of the virus of race prejudice. Rather, may this unified Saxondom, as the agent of that "divinity that shapes our ends rough-hew them how we will," choose the opening hours of its era for the purging from its great heart all the lingering vestiges of hatred of men, and with eyes ever on the heights above, begin the final climb of the human race toward the ideal state. May this trumpet call to a greatness of soul in keeping with its greatness of power, supplant the voice of Dixon the hater, summoning men to grovellings in the valleys of a thousand years agone.

Mr. Dixon's Borrowed Power

WE SHALL NOW MAKE MENTION of a force within Mr. Dixon which, from our point of view, enabled him to seize the passing opportunity and challenge the attention of so great a constituency. There is nothing more patent to an observer of life in the South than the fact that the Anglo-Saxon and Negro races are producing in each other modifications of many of their racial characteristics. The erstwhile, abounding humor of the Negro has found its echo in the white race of the South and we find the dignified L. Q. C. Lamar, of Mississippi, succeeded in his grasp upon public attention by the witty, fun-loving John Sharp Williams, while the great American humorist, Mark Twain is likewise a product of the South.

The unquestioning faith of the Negro in the Bible is largely responsible for the militant orthodoxy of the white Christian ministry of the South, which makes life miserable for any mind retaining and applying to religious matters the old Anglo-Saxon habit of investigating. "The hand that rocks the cradle is the hand that rules the world," even if that hand is a black hand. It is the boast of the Southern white preacher that he was nursed by a black mammy.

Along emotional lines there is appearing a marked difference between the white people of the South and those of the North. It was remarked of the National Democratic Convention, held in the city of St. Louis in 1904, that such an emotional convention could only have been held somewhere in the South. The Negro race is noted for its highly emotional nature, and while contact with the Anglo-Saxon race is toning it down, there is also evidence that the Negro race is affecting the Anglo-Saxon.

Now, Mr. Dixon's publishers, in announcing a second book from his pen, singled out for purposes of parade what they regarded as the most powerful element in his work, namely, his grasp upon the emotions of men, his ability to arouse and sway their feelings. In the long line of men of letters of the Anglo-Saxon race we find no counterpart of Mr. Dixon. So the question is very pertinent as to what influence has given power to this pale-face shout exciter, this expert player upon men's emotions, this literary (we beg a thousand pardons for seeming billingsgate) demagogue and exotic in Anglo-Saxondom. The irony of fate! Mr. Thomas Dixon, Jr., beyond doubt owes his emotional power to the very race which he has elected to scourge.

Mr. Dixon has not breathed the Negro air of emotionalism without being affected thereby. The Negro minister whom Mr. Dixon derides in his book is beyond all doubt Mr. Dixon's spiritual parent so far as power is concerned. The fact that Mr. Dixon has chosen the discomfiture of the Negro race as the chief end of his existence is not inconsistent with the fact that the predominating element in his power is the gift of that race. It is perhaps this subconscious feeling on the part of Mr. Dixon that he is in the grasp of a power not Anglo-Saxon that causes him to rant and cry for a freedom that his own Southern brethren less affected do not understand.

The Real Problem

AH, GOOD PEOPLE OF AMERICA, here is your real problem! Southern self-interest may be relied upon to keep the Negro here; being here, no human power can prevent him from contributing his quota to the atmosphere of the group in which all the sons of the South must find their environing inheritance. In the contact of the street workman with his boss; in the cook kitchen; in the nursery room; in the concubine chamber; in the street song; in the brothel; in the philosophizings of the minstrel performer; in the literature which he will ere long create, by means of which there can be contact not personal; in myriad ways the Negro will write something upon the soul of the white man. It should be the care of the American people that he write well.

Mr. Dixon trembles at a possible physical amalgamation and would have the races separated. The "nay" which the nation renders to his cause so badly plead makes the spiritual amalgamation a certainty.

That the contribution of the Negro to the coming composite Americanism may be of the highest quality is the nation's problem.

Just now the American people seem much engrossed with the training of the hand of the Negro, confessedly a work of tremendous moment. *But be it known unto you, oh Americans, that it is through his mind, his spirit, the exhalations of his soul, his dreams or lack of dreams, that the Negro is to leave his most marked influence on American life.* Let the use to which Mr. Dixon is putting his borrowed emotional power recall the nation to the slumbering Negro mind that must ere long awake to power. May the coming, then, of Mr. Dixon, the literary exotic, serve as a reminder to the American people that they give the Negro a healthy place, a helpful atmosphere in which to evolve all that is good within himself and eliminate all the bad. If this be done, even Mr. Dixon will not have lived and frothed in vain.

A Final Word

A FINAL WORD WITH REGARD to Mr. Dixon. The appearance of such a man with such a spirit might incline one to think that the world is going backward rather than forward. But there is this redeeming thought. Mr. Dixon represents the ultra radical element of Southern whites. The coming of this radical of radicals before the bar of public opinion, clothed in his garb of avowed prejudice of the rankest sort, means that the self-satisfied isolation of the past is over, that even the radicals desire or see the need of sympathetic consideration from other portions of the human family—decidedly a step forward for them. The coming to the light of this type where civilization may work upon it is in this respect one of the most hopeful signs of America's future. Soberly the great world consciousness will deal with this enemy of the human race, and the universal finger of scorn that will surely in the end be pointed toward him will render it certain that no other like unto him shall ever arise.

If, when his services are in demand, the chiseler of the epitaph for Mr. Dixon's tombstone desires to carve words that will be read with patience in the coming better days of the world, let him carve thus:

"This misguided soul ignored all of the good in the aspiring Negro; made every vicious offshoot that he pictured typical of the entire race; presented all mistakes independent of their environments and provocations; ignored or minimized all the evil in the more vicious element of whites; said and did all things which he deemed necessary to leave behind him the greatest heritage of hatred the world has ever known. Humanity claims him not as one of her children."

SUTTON E. GRIGGS

A Note About the Author

Sutton E. Griggs (1872–1933) was an African American novelist, activist, and Baptist minister. Born in Chatfield, Texas, Griggs was the second of eight children. His father, Rev. Allen R. Griggs, was a former slave who became an influential minister and founded the first newspaper and high school for African Americans in Texas. Upon graduating from Bishop College and Richmond Theological Seminary, Griggs followed in his father's footsteps to become a pastor in Berkley, Virginia, where he married Emma Williams in 1897. In 1899, while serving as pastor of Tabernacle Baptist Church in East Nashville, Griggs published his novel *Imperium in Imperio*, a powerful story of a separate African American state. Recognized as a pioneering work of utopian literature and science fiction, the novel launched Griggs' literary career and allowed him to open the Orion Publishing Company in 1901. Devoted to alleviating social issues within the Black community, Griggs supported the Niagara Movement and the NAACP, educated himself through the words of W. E. B. Du Bois, and advocated for both separatism and integration in his literary works. Towards the end of his life, having published several novels and dozens of political and religious pamphlets, Griggs devoted himself to his work in the Baptist Church, serving for 19 years as a pastor in Memphis and for one year as president of the American Baptist Theological Seminary.

A Note from the Publisher

Spanning many genres, from non-fiction essays to literature classics to children's books and lyric poetry, Mint Edition books showcase the master works of our time in a modern new package. The text is freshly typeset, is clean and easy to read, and features a new note about the author in each volume. Many books also include exclusive new introductory material. Every book boasts a striking new cover, which makes it as appropriate for collecting as it is for gift giving. Mint Edition books are only printed when a reader orders them, so natural resources are not wasted. We're proud that our books are never manufactured in excess and exist only in the exact quantity they need to be read and enjoyed.

bookfinity™

Discover more of your favorite classics with Bookfinity™.

- Track your reading with custom book lists.
- Get great book recommendations for your personalized Reader Type.
- Add reviews for your favorite books.
- AND MUCH MORE!

Visit **bookfinity.com** and take the fun Reader Type quiz to get started.

Enjoy our classic and modern companion pairings!

Classic & Modern

Printed in the USA
CPSIA information can be obtained
at www.ICGtesting.com
JSHW022334140824
68134JS00019B/1481